Daughter Of Fire

Jennifer R. Povey

1

"For crying out loud." The voice carried across the canteen, raised to a pitch that turned several heads. It came from a young brunette woman, but then, most of the people there were young. Tables and chairs were scattered across the room, and the posters on the walls advertised student associations.

She glared at her cell as if it had bitten her. "If this...boy...doesn't leave me alone, I'll..."

One of the other girls nearby made a suggestion, "Push him in the lake, Laura?"

"I wouldn't want to poison the fish." Laura flickered a grin at her.

"Like there are any fish in the lake. The chemistry department took care of those years ago."

That was an article of faith at the small college...that the state of the artificial lake (namely completely free of life,) was a result of chemicals leaking from the science building. Laura privately thought it more likely that nobody had ever got around to stocking it. There was also supposed to be a car in it, but she knew full well its depth was not sufficient for anything but, maybe, one of those new smart cars to be hidden. Besides, there was supposed to be a car in every single small lake in North America and most of the ones in Europe.

"Point, Dana," was all she said, not voicing all of those thoughts. "Still. He won't stop texting me."

"Block him?"

"I tried. He changed his freaking number. I'm this close to just calling the..."

"Police?" Dana flicked a finger towards the canteen entrance.

Two men came into the room. They were strangers in suits that screamed police to anyone who was used to being arrested or watching arrests. And this was a college campus.

Laura rolled her eyes. "Okay, who got caught with drugs again?"

Dana laughed. "Probably Dennis. He's going to be expelled if so...he's already on probation over it."

"At least it's only pot." Laura twisted in her seat to see the cops. "They're heading this way. Anything you want to tell me?"

"I am absolutely innocent of all charges." Dana batted her eyelashes at her friend. "Maybe you can ask them what it would take to get a restraining order against Petey-boy."

Laura laughed. "Well, it's not Dennis, they walked right past him. I hope it's not something...really bad."

Like, say, a parent or sibling being murdered, or... She shivered a bit. Her parents were safe. Safe in their exclusive gated community. Where they had bought everything they wanted...the perfect house, the perfect car. She wished she could be the perfect daughter, but she never quite managed that.

Well, no, they had not bought Laura. That was illegal. But she had known most of her life that she was adopted. That her mother was not capable of producing children. Clarice Maxwell saw it as a way of walking the pro-life talk. She wondered if her mother was satisfied with what she had: A daughter who did not want to be rich, could care less about the money. A daughter who wanted to teach school.

But the cops were definitely there, and something in her stomach sank. Had they found out that she had illegally downloaded some music? Or was it Dana who was in trouble?

"Laura Maxwell." The leader of the two cops put only the slightest trace of question in his voice.

"Am I under arrest?" She could not think what for. Yes, she had done a couple of illegal downloads, but they did not send the cops after you for that. They just sent you nasty letters demanding money.

"No. We need to talk to you, that's all. You're not in any trouble."

"You might have called me," she started to say, then recalled that she had turned her phone off because of 'Petey-boy' and only just turned it back on. She turned it off again. "Never mind. You know anything about restraining orders? And...people are going to think I did get arrested."

"I'll take care of that." The cop sounded gentle, even sympathetic.

Laura kept her head high as she followed the two men out. Hopefully not everyone would realize she had left with the police.

They opened the back door of an unmarked car for her. Inside, she turned on her phone again. Ten voice messages from Petey-boy...she was going to have to ask her mother to introduce her to a lawyer. Three from her mother, yelling at her to turn her phone back on and to cooperate with the cops. One from a Detective Ross, telling her to come to the station.

He'd apparently lost patience. Her phone had been off for a while. The hundred plus texts from Petey were enough to make her very glad she had an unlimited plan. She deleted them as she got her head together.

Why would the cops want her? Her mother had not said anything, her voice holding worry, not information. But she did not feel up to asking questions yet.

* * *

Laura had never been inside a police station. She had always avoided such. She was not the type to do drugs or start fights. It didn't look much like it did in the cop dramas.

A lot more modern. Maybe the cop dramas went for a retro look. The squad room was open with cubicles, but the two led her through it to an office with "Detective Ross" on the door.

An older man sat behind the desk. With little talk - she had wondered if any of them other than the lead one had tongues - her escorts left. She studied him for a moment. Greying, a little weather beaten. Too overweight for the television image of a detective, but not what she would call fat.

She sat down without waiting to be asked, claiming a little bit of power over the situation. Just a little, to keep her from losing all control.

"Miss Maxwell..." His gaze turned towards her. She saw the bags under his eyes and the way his skin drooped.

The poor man looked exhausted. She kept her gaze even, though. She had come here willingly. He had no power over her. But she was in a police station, and her father would never forgive her for embarrassing him. He still hadn't forgiven her for the butterfly tattoo she now had on her left shoulder. It made her less of a perfect daughter. Not that he would punish her. Just give her those disapproving looks. Her mother, of course, liked the tattoo.

She always wore long sleeves at home. "What's...up?"

Her voice sounded uncertain in her own ears. The words seemed ill chosen for the occasion. She was in the freaking cop shop! Her life was not going to recover from this immediately. How could it?

"This is not going to be easy." His voice was gentle as he opened one of the files on his desk. There was a photo inside; he slid it over to her.

A dark-haired woman, dark eyes, exquisitely attractive. Not young, Laura could tell that. Forty, maybe, but a forty that knew how to defeat age. It looked almost like a promotion or glamor shot.

It was, almost, her own face that looked back at her. Older, the nose set a little differently, the hair in a different style. But those were her eyes, and a shock ran through her. Who was this woman? The wilder side of her envisioned some kind of time travel plot. Time travel was, of course, impossible. She focused on the nose, which was not quite her nose. It was clearly a relative of hers. One she did not know about.

"Have you ever met that woman?" The cop's tone was sympathetic, no hint that she was suspected of anything.

"No." The word came out despite the fact that she was not sure. She knew her. She did know her, but they had not met. The sense of familiarity had to come from some other source.

"Have you ever been contacted...phone, email or text...by a woman calling herself either Jane Lawson or Ella Miracle?" The cop rested his hands on the desk. His entire manner radiated intimidation, but closely held, leashed. As if he was more used to interrogating suspects than innocents.

"No..." Her voice tailed off. Realization flowed through and into her. "She's my mother." Her birth mother. The physical resemblance, the near recognition. The woman she had never been permitted to learn anything about. Had been protected from.

"According to adoption records, yes." The detective took off his glasses. He reached for a wipe, cleaned them.

"I don't know where she is." So that was what this was about. Ella Miracle. That was...well. She supposed she should not be surprised. Her birth mother being a hooker was one of the high probability possibilities she had considered. It would explain her father's attitude toward the matter...that odd mix of forgiveness and disgust that had always accompanied her requests to learn about her. She folded her hands into her lap.

"We do." The glasses were perched back on his nose. It took him two attempts. "Jane Lawson was murdered two weeks ago."

Laura tried to find the sort of pain that should have accompanied that news. She could not. This woman was not her real mother. She had given her up...perhaps for good motivations, perhaps bad. But still, she had given up the right to be her 'mom' when she made that choice.

Two weeks ago. He'd said two weeks ago. She shivered.Two weeks ago she had woken up at five am in a cold sweat for no reason. She had forced her way from a dream in which she had been fighting against faceless enemies with a sword, something she had never done. Something she would not know how to do. But that she would not mention to the cop. He would assume it meant she knew something, when she did not. Of course, she had heard of such incidents, such apparent precognition. She knew that it was a psychological illusion. She would have forgotten the nightmare had it not been for the coincidence. One remembered only the predictions which 'came true'.

Or was it? Sometimes she seemed to have an awareness most people did not. This was not the first nightmare, the first dream of fire and war that had turned out to reflect something in reality. And she had heard all kinds of stories about mother-daughter connections. It was entirely possible she had somehow felt her mother's death. She was still not going to mention it.

"I don't know anything. She gave up her right to be my mother." Her voice was even. There was no pain, but there was a hint of sorrow. That she had never met her. Regret. That was the word she was looking for. She felt only regret.

She expected that to be the end of it. The cop hoped she made contact, heard something that might lead them to the killer. "Although," she added. "I was planning on contacting the agency and trying to get the records this summer. When I didn't have school to worry about." Her father would not have approved. Her father thought that his perfect daughter should not reach for her obviously common roots. Her mother... They disagreed on that, too, but disagreements were, it seemed, part of marriage.

It was not over, though. "The thing is...before the murder two men were seen asking around after Lawson. They specifically asked about a 'boy' or a 'child'. According to all the records we can find, Lawson only had one child..."

"Oh come on. They're not going to come after me." That was the kind of thing that happened in thrillers. Badly written thrillers. Although, if she was inclined to write, it would make a good start for one.

"Most likely not. But we may want to put some protection on you. We asked the agency to destroy the computer records of your adoption, but it is against their policy and by the time we got a court order..." His voice was as serious as handcuffs and bullets.

"Can you tell me who my father was?" She had to ask, had to know.

He frowned. "Lawson apparently didn't know or didn't want to say. There's no father listed on the birth certificate. Given..."

"Given her profession," Laura interrupted, "She most likely had no clue." Even with condoms and the pill, pregnancy had to be an occupational hazard of hooking. Either she had felt Laura would cramp her style or, more charitably, that it was unfair to raise a child in a brothel. Or perhaps she even truly believed a child needed two parents.

"Most likely not." The detective studied her. "You're taking this too well."

"I didn't know her. But...is there any chance I could have a copy of that picture?" She suspected the answer would be no.

"I'll see what I can do." Not a direct no. A polite I don't think so. It tempted her to snatch the one in front of her, evidence or no evidence.

There was an odd, almost empty feeling within her. Her birth mother was dead. "One more thing. Do you know anything about restraining orders?" She shouldn't ask. She couldn't quite resist.

2

Going home for spring break instead of away would not have been Laura's choice. But spring break started a day after the incident, and she canceled her plans. No Cancun for her, not this year, the flight tickets paid for, but unused. She felt as if she would be too exposed. Besides, Petey-Boy said he was going there. He was bad enough sober. She did not want to even be in the same country as him when he was drunk.

Laura went home. Home was protected and safe. If there really were bad guys after her, she felt it was a fortress in which they could not touch her. Of course, it had been made that way.

Truthfully, the security could not have kept out anyone determined. It would, though, keep out Petey-boy...and by the time she got back, she would be armed with a restraining order, thanks to her mother's lawyers. She hoped he really was going to Cancun.

Her real mother. Ella Miracle, or Jane Lawson or whoever she really was, was not her real mother. She was a gene donor. And whoever her father was had been even less. He did not even know she existed.

That finally hit her as she sat in her old room. She had not had it redecorated since she started college, and it was amazing how her tastes had changed in that year. It seemed quaint, young. A girl's room, not a woman's. A place where her childhood daydreams had flowed through her mind. A child, when mad with her parents, when she felt her childhood injustice, might fantasize. Laura had imagined her distant mother swooping in, taking her away. Giving her a new life, one better and more exciting than the life she had. As a woman, she knew better, knew it was a silly fantasy. Yet, as it dawned on her that her mother was dead, the regret came back.

She would never be able to ask Ella Miracle who she was, whether *she* had any regrets. She was dead and somebody had killed her.

Laura's emotions ran in mixed currents, swirling around and over one another. There was grief and guilt in there, but not as much as there might have been. Not as much as if it had been her the mother who raised her. There was a faint smoldering anger that somebody had messed with her family. There was relief...that she would never have to face that woman. She knew now that her initial reaction in the office had been protective numbness.

She opened her bag. The detective had sent her a copy after all. Ella Miracle. Jane Lawson. She was beautiful, Laura thought. Not all of it was real beauty, though. Some, she could tell, was stage beauty. The false loveliness of well applied makeup and a careful coiffure.

Ella Miracle had not been a cheap prostitute. That was the other emotion. Curiosity. The desire, strong and clear, to find out exactly who Jane Lawson had been. It warred with fear of what the cops had said.

Laura was not used to feeling afraid. Was it really fear she felt, or something else? All her life, she had been good at everything she tried, attractive, always that bit ahead of her peers. Her teachers expected her to end up CEO of something. None thought she should waste herself teaching.

But she also remembered the spike of cold. She had known her mother was dead. No. Jane was not her mother. Her father? Somebody reasonably wealthy, somebody who could afford such a woman. Somebody who was not satisfied with wife and home or, perhaps, had none. Not important.

She got up, left the room, left the house. There was a model farm in the middle of the community. Black and white dairy cows grazed peacefully, intermingled with black and white dairy goats. They sold the milk and cheese at a little store right there. Laura liked goat's cheese. It somehow came over, in her mind, as more like cheese than the cow's milk variety.

She leaned on the fence, watched them. They had no troubles. A cow could not possibly worry about anything but the next blade of grass and when milking time was. Did they, though, wonder about their calves, taken away so that humans could have the milk?

Great, this wasn't going to work. Right back...and as she turned away, she saw another reminder. Children in the playground next to the pasture.

"For crying out loud." Her mother's favorite euphemism. Nice girls did not swear. Somehow, Laura had never picked up the habit. Maybe that made her a nice girl. Pheh. No, it made her a girl who did not swear.

Nice girls did not get tattoos or hang out in night clubs, or own fake IDs so they could drink.

She turned to walk away from cows and children alike. There seemed to be some kind of argument going on at the gate. She glanced over. It was Petey-boy...the security guard refused to let him in. Good. Her mother said she had asked them not to. Turning away pointedly, she made her quick route home.

Her mother was cooking dinner. She did that a lot, Laura noticed. In some ways, her mother's kitchen was her self, her soul. She had always been disappointed that Laura cooked only for the results.

"Hi, Mom." Normal. Mundane. Still 'Mom'. Nothing could change that. As much as she had wanted to know who her birth mother was, this was her real mother. She was the woman who had made her who she was. Not some high-class hooker.

Clarice Maxwell turned and then put a wooden spoon down to hug her daughter. "I'm glad you still call me that."

"She gave me up. She probably had her reasons, but she gave up the right to be Mom." That, Laura clung to, even if she wished she had met the woman. Even if she grieved for her, in an odd way. A twisted way.

Clarice moved over to the kitchen table. "Sit down."

Laura did so, fidgeting with her hands, with the couple of silver rings she wore. "What's cooking?"

"Stew. But we need to talk." Clarice sat down, resting her hands on the table. She positioned herself where she could see the stew pot. Just in case.

"I don't think we need to be worried. Whoever that nut job was, he's not coming here." There was security. There was anonymity. The records would be destroyed. She did not need them. She needed this, her family.

"That's not what I want to talk about." Clarice folded her hands, dusted with flour, into her aproned lap. "I'm honestly not worried either. I wanted to make sure you were alright."

"I'm not." Laura did not lie to her mother. "I will be, but I'm not right now." She wondered if she should have stuck with her original plans and gone to Mexico. Of course her mother was worried. She would have been.

"Honestly, I'd be worried if you were. I was always honest with you because my therapist told me that would be best. That kids end up feeling very betrayed if they find out they were adopted as adults. But this..." Clarice tailed off.

"It's a gut blow. I was going to try and find her this summer. Just to say hello, let her know I turned out okay. Of course, I kinda thought she was like fifteen when she had me or something." Not that she had assumed anything. She had not even assumed her mother would still be alive. One of her lead scenarios had been that the woman had died of a drug overdose years ago.

Clarice opened her mouth, but at that moment the phone rang. She stood, crossing to get it quickly, lifting the receiver.

"It's for you."

For me? Laura wondered. She picked it up. A voice on the other end, a male voice, an unfamiliar one. Her stomach sank.

It was the police again. "What...what do you want?"

"Your help. I promise, it won't be horribly dangerous."

She glanced at her mother. She took a deep breath. "What do you need me to do?"

3

Laura walked along the street quickly. She did not know the man next to her beyond his name....Patrick...and the fact that he was a cop. "Are we sure this is a set up?" The street ran through a canyon of skyscrapers, their glass walls towering above her. It was a place she was not familiar with, or comfortable in.

Patrick shook his head. "No, but we have good reason to think so. Yes, Jane Lawson had money, and her leaving it to you is feasible, but this particular lawyer doesn't seem like one she'd use."

Laura nodded. A dark feeling came over her, something in the pit of her stomach. Was afraid the right word? He was talking again.

"Let's go over this again. If possible, I'll stay inside with you. If not, I'll be right outside." He was fairly tall, dark hair, a face and manner that indicated he would not drink green beer...because real Irish people did not. Everything about his tone and body language gave a strong air of business as usual. As if he did this kind of thing all the time.

" Maybe she really did leave me a small fortune. Not that I need one, but..." Laura tailed off. If there was a fortune, there was nobody else to inherit it. Ella or Jane had given up parental rights, but somebody could leave their money to whoever they wanted to have it.

"It could be. I wish I could say for sure that it was. What I really wonder is the why of all this...maybe we can get that out of them." The detective studied her for a moment. "You're very brave, Miss Maxwell."

"I want to know why they killed her, too." And frankly, although Laura didn't want or need Jane Lawson's money...she might have some nice clothes and jewelry. Laura was not above dressing up, although right now she had dressed as if for a night after school. The cops had suggested looking like she did need the money. Not desperate, but not well off, either.

So, her jeans were designer ripped and she had left the expensive jewelry at home. She wore a tank top that showed off her tattoo. The outfit was dominated by black, with a bit of silver costume jewelry. Almost the goth look. She was even close to having the hair for it.

The lawyer's office, at least, had checked out. Expensive, and, worse, in one of those skyscrapers. Laura did not like that, if she had to run. The cop had a gun, but she did not want him to use it. A lump formed in her throat. It was fear, after all, but it was not fear of what might happen to her. Fear of what she might have to be involved in. Of what she might have to do. Of whether she could do it, and the yes was far worse than the no.

An elevator, upwards, and she felt time seem to slow a little. She had experienced that before. Most likely, it was a result of her being stressed. She glanced at Patrick again. Perfectly relaxed, his hands loose at his sides, his eyes staring at the door as people did in elevators. He was probably remembering that there were a lot of cops, undercover, in the area for when things went south.

Laura was wondering what they could do when the doors opened on the twentieth floor.

Rich lawyers. Like her mother's lawyers. Had it been the same one, she might not have suspected a trap. She knew she did not look like she belonged here. The carpet felt thick under the boots she was wearing. Boots were good for kicking people with.

There were three men in suits leaning against one of the walls, loitering. Laura knew at that moment that it was exactly the trap she feared. She could see no guns, but her awareness shot into a heightened state she had experienced only once before...when somebody had tried to mug her. He had failed because of it, because she had instinctively moved out of his grasp and then fled.

She said nothing to Patrick, but rather reached to grip his hand for a moment. How did she tell him she was worried?

The elevator doors slid closed. She saw no other access...the fire exit had to be somewhere, but it was not visible to her. Where was it likely to be? The map of the building flashed into her mind, clearer than memory normally was.

This lobby area had no windows to the outside. She wondered if the wire she was wearing even worked, or if the thickness of the walls would block it.

Then she was on the deck. There had been no conscious thought involved. Solid object. You were supposed to get behind solid objects. The gunshot had sounded a moment after she moved. She did not know exactly why. Almost as if she had known what would happen, known it and felt it.

"Fuck." That was Patrick. Had he been hit, or was he just pissed off at the general situation? She did not know and could not spare the energy to care.

Receptionist's desk. Solid oak. She was moving to pull herself behind it, except...too obvious. Another bullet, and her shoulder was suddenly on fire. "Fuck." She never used language like that, but it seemed to fit the moment. Weapon. She needed a weapon. A weapon she was not sure she would know how to use. They had said she should not carry one for that reason. Because she would be too tempted to use it.

She had none, thus, except her fists. The snap of another shot impacted on her ears. Patrick was trying to shield her with his own body. No. She could not face the thought that he might die for her.

Two men now. He had, perhaps, already killed for her.

Time slowed even further. Her combat training was limited to a self-defense class, but they were focused on the threat. On Patrick. Another shot. Her shoulder still burned, but the arm worked. It could not be that bad, surely, and then she was on one of them, forcing him to the ground with the strength of desperation. The gun.

Her hand closed around the gun, wrenched it from his. His face was startled, then afraid. Another shot. And she was kneeling over him in a position that might have been, at other times, suggestive.

Everything was quiet. "Patrick?"

"Ugh. Are you hurt?" Genuine, if professional, concern for her.

"Yes, but I don't think it's bad." She could be wrong. She had never been shot before, and the shoulder felt like a dull fire, as if somebody was rubbing a cigarette butt into it.

"My radio's not working. I need to find a window."

The other two men were dead. She trained the gun on the face of the one she had pinned. "You guys thought I was just a little girl, didn't you?"

"Supposed...to be a boy." He stared at the barrel of the gun, each word he spoke pulled out of him by it.

"There's nothing I can't do that a boy can, other than go to the bathroom standing up." She'd always believed that, although normally she would not have put it so crudely. Now she had the power. It felt good, despite the pain in her shoulder. Too good. Something she might get used to, given the chance. Even come to truly enjoy. She shook her head, but she could not let him up. He was the one who knew something and only in stories did people like this have cyanide teeth, surely.

She wondered if the fact that they had, somehow, thought Ella Miracle's baby was a son had slowed them down. Or maybe they had...

...waited until she turned eighteen. Waited until the adoption agency would release the records. Perhaps Ella/Jane had asked for them. Perhaps they had killed her to take them.

Damn. Could it be all about her?

4

The hospital emergency room was not a place she wanted to end up. She'd been there before, and every time she promised she would avoid it. The bullet had grazed across her shoulder, leaving a relatively shallow, but long, cut. It needed stitches. It would probably scar.

Somehow, that didn't bother her. Her mother would freak, and then pay for plastic surgery to remove said scar. Fine. Then they forced her to talk to the ER counselor. She tried to insist she was okay.

She felt fine, even as the last vestiges of the adrenalin rush faded out of her system...or perhaps were driven out by the local anesthetic, by the smell of medicine and death.

They had really tried to kill her. All she felt about that was anger. The one man who had lived refused to talk. The 'supposed to be a boy' line was all, it seemed, that they were going to get out of him.

Patrick came over. He had two cups of bad hospital coffee. "Never thought a slip of a girl like you could move that fast."

She scowled at him. "I refuse to dodge bullets for the rest of my life."

"Witness protection..."

"Throws away everything. That's letting them win." There was a cold feeling inside her at the thought. She would not graduate, would lose all the money she had, would end up waitressing somewhere. She would never hear her mother's voice again. She would not exactly rather die, but...

"Better than dying."

"I'm not backing down to these people. I just have to demonstrate I'm not who they're looking for. Do you think it's possible that they think I'm the offspring of some regular of hers?"

"Or they..." Patrick frowned. "This one's beyond me. None of it quite makes sense."

Including what I did, Laura thought. Of course, she had never had any problems doing whatever she wanted to do, physically. But she had never pushed herself that hard. "The one we captured?"

"Nothing. He's not talking, no matter what interrogation techniques we try."

"Heck, maybe they think I'm some kind of ubermensch." She hadn't realized she was speaking out loud until it was too late.

"No such thing." The cop's tone was firm. "Let's get you somewhere safe."

Laura realized she might well not make it back to school for the rest of the semester.

* * *

In fact, the police now seemed determined not to let her go anywhere or do anything.

Her style was beyond cramped. At this point, she was sitting in a corner of the freaking squad room, wondering why anyone became a cop. Certainly, the food was no reason. She'd bet the prisoners in the jail ate better.

She still had not declared a major. But criminal justice was most definitely not on her list. She would teach, but she had yet to decide what, where, and to whom. History, perhaps.

Nobody was looking at her. She wondered if she could at least sneak out into the street, get some air. Standing, she made her way to the door. The cops were all focused on computer screens, those that were here. Most were out on the beat.

She made it to the door and stepped outside. The building was set back from the plaza, screened by a bit of grass and trees. She wanted to go home. She wanted to go to Mexico.

She wanted to be anywhere but here, hiding from some unknown enemy. From somebody who sought her life. For no reason. The sky was very clear, and the faint scent of some kind of flower reached her nostrils. She didn't seek it out. Something in the colored bed that rested along the wall.

Think, woman. There had to be a reason. Could it be her...well, there was one obvious possibility. Somebody thought she was their half-sister, competition for a father's fortune.

That could be easy to prove one way or another. And if she was that person's sibling, she could well demonstrate that she had no need of the family money. Buy them off with words that were no more than the truth. It should not be hard.

That was the most logical explanation, but nothing explained...and her thought was interrupted.

The woman who approached, stepping into the plaza, did not exactly look familiar. The vibe that swept through Laura was not recognition, it was something else.

Laura shook her head. Almost sexual, but she was seldom attracted to women, and this woman did not fall into that narrow type. She wanted to flee back into the building. She knew that this woman was a threat by deep instinct. Or an ally. One or the other, certainly nobody to disregard.

No. She would not let them win. "Hello?" The woman had not reached her.

"Good to see that you're alive." The woman's long dark hair fell in curls over her slender shoulders. She was truly attractive, even her voice, which was deep and rich. Her eyes were almost black and pierced right through Laura. Not quite enough to intimidate, but enough to give... Vibes, yes. Laura was definitely getting vibes.

"It's a good state to stay in," Laura informed the stranger, keeping her tone as light as possible. So, was this some kind of trick, or did she have allies as well as enemies?

"I was a little worried I would be too late."

Laura reached up to rub her shoulder. It itched. Probably meant it was healing. "Look, whatever you have to say, say it. I'm not in the mood for any more games."

She half expected the stranger to pull a gun.

"Only that you need to stay alive. Whatever it takes. There will be somebody coming for you."

"Right, and how will I know he's not another trap." Laura regarded the other woman. She wished she had a joint. The pot would have settled her nerves. And got her arrested.

"How do you know I'm not one?"

Laura frowned, then, "I don't. I want to believe you're not, but...I need more information."

"Of course you do." The woman turned to walk away, without a further word or providing said information. She flicked her hair arrogantly.

"Bitch," Laura called after her. Well, see if she cooperated with people who gave cryptic statements and then left.

No, she was going to find the people who wanted her dead, turn them over to the cops, and then she was going to go back to school. Study something harmless, find a place in the world. Forget this had happened. Forget about Ella Miracle.

Yet, whoever that was had not hurt her. Just played with her head.

She went back inside, feeling no better than before. The next person to anger off was likely to get hurt. Badly hurt.

Had that been the woman's intent? Make her angry? Sharpen her up? It might have worked, but Laura did not take kindly to being manipulated. By anyone.

"You shouldn't go outside." That was Patrick.

"I'm going stir crazy. This is so letting them win. You know that. I can't hide forever."

"Just until we catch the guy."

"Oh, for... I know what you're going to try to push me into. Witness protection, never using my own name, losing my family, my friends, and what? Waitressing?" She finally voiced her fears.

"You'd be alive, which is more than we can say for your mother."

"She's not my mother. She wasn't my mother."

"She gave birth to you. For some reason, that puts you in their crosshairs. Would you rather put your parents through you dying?"

"Than them never seeing me again, never knowing whether I was alive, never seeing their grandchildren?" It wasn't fair. She hadn't met Ella Miracle, she hadn't asked for her life to be torn apart like this. She certainly hadn't done anything to deserve dying.

"It might be temporary."

"It might not." She regarded him, feeling the anger rise within her. She should not target him; he had been willing to kill for her. The problem was, he was the only one there. The only one she could reach.

"The important thing is your life."

"I don't think we're disagreeing there."

"We'll catch the guy. In the meantime, don't wander."

Don't wander. Like she was a little girl. A child. She watched him go, her eyes narrowed a little. Her breath came in, out; she forced it to be slower, steadier. More even. She even went as far as to close her eyes.

The sounds around her were purely human sounds, and the urge to escape returned. The urge to get out of here, to go somewhere there was sun and green grass. There had been something about that woman that had spoken of that to her.

Sun and green grass. "I need to get out of here."

She did not realize she had spoken out loud until she was answered.

"Cabin fever?" A female voice.

She turned. A blonde woman in a grey suit faced her, her hair drawn back from a severe face. "I guess you could call it that. I don't feel safe, I feel imprisoned."

"Oh, come with me." The woman reached to take her hand. "I have a prescription for that."

"Are you a doctor?" Those words came out without any conscious thought attached to them. Of course, this person was not a doctor. She was a cop.

"No, but I know exactly how you feel." There was a small canteen at the rear of the building. "I'd lose my job if I gave you booze, but let's get some iced cocoa and go out back."

It was warm enough to want one's cocoa iced, for sure, and the chocolate did help Laura's mood. "I just feel as if... I'm not a run and hide kind of person, you know?"

"They've already shot you once." The policewoman pointed it out gently. "I'm Barbara." Out back was a sort of yard garden, partly greened, mostly paved, with a couple of tables.

"I always figured cop stations as small and dark."

"The old one was. We got lucky when they gave us the new building. So, what's your college major?"

"I'm still deciding. And no, I am not considering criminal justice."

Barbara laughed. "You'd always be employed...sadly."

Laura thought about it and decided that was a sad thing indeed. As long as there were human beings, there would be a need for police...short of eliminating humanity or human free will. "Actually, I'm considering schoolteacher."

"Also always employed, but for a better reason." Barbara flickered a grin. "Doesn't pay as well as it might, though."

"My dad's rich, remember. There's enough money in my trust fund that I don't need to work, so I'm looking for something that will make me...well...feel like I'm worth having around." Doctor was too scientific. Besides, she'd always gotten along with younger kids.

"Then why work at all?"

"I'd get bored," Laura admits. "Maybe that's the real problem. Heh, I should get you guys to put me to work."

"Maybe. We probably have some civilian level stuff you could do. But we're going to move you tonight anyway. Safe house."

Laura sighed. "Where I'll do what? Sit around, do nothing, hide? I need to do something." Maybe she just wanted to feel that adrenalin rush again, but she knew she could not just sit there. "And don't give me the 'It's not my job'. It's me who got shot. It's me they want dead. It's me..." She tailed off.

"Maybe you should consider criminal justice after all."

5

The safe house was a big old Victorian out in the suburbs, with a high wall around the ill-kempt grounds. It crumbled a little, ivy covering the wall and reaching up between the windows of the house. They looked out with inner lids closed in the form of heavy curtains.

Laura felt the garden wall loom around her. She could not even call her parents. They were getting reassuring messages. Her thought of them caused a cold shaft to pass through her, not unlike that she had felt when Ella Miracle had died. No, not her parents. She turned. "I thought of something. Are my parents protected?"

"I believe they hired some pretty competent bodyguards. We have no reason..." Patrick had accompanied her. "...to think they're in any danger."

Of course not. "Well, if people will abduct kids to get to the parents... Maybe I'm just paranoid." She knew she should not have backed down so easily, but she was oddly tired. She needed rest, sleep. Time. Fresh air.

"Are you sure this place is safe?" She could feel her breathing increase; it did not seem as if she could get quite enough oxygen.

"As close to perfectly safe as anything short of a concrete bunker. Even most of the cops don't know where it is." Patrick's tone held practiced reassurance. He had done this before.

And they had not been followed, or had they? She felt cold again, unsafe. Exposed and contained all at the same time. I can look after myself. A litany, that, she knew, was not true. Not anymore. It would be again. She would make it so.

She would kick their butts again, and the next time she would do so in a way that was decisive. If she had to kill them, she would. She would do whatever she had to do to be left alone.

Patrick perhaps noted the setting of her jaw, for he spoke up, "And be careful. I know..."

"You don't know anything. Have you ever been in this situation?" Laura tried to bite back the words, but they escaped anyway, dogs off the leash.

"I have." The voice came from within the house. A man no longer young spoke. "Come in, please." He had grey hair, but did not stoop.

She felt, not familiarity this time, but a sudden sense of threat. That if she walked into this house, she would never walk back out. Unreasonable fear flowed through her. Why was there anyone there? Shouldn't the place be empty? Was he a caretaker?

Instinct took over and she broke and ran. She could hear Patrick calling her name, but what could she tell him? He was not the type to believe in hunches. Or...what? Did he know the guy? He hadn't said there would be anyone there. He hadn't warned her. He hadn't introduced them. Everything began to say past instinct and into logic that the man should not be there.

She had to put as much distance between herself and that house and that man as she possibly could. On foot, that would not be easy.

She needed a vehicle, but saw no way other than stealing one. Then a red convertible was pulling up at the curb. "Get in!"

Reason told her that was not wise. Reason had, though, told her to go into the safe house. Instinct told her to get in the car. Maybe it was a Transformer.

Leather seats. Driven by a young man whose eyes were hidden by shades. "Just in the nick of time."

"Who are you? And don't say a friend or..." She was starting to get tired of the cloak and dagger tricks.

"Clark."

"As in Kent?" She couldn't help it. But his presence somehow relaxed her. "Screw this. I want to go home." So much for the girl who did not swear. She had used more foul language in the last week than ever in her life. She glanced over. He did not look like Clark Kent. He had dirty blonde hair and features that spoke of England or maybe Scandinavia. He was not a small man, either, she noted.

"Are you sure? Home might not be safe." His voice carried a slight accent she could not place, despite the American name.

"If home isn't safe then my parents aren't safe. And if a safe house isn't safe, where is?" She forced her voice to slow down, aware she was babbling.

"Nowhere." Clark's tone was matter-of-fact.

She scowled at him. "That's not good enough. I want out of all of this."

"You don't have that choice. You'll understand once you find out everything." His tone had not changed, his emotions unreadable.

"Which you can't tell me, or don't know, or...how do I even know which side to be on?" She was aware of her voice raising again, becoming sharp, but she found she did not care.

"The one not shooting at you." He made it sound very simple. "You're on your own side, like everyone else. There's no real sides. But I'm not going to try and kill you and they are."

"And your friend from the cop station? Miss mystery girl?" She knew she was jumping to a conclusion.

"Oh, I'll talk to her. Did she scare you?" For a moment he offered a touch of concern.

"No, she pissed me off." He was not hiding the connection. Thus, he was the one who would be coming for her. It fit together too neatly.

"Good." Just that one word, his eyes turning back to the road.

Good that she was pissed off? No, she decided. Good that she didn't scare easy. That was, at least, one thing she had going for her. "I'm at the point where I just want answers. Now. Give them to me."

She knew she sounded like a total bitch. "Answers, or stop this car and let me out." She could dial 911, claim to have been kidnapped. Except she could not trust the police.

Or the police could not trust their own. The safe house had been compromised.

He spun the car up a side street. "Hold on."

He pulled off the side of the road, across a locked gate. "I'm supposed to keep you alive at all costs."

"So, who hired you?" He didn't look like a bodyguard, but she'd seen bodyguards who didn't look the part before. He was big enough, but there was something in his face and manner that was not quite right. She did not sense danger from him, but neither did she sense honesty.

"Nobody hired me. Let's just say I know your father." He removed the shades, revealing eyes of a clear grey-blue

"Can't be sure he is my father, given..." She tailed off. "Short of a blood test." And appearance-wise, she knew now that she favored her mother. "My father could be one of any number of men."

Clark shook his head. "There's ways of knowing."

She could see his chest rise and fall. He didn't want to tell her, that much was clear. He knew something. He knew who she was and he wouldn't tell her. She wanted, for a moment, to hit him. Might have, if he hadn't just rescued her. 'You were supposed to be a boy'. An heir, fathered on a woman who would never want to marry him, tucked away in safety? "Look. I know you don't want to tell me, but I am not going any further until I know what's going on. And who he is."

"I'll tell you what I can. I'm more worried about freaking you out than getting into trouble." He turned to face her, one hand still on the wheel. "The people trying to kill you are afraid of you."

"Even if I am a girl." Why did he think she would freak out if she knew who her father was? He was clearly not going to tell her.

He snorted. "I reckon it probably makes you more dangerous, but then, I've had my ass kicked by more than one woman."

She could not help but laugh at that. "Go on, unless you want to add another one." She was not sure she could kick his ass, but the words came out anyway. She felt angry, but also more alive. Did she really want to go home? Yes and no.

"By killing you they would significantly weaken your father's position. And potentially solve some other problems."

"He's fucking mob, isn't he." Maybe she could convince them she wanted and needed no part of this. Given what she knew of the mob, the only use they had for women was to look pretty on somebody's arm. Supposed to be a boy. Boys were useful. Girls...but this wasn't a thriller. She shouldn't immediately think organized crime.

"Not exactly." Clark was not quite looking at her.

"He's not Triad, or I'd have different eyes, and I doubt he's Russian."

"He's not a criminal. That much I can promise you. Although he wouldn't be above breaking the law to protect you until you can protect yourself."

"I've done a decent job so far."

"For an untrained girl, yes. We can't fix the girl part, but we can sure as heck fix the untrained part. Do you really want to go home?" The grey eyes turned back towards her. There was something in them that she could not read.

"I want to know my parents are alright...and don't tell me they're not my parents. My mother was a hooker and I never met my father. If he knew I existed, he could have..." She tailed off. "Led his enemies to me."

"You're learning. Unfortunately..." His hands had fallen into his lap, off the wheel, at some point. Now they started to lift again.

"I'm guessing that Ella requested my records, they had been watching her and broke in to steal them. She got in the way." It was a guess, but she could think of no other option.

"That's our guess too. So. What do you want to do?" As if she had the choice, his tone still entirely too calm.

"Erase the last few weeks. Failing that...I want to kick their butts and teach them a lesson. And keep my parents safe." She knew now she was going with him, even if he would not tell her the truth.

"I'll find out about them."

He did not sound sure or certain, though. Perhaps he was worried too, now the thought had been brought up. Well, good. His attitude was wearing on her. He didn't seem afraid at all. He didn't seem as if...well. He didn't seem to care. As if this was all a fun adventure for him.

Maybe it would be a fun adventure in the future, when she looked back on it and told her children. Right now, she was learning all about how uncomfortable adventures could be.

"Let's go, I guess." She had nowhere else she could go.

He hit the gas, the car roaring away with scant regard for such niceties as speed limits. Laura sat back. Her head had started to ache. The police would be looking for her. They would never understand why she had broken and run.

But she wasn't about to say any more to Clark, whoever he was. Strengthened and weakened positions. She wanted to tell Daddy dearest that all she wanted to do was graduate and teach school. Or some other quiet profession. That she would neither help him nor hinder him.

The wind roaring past lulled her, though, if not to sleep then at least to a quieter frame of mind. It made everything bearable.

Eventually, she slept.

* * *

Laura woke with a start, realizing that the car was pulling to a stop. Her thoughts were clearer now. The only evidence she had that Clark didn't intend to kill her was that he hadn't. Most likely, he wanted her alive, as that side road would have been a far better place to do it.

Now, they had stopped outside a house. An old farmhouse, around which a subdivision had sprouted like mushrooms. She was surprised it was not the middle of nowhere. Then again, maybe the middle of nowhere would have been checked first.

Clark got out, then opened the door for her like a gentleman. The air seemed clearer than the city, but not that clear. She wondered where she was. If she asked, would she get an answer?

It occurred to her that they had brought her to a place from which she could walk away. She could hear the sounds of children playing not that far away. It was a real subdivision in a real city. Her cell would probably work, but it would let the cops track her. She decided to leave it turned off. If all else failed, she could go to one of the houses. Say she had been kidnapped, ask to use the phone.

They were giving her an escape route...or the illusion of one. An excuse, perhaps, to say later that she had stayed of her own free will.

Clark pulled out a key and opened the door. Inside, there was a tank full of sea horses on one side of the door. They floated peacefully amongst thin strands of weed, tiny jeweled creatures.

She stopped to watch them. Living art, she thought, for they could have no other purpose. Untouchable, forever apart in their world of water. She felt apart herself. The odd sensation that even if she went home, she would never be able to go back.

Maybe being shot did that to you. The ache in her shoulder had faded away much sooner than the doctors had promised. That disturbed her a little, but maybe it was the adrenalin.

There seemed, right now, to be nobody else here. Nobody but her and the seahorses. Above the tank was the picture of a dark-skinned woman.

Finally Clark stepped inside. "Nancy's probably upstairs."

"Let me take a look at you." That would, she presumed, be Nancy, coming down from upstairs. "Hrm. Good condition, at least."

She turned. Nancy was a woman of Asian descent, who might have been twenty or fifty. Laura couldn't have told exactly what ethnicity she was, but the woman was large and muscular, quite the contrast to the normal image of Asian women as pretty and petite. She was also definitely not the woman in the picture. "You'll do. But we need to get some food into you."

Laura found herself following Nancy into a kitchen very like the one she was familiar with at home.

"Clark...could you make another supply run?"

Laura knew that was a way to get rid of him, but he flickered a grin, saluted her and left. "So, do I get the rest of the story yet?"

Nancy was rummaging in the fridge. "For now, you get a cheese sandwich."

Laura made a face. "I can walk out of here, you know."

"You'd last a week. Less if you went back into police protection."

"Well, you guys need me alive. I'm leaving unless I get answers."

Nancy's eyebrow arched, as she turned from the fridge with bricks of cheddar and Swiss. "You'd rather die than stay ignorant...but what if what you're ignorant of would be just as dangerous?"

"Look. I've been shot at and now all but kidnapped. I'm missing school. And I only have your assurances that this doesn't involve the mafia." Not that she really thought it did. Not quite. Why would they lie to her if they thought she was some mob princess?

"Your imagination is so narrow. The mob? Really? But then, perhaps that's a good thing. It keeps you safe."

"I'm not safe anymore." Laura was trying not to scowl at the woman.

The woman nodded. "Come."

She handed Laura her sandwich, then padded out of the room and down a short corridor. There was a door at the end. Beyond it was a dojo.

A full scale, wooden dojo. Maybe the original designers of the house had intended the room to be, oh, a ballroom or something. Now it had a Buddhist shrine at one end and various weapons arranged along the walls.

"I feel like I'm in one of those martial arts movies where the ignorant gaijin is trained by the master to face his enemies." Or her enemies, in this case.

Nancy's laugh echoed from the walls. "It does seem a cliché, doesn't it?."

"You give me some cliché about facing myself and I'll hit you with one of those staffs." Laura realized she was being smoothly diverted, but she knew she was going to get nothing from this woman.

Nancy just smiled. "Go ahead. Try."

* * *

Laura learned rapidly that trying to hit Nancy with one of those staffs was beyond her. She rather thought this was a horrible cliché. "This is ridiculous. Lawyers setting me up, bent cops, and now Asian martial arts experts?"

Nancy laughed. "Come, let's eat." She offered her a hand up. "And yes, I am an Asian combat expert, but don't expect to be winning any tournaments or learning..." She air quoted. "Kung fu."

"Then what am I?"

"The daughter of somebody I don't entirely trust."

Laura knew she did not mean Ella Miracle. "And you aren't going to tell me." Anger bristled through her words. "I'm not a child anymore."

Maybe to this woman, older, she was exactly that. If not a child, then at least young enough to appear to be one. As you got older, supposedly that happened.

"Not yet. There's a reason for it."

"To keep me safe. I'm not safe. I'm not safe here, I'm not safe anywhere."

Nancy lifted a hand. "True. Which is why we need to ensure your safety. And there's only one way to do that."

She was rummaging in the fridge. She did not pull out any kind of Chinese food, but rather leftover pizza, which she put in the oven.

"What is it?"

"Teach you how to ensure it yourself."

"Great. What's next? The training montage?" she found herself asking.

Nancy laughed. "It is a ridiculous cliché. But yes, we need to train you. To teach you how to be what you were born to be."

"Without telling me what that is."

"If I told you now...could you honestly say you wouldn't go looking for your father?"

Laura scowled. Because Nancy was right. She would. "You're implying I'd get myself killed."

"You would. For sure. You don't have the training yet, and the experience would take more time than we have."

She slid a slice of pizza over to Laura. "Eat."

Laura didn't want to eat. She didn't want to back down. Organized crime? Something else?

* * *

Laura really did feel as if she'd fallen into a martial arts movie, except that Nancy seemed not to be the classic sensei. More likely the movies were just plain wrong. In any case, she was not learning kung fu. Nancy said that in real fighting, you learned from everything...from krav maga, from capoeira, from western boxing, from whatever worked. You used what weapons you had. "Again," Nancy said, calmly. "And as if you mean it this time. You will not hurt me."

The padded floor had a spring to it. Laura already knew hitting it was unpleasant but not damaging. On the other hand. "Okay." The smell of wood and sweat filled her nostrils.

A step inwards, reaching for Nancy's wrist...and missing yet again. The woman was not holding back against her.

Laura already ached all over, but she had learned that her speed of movement in the fight had been no fluke. Maybe her father was Captain America, she thought ruefully, dodging Nancy's counter attack.

No weapons, right now. She circled to the side, bare feet feeling the floor as surprisingly comfortable. With little effort, she drove all awareness of anything but the fight out of her.

No weapons. Most of the time, no weapons, although she had also been working with a gun, out back, a solid target. The neighbors either did not know or did not care.

"Again." That was all Nancy said, dark eyes focused on her.

This time, she managed to get a grip, feeling the other woman's strength. An intimacy of sorts, but then it was Laura who hit the ground, bouncing from the floor. Automatically, she rolled back to her feet. Aiming a strike towards Nancy's midsection this time. It landed lightly.

"Better. Remember, in a real fight, the opponent seeks your life. Always remember that."

"Not always." She circled again, looking for an opening.

"One way or another. Your death or your life. Remember that." Her voice never rose from those soft tones.

Laura had seen her angry only once. She sought never to repeat the experience. There was something powerful and old about the woman, something which would have made her look for fangs had she not seen her out in daylight. The herbs in the kitchen, not all of which were culinary...or even safe.

She tried for a sweep. The Asian hit the ground, rolled back to her feet. Your death or your life echoed.

Nancy had her life. Wanted more from it still. Focus on the fight, she told herself.

It was becoming harder and harder as time went on, as her awareness that time had passed intensified.

She did not want to focus on the fight any more. She wanted to know what she was fighting for. In the doorway, Clark was standing. Watching her. She was not sure what he wanted. She was not sure she wanted to know.

* * *

Clark and Laura walked through the woods. Away from the houses.

Somehow she knew that they would not be seen, even here. Nothing disturbed this, this bubble of space and time. How long had it been? A month? Two?

"I have to...I can't stay here, Clark."

"Sure you can. Where else are you going to go?"

She turned slightly towards him. Home, she wanted to say. Should she go home? Her mother, always there for her. Her father, rarely present, but supportive even during his absences. She knew he had to make the money to sustain their lifestyle. She knew that was his one priority, and she knew that was not going to change.

Home.

What would happen if she went home? "They're probably looking for my body."

"Big deal," Clark said. "You'll lead your enemies to them. Besides..." He tailed off.

He didn't admit to what Laura worried he was about to admit to. Always on the edge of things, always watching. Seldom intervening. She wondered why he stayed.

Maybe he was the lookout.

Maybe he was staying for some other reason. "Clark...I can't keep doing this. It's been weeks, and I need to know what's going on in the wider world."

"The same that's always going on, Laura. Humanity continuing on its road of destruction. And not enough of us to stop it. Just me, just you, because everyone leaves. They always leave."

"Maybe I'm not as cynical as you are." She turned from him, walked back up the hill to the house. The house that did not fit amongst its neighbors. She didn't ask herself what he meant by everyone leaving. She didn't want to know, or she told herself that.

Clark was not like Petey. He was not gross, he was not pushing her. But he wanted her to be like him. He wanted to change her. Maybe he wanted to fix her.

She needed out. Not wanted, at this point. Needed.

What had started out as a way to be safe was rapidly becoming a prison.

6

Her parents could not be contacted. They were not answering their phone. "Now I know how Luke felt on whatever that planet was."

"Dagobah," came Nancy's voice from behind. "But I won't tell you anything about falling to the dark side. The only side you need to be on is your own."

"I prefer a little more actual morality than that." She turned to face the older woman. "I'd like to be one of the good guys. Whoever they are. I saw you in the garden. I saw the light. I..."

"You don't have to be. You're who you are regardless of what you do."

"And who the heck am I? Every time I ask, I get blown off. Do you think me knowing would bring the bad guys down on us? Or that I won't believe you? I know I'm not normal." She felt like she was in a comic book, now, more than a martial arts flick. She felt unreal for a moment, as if her tenuous grip on herself weakened with each strange event. Nancy standing with light around her, it vanishing immediately when she realized Laura was watching her. Magic? Superpowers?

"Laura..."

"Don't 'Laura' me. I want the truth, and I want it now." For a couple of months, she had been content, or at least too tired to question. She was learning, though. She felt now as if she could protect herself. She needed her whys not her whats.

"The truth is that you wouldn't believe me. I can tell what kind of person you are. You need your proof, your evidence for everything. But at least you can open your mind to other possibilities."

"Which is another brush off. What if I walked out of here and went it alone?"

"You'd probably survive at this point." Nancy reached out, rested one hand on her shoulder. "If I told you now, in your current state of mind, you probably wouldn't."

"I can take it. Whatever it is, I can take it."

"No," Nancy said sadly. "You can't."

"For crying out loud, Nancy..."

That was the last straw. Laura had few things here...a small bag was all she needed. She walked away, out into the bright suburban streets. For the first time in a weeks, she turned on her cell phone.

Her voice mail was long since full. She deleted the messages unheard as she walked along the street. Then, she thought to look back. The house was gone. In its place was a clapboard semi, just like all the others on the street.

What flowed through her was not quite fear. It was an uncertainty, reality seeming to ripple around her. The ground no longer solid under her feet. Nancy was real. The house was real. Clark and the car, real.

Or she was hallucinating, but in that case...then again, she might have hallucinated the last two months. She looked at the time and date on her cell phone. It had been two months alright.

Two months. Could she really have left at any time? A bus stop. No schedule attached to it. Nobody to call.

Her friends all thought she had dropped out, no doubt. Maybe she should have listened to those messages.

Had her enemies got what they wanted, in the end? Her life was interrupted, over. A bus came, rattling along the street. She had no clue where it came from or where it went to, other than away from here.

She climbed aboard anyway. What did it matter where she was going when she had nowhere to go? The bus seemed normal. Full of ordinary people on ordinary errands. She sat at the back and pressed her face to the window.

Magic. Maybe her father was a magician. No...it seemed to be something deeper than that. If there was real magic, then it would have to be taught, surely. What she could do seemed far more inherent.

A shiver suddenly ran through her...possibilities that she had not considered. The lead one was that her father was a vampire. Kinda like Blade. That would explain a lot. There was something going on that went past the merely natural. Including how much she had learned in two months, although she knew Nancy knew far more. Far more than one woman had a right to do, and Nancy herself had scoffed at any of the quips Laura had made about ancient, immortal sages in a way which made her wonder if she really was one.

The bus rumbled past more subdivisions and finally came to a halt at the edge of what seemed to pass for downtown here. She thought she was somewhere in the sprawl between New York and Philadelphia and DC. However, for all she knew, it could have been Illinois.

For all she knew. She stepped out into the light, followed by a black man who immediately lit a cigarette. The smoke blew into her face and she turned away.

She should not have gone with them. Except the alternative...

Her cell rang. She answered it without looking, but with a short hello, rather than her name.

"Laura? Is that you?"

She recognized the voice. Oh gods. It was Petey.

"It's me." She had wanted to say no, but even he deserved to know she was, at least, not dead.

"Where the hell have you been?"

"I can't tell you that. It's a long story and..." In all the movies, they warned people not to say stuff over cell phones. "Look. I'm alive, I'm okay, and that's all I'm saying right now." She let her old anger with him flow, hoping it would drive him away.

"Laura..."

"Just tell everyone I'm alive." She hung up on him, turned the phone back off with a click. She should not be using it anyway, and if the only person calling her... She hated him, but she did not want him dead. Not anymore.

Was she a better person? No, just a stronger one. How did she become a better one?

She did not know. But she saw a sign that told her where she was. Frederick, Maryland. Nowhere important.

A long way to New York from here, but far from unattainable. She just needed to find a bus to a train station, then get the local up. They had left her somewhere she would not be stranded.

She wondered if the house had even been in the same place all the months she had been there. Magic was real...there was no other explanation, even if her mind wanted to recoil from it. To flee back into rationality.

The wind caught her hair, and across the street she saw a man in a suit. He drew her eye, and not in a good way.

How had they found her so quickly? She ignored him, not so much in the hope that he would go away as in the hope that he would not act on his own. Did he detect any difference in her?

She wished she had a gun herself. Nancy had had guns, she should have taken one. They wanted her to stay alive, would they begrudge her a weapon?

It was crowded. She felt that as a burden. If there was a fight here, somebody else might get hurt. She did not want anyone to get hurt except the enemy.

The enemy, she would take out. Not cheerfully, but without hesitation or uncertainty. 'You don't have to be on any side other than your own'. Maybe she would add Nancy and Clark to the list.

No. They had genuinely helped her, even if they had done so under false pretenses. Why had they not simply...

Because she wouldn't have believed them. Her perception seemed to expand for a moment. Three more men. All wearing the same suits, one of them already reaching for a gun.

"Game's on," she murmured to herself.

And the first round was to lead them somewhere they would not be able to bring harm to anyone else.

* * *

The second round was to take them down. She wasn't armed, but as she moved into the deserted parking garage, she could already see options. Anything can be a weapon. If you have no other weapon, you always have your own body. The lights flickered a little, as if the power to them was fluctuating.

And then the men were there. "I see you wanted to take it outside," one of them said.

"I don't see any point in involving anyone else." She felt familiar heightened awareness flow over her. These people would not take her down. They would go down themselves. Four against one?

Bad odds, and she did wish for a bit of assistance. Then she saw it. A motorcycle.

More to the point, a motorcycle with the keys in. Anything can be a weapon. She had noticed it. They, it seemed had not. The guns came out.

"Oh, come on, how about making this fair. Four on one, you think you can't take me unarmed?" Could she dodge a bullet?

"I'm sorry. I actually am sorry," their leader said. "I realize you haven't done anything yet."

"Yet. Ever occur to you that trying to kill me was the best way to make sure I did something? I didn't think so." Words delayed action.

The motorbike. She measured the distance with her eyes. The wound from before had healed without a scar. If she got shot again, she might not be so lucky.

They fired as she moved, all four of them. She could almost see the bullets, sense them move through the air.

She dodged three. The fourth lodged in her thigh, missing the vital artery. She hissed but leapt for the bike anyway. "Not bad shooting. My turn."

The pain flowed through her leg, not as bad as it would be, but enough to cause her to grit her teeth. She forced herself to focus. Great. Another trip to the hospital, and this time with no ID she could show. She gunned the bike towards them. It was a nice machine. She felt few qualms about stealing it.

The men scattered, firing. But this time they did not hit anything other than the fairing, sending spider cracks through it. She ducked, and then the bike hit one of them. The impact threw her to one side.

Drop and roll. That was actually a conscious thought, albeit a vague one. It was not completed before she was back on her feet...then dropping again, this time to snag the gun the impact had knocked clear.

More conscious thoughts intruding. Stance, recoil. She aimed it at the one who had been doing the talking. The man she hit was unconscious, but not dead. "I'm not afraid to kill you."

"Then there will simply be more. You can't get away, Laura Maxwell."

"Yes, I can." She fired, feeling the recoil in her hands, smelling the faint hint of gunpowder. She did not aim to kill him. She aimed for his knee.

She had never shot anyone. She had never imagined herself capable of doing so. The gun bucked in her hand, the sound louder than anything she had ever heard. He fell in apparent slow motion, clutching his knee.

She had probably just crippled him for life. She could not bring herself to care.

The others had, though, backed away. They had not thought her capable of it. They just wanted her dead.

"Hell, guys, I'm probably not even the person you're looking for." One last try at words.

No response. She broke, diving for the bike, using the gun to sweep a path ahead of her. Her leg burned and itched, less pain and more...she could not be sure what. Firing again, this time not trying to hit the man, just to get him back, get him away. Onto the motorbike and firing it up. It was damaged, but not beyond repair. She rode straight at them, and they scattered like deer. Shots followed her as she left, but she felt no impact, no red heat and cold pain.

Then she was out in the open street where, surely, they would not follow. Her heartbeat was loud in her ears, her breathing had become difficult. Her blood seemed to be roaring.

Breathe, she told herself. Breathe. She still had the gun tucked into her pocket. Safety. She turned the safety on, before she accidentally shot herself. That would be a great end to the day.

Only then did it occur to her that she might have stepped outside the law. Would the police accept self-defense if that man brought assault charges.

Her life would never return to normal now. No, that ship had already sailed when she had vanished from witness protection, vanished from life for two months. It was mere fantasy that she could pick up the pieces. Now...

7

Home was the one place Laura knew she should not go. By that point, it was where she needed to be. Her parents would be the next target, she was sure of that. Or, rather, she was trying to think like her enemies. Was that how the cops did those things? Her leg still throbbed, but only faintly. It already looked as if she had been injured a week ago, not a matter of a few short hours. She thought about the spars, about the way her bruises had seemed to vanish. She had never taken real injury before. Her mother, wrapping her in cotton wool. Inadvertently hiding this from her? Or was this why? She turned in her mind to face reality. She had super powers. So, she was sure, did Nancy.

She rode the stolen bike through the gate, security not questioning her beyond one call of 'Helmet'.

Yeah, she needed to get hold of one of those. She was going to make sure her parents were still alive, and then she was going to get her butt well away from here.

They did have competent bodyguards, after all. Far more competent than her. One of them would probably have handled the ambush without kneecapping somebody. For...

Yet, she felt no twinge in her conscience about the matter. She felt nothing for the man she had crippled. He was the enemy. He had been trying to kill her, and she could easily have killed him.

Maybe she should have...that would have guaranteed not having to worry about him again. Killing them all would have sent a message, and part of her feared she was capable of just that.

Maybe blood was telling. Nature over nurture. She stopped across the street from her parents' house. If she went in, they would order her to stay. Demand that she be within whatever security cordon they could afford.

That would not be enough. Whoever was behind this would not stop until she convinced them she was not who they wanted. Or took them out.

That was a cold thought. She stayed there, wishing for a helmet to hide her hair and face.

If she went inside...and her scalp prickled. Too late, she knew she had made her worst mistake. She had, like as not, led them here.

Then she knew she had not. They were here already. A shadow in the back yard, and she reached for the gun. Quickly, too automatically. She felt time slow again. As if she was born for this.

A shadow, moving away from the house. She feared the person's work was done. Feared that it was far, far too late for her parents.

And she moved towards the house, the bike left where it was. Her leg twinged again, protesting its treatment, but it was too late. The world exploded into light and sound.

An impact in her back was all she remembered of the next few seconds, and then nothing until she was slowly picking herself up.

The house was on fire. Flames licked around it, devouring it. She would not cry. She would not scream. They might not be home. Whether they were or not, there was nothing here for her except bruises and pain and fear. Something within her locked into place. Something cold and certain. She could not permit this to slow her down or even stop her.

Cell phone. She pulled it out, turned it on, dialed 911. She heard her own voice as if from a distance calling for firefighters and an ambulance. Would they think she had caused this? She was a hardened criminal by now, she thought.

Her parents might be dead. Her life was over. Going into witness protection...would not have saved them.

It occurred to her to hide the stolen bike, but she could not leave. Could not bring herself to. She put it in the yard of a house that had been for sale, empty, for the last three months, and then stood there, watching the fire as if it held her mind. As if it was pure fascination...like a pyromaniac. She could not take her eyes away from it.

Sirens were ablaze in her ears, taking away what remained of her thought. She was a frozen statue of a woman as they started to pour water onto the flames. The flames began to die, fading away.

Half of her stuff had been in there. Most of it, even. All gone, but stuff was not as important as...

She just watched. Firefighters hunting through the house, and she knew what for. More sirens, the police, forming a blue line around the house.

One of them walked over to her. "What did you see?"

"A man...I'm pretty sure man, not woman, but I can't tell you more than that, sneaking out of their back yard. Then the explosion."

"Your eyebrows are singed."

She reached up. They were. "I guess I was a little close."

He was going to arrest her. She could just feel it. Was she being paranoid?

"What's your name?"

She hesitated a moment, not wanting to give it, but knowing she had to. "Laura Maxwell. I lived there."

The cop fell worryingly silent. It was clear to anyone that had anyone been in the house, they would be gone. "Well, we don't have any proof it wasn't a gas explosion yet."

"I saw an intruder, but you're right. It could have been a neighbor cutting through the back yard." Not at all unfeasible. "This place has all kinds of security, after all."

The cop frowned. "We're going to need to talk to you."

She lifted her hand again. She hated herself for the odd distance she felt from the situation. These were her parents, probably dead, the people she loved, and she felt nothing.

Shock, perhaps. Certainly it qualified as that. Her breath came in, then out as the cop walked away. Leaving her standing there, watching. If there was foul play, then she would find out who did it...and she had that gun.

Or maybe it would be crueler to get him arrested. Let him spend all of those years in jail. She had no moral high ground left, and she wanted to walk away. She could not, not without knowing.

She hated herself, her enemies, her birth mother for putting her in this situation, then hated herself more for thinking like that.

The cop was back after a brief moment, reaching a hand towards her. The other was on his radio. His eyes were cold, brown, uncaring.

She knew for sure, then, she was about to be arrested. Her parents were dead and she was going to jail for their murder. Without thinking about the logic of the matter, she turned and fled.

* * *

Her credit card still worked. She used it to buy a helmet and leathers at a biker store. Ironic, that, given she had stolen the bike. She would have returned it if she could, but she could not. She needed it, and doubted her funds ran to replacing it. Then it occurred to her...the police would trace the card. Use it to follow her. She tossed it in the ditch before she left.

At first, she was just getting out of the way. The police might think she did it. They might think that the people from the lawyers' office did it. Either way, they would be looking for her, whether to arrest her or to fail to protect her. Nancy had said to avoid police custody. Of course, how much could she trust Nancy?

There was no way she could go back from here. Laura Maxwell was as dead as her parents.

All she could do was survive. She rode towards downtown. This had been her home, her world for the years of her childhood. There was the playground, just inside the gates, where they let her play on her own. She could see the squat shape of the elementary school. The high school had been demolished and rebuilt right after she graduated. A good thing, to. That building had felt like a prison. Her parents had not felt the need for private school. Not when the public school was considered one of the best in the state.

Memories flowed around her. She did not, however, go past the high school, but rather glided onto Main Street. A modernized Main Street. Chain restaurants, a McDonald's, a couple of boutiques. The doggy day care was new. She stopped, looked through the window, saw two young dogs playing. Wished she could take one of them with her.

Her parents had never let her have a dog. Her parents were dead. It was her fault. No, not her fault. She could not blame herself for the actions of the bad guys. If she went down that road, she would break down.

It had been done to hurt her, to anger her.

It had succeeded. She pulled up outside a cafe where she had eaten lunch with her mother so many times. Talked about women's stuff. She wondered if she would ever now be able to contemplate marriage and children.

Or if she would be inside a federal penitentiary. She had committed a number of crimes, after all, good for a few years behind bars. Had she killed anyone? She was not sure. If she had not, she likely would before this was over.

She would rather die than go to prison. She would rather live on the lam...but wasn't that the same thing as witness protection?

Certainly, she could not stay here, where she might be recognized. Likely would be at any moment, but she felt too out of it to ride. Too...drained was the word that came to mind. Emptied.

She walked, instead, wheeling the bike. Knowing she would have to run if she saw the cops. Or should she run? It might make her look guilty.

She had been seen there, riding a hot motorcycle, no helmet. Everything looked worse than bad.

"Dammit," she muttered. She would give anything at this point for her parents back. Failing that, for all of this to be somehow forgotten.

Almost anything. She would not become an assassin...even though she feared she was well suited to it. Perhaps especially. She knew exactly what she could turn into. She'd seen it in the movies, those men who could kill, straighten their ties, and go about their business. Unaffected. The James Bond effect.

She was certainly not unaffected, but she could build towards that. Train towards it. Become it. She shuddered. No. She would keep her conscience.

She saw Patty Barnes before, thankfully, the other woman saw her. Did she run? She could hope that she would not be seen, but instead, she ducked inside a cafe, into a ladies room. Not that Patty wouldn't squeeze her bulk after her if she had recognized her.

If Patty knew what had happened and saw Laura relatively calm...well, she could jump to all kinds of conclusions. Hopefully, she would consider that maybe, just maybe, over even this she would not make a scene in public. That was a big part of what was keeping her from turning into a sobbing mess.

When she came out, though, Patty had not moved. Blue eyes rested on her from underneath white hair that benefitted from curlers. "Laura...what's going on?"

She wanted to snap out nothing. Or none of your business. "Don't worry about it," was what she managed, in a reasonably civil tone of voice. Anything she told Patty would be the common property of the neighborhood within a day.

Her presence would be known within an hour. Patty was the last straw. She had to leave, and she had to leave now. "I'm fine."

"You don't look fine. What happened?"

Laura would once have simply acquiesced to the gossip. Now she looked at her. "I'm not telling you anything. I don't want it getting back to certain people." Edited truth. She didn't want her presence getting to the cops or to Nancy or to anyone involved.

"You're in trouble, aren't you?"

"Patty. Go away." She had never spoken with actual authority in her life. Now she did, regarding the older woman with an expression that actually made her pale, then turn and hurry away.

Great. She would still tell everyone what happened, except it would now be about how Laura Maxwell had gone insane. No, she thought, where Patty was concerned, she had gone sane. The woman needed a bit of harsh treatment, to learn where her nose was not wanted or welcomed.

Laura ran back towards the bike. At least she looked like she owned it now. And besides, she did not want to fall on her head. She stood there, looking up and down Main Street. She heard sirens in the distance.

She had never planned on coming back here for good, once college was done with. Now, she felt even more distance. Bland suburbia enveloped her. Their concerns were petty compared with somebody trying to kill her. She did not care about who was sleeping with whom.

The skies were turning grey. She knew she should leave, but instead she cruised along the length of Main Street. Now that coming back was not an option, she sought to savor all of it in her memory. To store it up where nobody could take it from her.

A sudden sense of urgency alerted her. She did not know its origin, only that instinct took over. She gunned the accelerator...just in time.

They were on foot, thankfully, but they had her in a cross fire. She crouched low over the bike, praying nothing hit her. She could think of no defense other than prayer and speed. Shooting back was not something she could countenance. Not here. A bullet could so easily go through a window into a restaurant, into a store. Into the flesh and bone of an innocent.

Now she wondered where the cops were. Out investigating the fire? This was not a place that had or needed cops in any force, no doubt the only reason she hadn't bumped into them yet.

She swept by the mall, clear of the ambush, and kept going. What else could she do? They might get ahead of her, except for one thing. She was sure that she knew this place better than she did. A quick swing to the right, through a cheaper neighborhood.

No gates here. Smaller houses, people watching her from their porches. Children looking up. If they followed her here...

They did not, and slowly her heart rate returned to normal. She did not know quite how she had not been hit, like something in the movies. Plot immortality, her friend had called it. You know he won't die, he's too important. She's too pretty.

This was not a movie. She did not have the protection of the almighty writers. A bit of laughter came out at that thought. The only person, in the end, who could keep her alive was herself. She hoped she could manage it, suspected she would not. She might not want to die, but she was not entirely sure she feared it. Whatever was going on, her view of the world had to change. It had to grow to encompass this, or else she would cease to be the person she was. Well, no. It was too late on that.

She saw the cops before they saw her. They had no reason to stop her, she told herself, riding casually past them...but two of them jumped onto bikes and took off after her.

She could run, she could give up, or she could fight. The last was not something she was willing to countenance. She would not hurt the police, who were only doing their jobs. Who had no quarrel with her, nor she with them.

"Please pull over."

"What's the trouble, Officer?" she called. She would feel both stupid and angry if it was a broken light or something similar. Some damage done during the firefight.

"We're looking for a young woman. I just need to see your ID." His tone was gentle, but firm.

Run. That was the only option. Her ID would tell them who she was. She had no license or registration for the bike. She gunned the accelerator. Now they would know she was guilty. She had proven it, but she had to. She would die in a cell; the enemy could find her too easily there. They would have killed her in the safe house. In any safe house the police had.

She was not willing, yet, to die. She had, for now, to get away from this poor cop. It was not his fault, none of it, and she did not wish to risk hurting him.

A high-speed chase was dangerous, and he was pushing on her tail, forcing her to ride faster and faster. At least he was not shooting. Of course, that would endanger everyone around, not just her. Not just him. She had a gun, but she was not going to use it.

How the heck did she get away from him? She swung down another narrow road. An orange cat fled under a car as they approached, she briefly saw yellow eyes glaring at her. Not a happy feline at all. But a safe feline, as long as he stayed out of the way.

At the main road, she turned left, cutting across traffic. What was she doing? This was not the way to handle this, but if she stopped and got off, she was toast.

If she...how did she lose him? Then she heard the gunshot. It came from somewhere up ahead, crackling into the air, striking nothing. Instead of running, she crouched as close to the windshield as she could and sped up. She rode right towards them, right into the fire.

The gunfire faltered. Good. They were as thrown by it as she would have been. The cop peeled off. He probably thought they were together.

She prayed he would not be hit...and there. There was the gunman, thinking he was hidden in a hedge. Rather than pull her own gun, she simply turned the bike towards him as if to ride him down. At the last moment, she turned and sped away.

Neither the man nor any bullets followed her.

8

Out of town, the road under her wheels and the wind blowing through what of her hair stuck out under the helmet. Her emptiness filled with grief. She could not stop. They would pursue her forever now. Filling gas at a two-bit station in the middle of nowhere, she found herself removing her helmet so she could better see. No enemies or friends seemed to be in sight, only the scrawny red-haired kid who worked there, his neck about eighty percent Adam's apple.

He watched her, as if assuming she would leave without paying. She paid with the very last of her cash. She would have to earn or steal more now...she did not dare use her credit cards again. They could track her that way.

Should she try and find Nancy again? Tell the woman she had been wrong and right. She had not saved her parents. They were dead and she was alone. She had turned her back on her only allies.

Idiot, she told herself as she got back on the bike. Any moment now, the cops would show up. Or the bad guys. Or the bad guys dressed as cops. What could she do?

Die, a small voice told her. Or live caged. Neither option was acceptable. The former might be better than the latter, but she wanted... She just wanted to be Laura Maxwell.

Faking her death looked more and more appealing with each mile she traveled. If she could work out a good way to do it. The obvious one was to be seen in a car, then have it show up with a charred corpse in it, but where did she get the corpse? And what if they tested her DNA? Was her DNA on file? She was not sure whether it was or not. She had not had a sample taken, although she would if it would prove innocence or guilt in terms of paternity. For now, though? She had dental records, and she would never be able to match those.

She thrust the idea aside. She focused on the road as it flowed past under her wheels. Sooner or later she would have to commit more crimes.

Or...no. She dared not use her own name, her own ID, but there were ways. The cash economy existed everywhere; she just had to find it.

The road enveloped her. She had no idea where she was going. West, into the mountains, a subconscious destination.

She stopped at a lookout, surrounded by forest. One entire swathe of trees was dead, stripped of all of their bark except for thin strips. Some pest, no doubt, but it made the grief hit her again. Grief and the desire for vengeance that warred with what remained of her better self.

'You don't have to be on any side but your own.'

Right now, she wasn't sure what her side even was or whether she should be on it or not.

"Dammit," she said to the air. Was she damned? No, she was just lost. Confused. Uncertain.

They would find her even here, where the air was clear and city problems seemed as far away as the distant ocean. They knew where she was now, they knew who she was. The image in her mind was of hounds having her scent.

Fighting being so natural, she wondered if they could actually take her. Was it...no, that was a crazy idea. Genes did not determine who you were. Who her father was did not affect who she was.

"Dammit." Her own voice sounded unpleasant to her ears, like the voice of a stranger. She was a stranger to herself. She did not know this woman who enjoyed fighting and was good at it, who walked through darkness and fire as if it was nothing. Where was Laura Maxwell? Still in there, somewhere, she told herself.

"Such language from a lady." The voice was male, it came from behind her.

The gun was inside her jacket. She moved a hand towards it as she half turned. "I'm not a lady."

It was another biker. She was not sure how she had missed his approach. He gave her the elevator stare. "Sure look like one to me."

Any other time, she would have slapped him. Right now, she just shifted her stance. "I don't know whether that's a compliment or an insult." He looked to her like a classic biker type. Jacket, helmet under one arm, hair not trimmed in months if not years. Beard, same note.

Hell's Angel. Was she already in hell? Maybe she had died and it was all a hallucination, like a really bad movie she once watched. No, that was solipsism, by the back door. She did not believe that, but this man...

She could take him in five seconds. That was the assessment, which held its own certainty. Nancy's training had awakened in her this...desire to fight as well as the skill to. It was tension within her right now. She did not really want to hurt him...she had no reason to. Not unless he started something with her.

"Pretty girl like you shouldn't travel alone." The flirtation seemed almost automatic. He did not seem to be as serious as she would have at first assumed him to be. As if it was part of the biker image to do this to every female he met. That did not make it any less patronizing or annoying.

"I can look after myself." Her gaze slid over him, an almost male belligerence. 'You were supposed to be a boy'.

Well, she wasn't. And her reaction to that was the same as it had been to start with.

"Yeah, right." He clearly did not believe her, genuine concern mingling with male arrogance.

She did not reach for the gun. Instead, she went with a move Nancy had taught her. Time slowed as she stepped forward, grabbed his wrist and spun...so that she was behind him holding his arm. The smell of his cheap aftershave filled her nostrils. A moment, and she released him. "Like I said."

"Damn, woman, maybe you can!" His tone was impressed as he stepped back, turning to face her again. "Heck with it." He offered her his hand. "Simon."

"Laura." She shook hands with no testing grip. No need for last names, either. He knew that if he wanted to rape her...it would prove difficult. She had established that, and she felt on safe footing. The unkempt hair was brown, secured with a leather thong. She supposed he was around thirty, perhaps a little more.

"So, what's your story? Don't tell me you don't have one. It's in your eyes." He stepped back a little, making some distance between the two of them.

"Nothing I need help with." She did not want to tell him she feared for his life if he got involved. She did, though. He was big and slow and...

...and she was interrupted by the roar of three more bikes coming up into the lookout. As she turned, they drew guns. Tinted helmets hid their faces and eyes. Unmarked leathers gave only anonymity.

"Down!" she yelled. Simon was already hitting the deck, almost as quickly as she did. She was trying to get her own weapon free of its makeshift holster. Not an easy task in a prone position, and they were approaching, preparing to fire again. The tarmac under her was gritty and it dug into her cheek.

Then she heard another shot. Simon had apparently been packing himself. It sounded like a sawed-off shotgun. She did not want to think of the damage done to human flesh and blood, but her own pistol was free. She fired, not really caring...the best aim she could manage was to actually hit the person. The bullet spun him around, slamming into his chest.

Hell. She had quite possibly just killed a man. Grief washed over her, but her body knew what it needed to do. No thought accompanied the second shot, hitting the second man in the arm. Two of the three were down. Then Simon managed to pump the shotgun, get off a second shot.

Now they were all down. The gun dropped against Simon's leg and a cell phone seemed to materialize in his hand. "We call 911, then we get out of here, and you tell me what's going on."

Laura wasn't going to argue with him. After all, he had been shot at. He was owed an explanation.

She stepped away as he made the call, on what looked like a cheap disposable phone. He tossed it into the bushes as they left.

"I owe you the price of a phone." She tried to keep her tone light, but her heart was still pounding. Her body was refusing to come out of fight or flight mode, and she could not convince it otherwise.

"Eh," he said. "I'm the one who chose to start shooting." The shotgun vanished back inside his jacket. Somehow.

She wondered how many men he had killed. As the adrenalin flowed away, it left a small knot in her stomach. She was not sure if it was guilt or fear of being caught. That, of course, scared her even more. If she did not feel guilt, did that make her a sociopath? Or did it just make her angry? She hopped onto the bike as he roared off, gunned it in his wake.

Not that she trusted him. But she did owe him...an explanation and quite a few favors. Those favors would be collected in time, she was sure of it.

'You don't have to be on any side but your own.' Bullshit, she told the echo in her head. But what side was she on? Her own...that was the truth of it. Beyond that? What place was there for a young woman who had discovered within herself the capability to kill? Would she end up working for the government? For the mob? How could she trust herself to teach school now? Around all of those kids?

Simon pulled off the road into a parking lot. A freeway roared past not far away, and a small building with 'Jane's Place' on the roof rested at the edge of the lot. It looked quite welcoming and homey. Not really a place where a couple of rough-edged bikers would be welcome.

A small country store, a few tubs of mass-produced ice cream. Fridge magnets and bumper stickers. Road snacks. It held an air of normalcy that she could not shake off, no matter how hard she tried.

A diner was attached to it. Cheap but clean, manned by waitresses in traditional red checked uniforms. It looked like a diner she might hallucinate. Booths and tables and a display case full of delicious looking pies.

No hostess. Simon moved over to a booth and sat down. She sat down opposite. There was a red plastic tablecloth on the table, placemats that advertised truck repair and fresh honey. The usual condiments. It made her feel more real and solid.

"I'd say you have a hold on me," Simon began. "But I think it's mutual. Who's after you?"

"I'm not entirely sure. There's weird shit going on." She let her hands rest on the table. Looked down at them. They were...clean. Somehow she thought they shouldn't be. "I want my life back, but I don't see it happening." She felt as if she owed him more truth than she might have otherwise given.

"In these mountains?" From his tone, the skepticism could have been for either.

She shook her head. "It started in New York. Weird ass shit." She knew she was repeating herself, but she sure as heck didn't care right now.

"Can't be any weirder than some of the stuff I've bumped into."

"Oh, I don't know. I've been wondering if any of it's real." She stopped as the waitress showed up. "Cheeseburger?" she ordered. Could she even afford it, or would she be forced to leave Simon with the bill? She could not bring herself to do that, but...

"Burger special," Simon said, turning back to her only when the young woman had left. "Save room for pie," he suggested.

Having seen the contents of the glass case, she was not about to argue. And at least the food here was cheap. Very cheap. "Well, first of all, they seem to be after me because my birth father was somebody important."

"Happens."

"Not when your birth mother's a prostitute and they can't even prove the guy concerned was your father." She regarded him evenly. She couldn't believe she was telling everything to this stranger, except that he could probably have just walked away. Left her to them. Could she even be sure she might not have done just that?

"Okay. So, maybe they're trying to remove any chance of an heir, legitimate or otherwise." He was frowning, now.

"Money?" Most things boiled down to money, good or bad. Only irrational instinct told her there was more to it. "Yeah, probably money."

"So, do you have an action plan?" He laced his fingers together, regarding her over them.

"Got the cops after me too," she admitted. "My initial plan was to prove to them I wasn't who they were looking for."

"And if you are?" The question had to be asked, and it was given in such even tones that she might wonder if he cared.

"Then I'll take them all out." That came out before she thought about it. It was definitely not words she had intended to use. Any response Simon intended was delayed by the waitress with burgers.

Good burgers, too. He had just come here for good food, and she felt herself relax a little. Not fully. Would she ever be relaxed again?

"On your own?" Not entirely skeptical, that. He had seen what she was capable of.

"If I have to." She had set her helmet down on the chair next to her, now she brushed back her hair and then...found her burger very interesting. She realized how she sounded. Like a spoiled rich kid, not used to being denied what she wanted. Well, she was one.

He did not answer for a while, taking a series of large bites out of his loaded burger. It seemed to have everything on it one might possibly put on a burger.

She realized that their booth had a decent view of the window and the parking lot. She watched it, expecting a cruiser to pull up any moment. Expecting cops to come pouring in.

"Relax." The word was slightly muffled, a bit of burger still in his mouth.

"This is rather a public place," she admitted. "Unless you have some reason to think the cops won't show up here."

"Cops raid Jane's? It might interfere with the pie baking." He finally looked at her, properly, his eyes seeking hers.

She laughed a bit, but it was humorless. "I think that what happened was serious enough."

"Do you trust me?"

"No." She was going to be honest with him. "Right now, I don't trust anyone. I've nearly been killed three times now. The second time involved a bent cop."

"Hell," Simon muttered. "Best bet probably is to convince them you aren't who they're looking for, yeah."

"Then I only have to worry about getting arrested. I should have taken the cops' offer to disappear, except..."

"If somebody was bent, they'd still have found you. Witness protection ain't foolproof."

"You sound like you know."

"My brother." He didn't explain further but demolished the rest of his burger. Either he wasn't paying attention to his own suggestion about pie, or he had a big appetite.

Laura stared out the window. She felt trapped. Things had gone from bad to worse, with no decision she made having changed anything.

She picked at her food, her own hyperawareness taking over again. It did not seem to improve the taste of the burger, however. Just that she could hear Simon breathing, could feel her own heartbeat. Could hear the waitress in the kitchen, talking to the line cooks. About pie and inconsequential things.

She saw no danger, though, and she tried to force herself to relax. No success. "I'm lousy company."

"Most people are after they get shot at. Get the apple pie." It hovered between a suggestion and a demand.

She followed his advice when the waitress showed up again. A la mode, vanilla ice cream. Pie, loaded with apples and cinnamon and walnuts. She thought it was the best pie she had had in her life.

"Feeling better?" Simon took a piece of his own pie, which was vanishing swiftly.

"A lot." Pie therapy, she thought with amusement. But she did feel more human again, and the hyperawareness had faded away. "But I need to find somewhere I can, well. Settle down and plan."

"Okay. Keeping moving is your best bet. Finding a sympathetic cop would be good too, but..." Simon tailed off, glancing at his empty pie plate.

"I killed somebody. They won't be sympathetic." They would nail her for manslaughter at the very least. Her life was ruined no matter what happened. She wanted to fade away, to cease to exist. To change into somebody else and at the same time to return to herself.

"Then you may need some protection that exists outside the law." His hands rested on the table. Large hands. Solid hands. Hands that wanted for only a gun.

"The mob, you mean?" The idea had occurred to her, but been dismissed immediately.

"That's a possibility, if this mystery father of yours is mob or similar..."

"I have to find out who he is. Except, what if I'm not his daughter?" Besides, they might make of her something she did not wish to be.

The room seemed to shift. Outside, the sky took on the slightest sheen of silver.

"Hell." She was not sure what she was seeing or perceiving. Instinctively, she grabbed for Simon's hand.

"What..."

He couldn't see it, she realized, couldn't see how the colors changed through rainbow hues, as if reality itself was fading. Pixelating, almost. Maybe she was in the Matrix and it was breaking down. It was like this was suddenly some kind of strange video game.

Was she the player character, if that was so? Then things settled down again...except that everyone there was frozen in place. The waitress, halfway through the door from the kitchen. The two men at another table, one mid chew, the other with his fork raised. Gravy dripped from it, and even the drops hung in mid-air. Time itself had halted.

Except for her. Simon was partly turned towards her. Frozen in space, his mouth open.

Magic again. Or more than that. Somebody was affecting the fabric of reality.

At the parking lot entrance stood the woman who had first tried to warn her.

"Come on. This won't last much longer." Then the woman's eyes fell on Simon. "Leave him."

"No." Now her tone was absolutely firm. "He saved my butt, I am not leaving him here. Release him." She could see, now, the cop cars that were in the process of pulling in, also affected by the time freeze. Their lights shone eerily.

"He's not part of this." Firm tones, even a little sharp. The voice of a woman accustomed to having authority.

"He saved my life. We're taking him with us." Defiant, turning to face her. Seeking some authority of her own, perhaps, a desire to face and to fight these people. All of them.

"He is *not* coming with us." The other's tone did not change.

"Then neither am I." Laura kept her voice very firm. She studied the other woman. Not that much older than her, although if she could affect time...then time, perhaps, did not affect her. This was not a comic book, she told herself.

"You get arrested, and the people trying to kill you win. He's not important." Uncaring and cold, those words, but perfectly logical.

Laura looked around her. Get arrested or leave a companion to take the fall. No side but her own.

But, dammit, she could decide what her own side was. "No. Both of us or neither. If I'm really that important..."

"You don't actually have the choice. I was hoping for your cooperation, but..."

And the woman reached forward to try and grab her. She twisted out of the way, barely avoiding her grasp. "Go away!"

She felt something, for a moment, flow through her, a sense of her own reality. Time returned to normal. The woman was gone.

"Crap. How we going to get past those cops?" Simon, oblivious to the exchange, let his fork fall to his plate.

"Does this place have a back door?"

"Only through the kitchen." He sounded resigned, for a moment, as if not sure what plan he had. As if he had really not expected them to come here.

The window, she thought, measuring it with her eyes. Not to mention... "And we wouldn't be able to get our wheels."

Breathe, she told herself. Breathe. As trapped as she felt, there had to be a way out.

A rather large woman in an apron emerged from the store, coming over to them. "Cops are looking for you guys. What ya do?"

"Somebody started a fight, we finished it," Simon said, simply.

"I can let you out the back." Half sympathetic, half worried. Not wanting to turn them in, not wanting them there.

Simon shook his head. "They're not stupid. Kitchen door will be watched, then they'll know we're here."

Laura closed her eyes. "If I turn myself in, they probably won't catch you."

She had not forgotten what the woman had said, but...she had involved these people too much.

"I..."

Laura cut Simon off. "I escaped from the cops before. I can do it again." With that, she turned and headed for the door, stepping out into the sunlight.

* * *

They had her handcuffed this time, in a bare interview room. The detective sitting opposite was a woman. An older woman, her hair flecked with steel. She even wore wire rimmed glasses. It did not make her more sympathetic.

"So, let's see. You bolt from protective custody, disappear for two months, reappear again to torch your parents. Then we find bodies in a turnout, right on your route."Her voice was surprisingly even, but it was clear that she was only comfortable being in Laura's presence with handcuffs involved. Laura kept her hands under the table. Could she get the cuffs off? It did not seem so.

"I'll admit to number one. Number two I didn't do. Number three..." Laura lifted her hands. "That wasn't me."

" What are we going to do with you? I really don't have any choice but to arrest you for murder and arson."

"I know. I doubt there's any good, solid evidence that I didn't do it. But what about motive?" Why would she kill her parents? What possible grounds could she have?

"Why did you bolt?" The detective leaned forward slightly.

"I felt as if the person in the safe house was dangerous." What else could she say? It was only the truth, and she could not find the energy to make up a good story. She would find her way out of here, and that moment of sympathy, that 'what are we going to do with you' was feigned. She might as well just tell the flat truth

"Also, who helped you kill those three men?" The question was inevitable. Somebody had seen something. Or it was a bluff. Most likely a bluff.

Laura closed her teeth together. She was not turning Simon in. Hopefully he had got back on his big Harley and ridden into the sunset.

The people trying to kill her would win. Without knowing who they were, she didn't know how much of a disaster that was for anyone but her. They had won. They could get to her in jail, she was sure of that. Yet...as long as she was alive...

"I might be..."

"Spare it. I'm not getting somebody arrested for saving my life." Nobody's side but her own. Well, she could make that side, couldn't she? If she ever got out of here.

If Laura ever got out of here alive. She had nothing to lose at this point. "Look. People are trying to kill me. They did kill my parents...I'm pretty sure they either thought I was in there or were hoping to set me up."

"If you hadn't left the scene..." Reasonable words, a reasonable tone.

"You'd have sent me back to that unsafe house." She emphasized the 'un' slightly.

"We could have made other arrangements. Instead, you bolt, lead a cop on a merry dance..."

"You'd still have had to bring me in under suspicion." She knew a little of how it worked. A little. Now, how did she convince this woman...she could convince her that she hadn't really killed those three guys, but that it had been an unknown Good Samaritan. Maybe.

She could break out. Maybe. She could...

"It really would help if you told us who your rescuer was. I mean, what loyalty do you owe the guy?" Sharp eyes caught hers.

None, was the obvious answer. "It's a matter of principle." She knew Simon had only helped her because he thought she was hot.

Was it reciprocated? No, not really, and if she ever saw him again, she would have to let him down easy. She was not the type of girl to string a man along. At the same time, she respected him. She could give him that much.

The detective scratched her head. "You're facing five murder raps and..."

"Oh, come on. Even if I did kill my parents...which I didn't...the other three."

"Without the other person, it's only your word that you weren't there, and your word doesn't look good." The detective stood, indicating that the interview was over.

Yes, the sympathy and understanding had been feigned, set aside once it was clear they were not an effective tactic. On the other hand, Laura wished she felt the cop was wrong, but she knew better. She was going down on every charge, and she would not cut a deal with

Simon's freedom. There was no help for it.

She was going to have to break out of jail.

* * *

Breaking out of jail is one of those things easier in movies and stories than in reality. It would also prove her guilt, but it seemed as if that had already been decided. Any jury would decide she was insane or worse. Insane? That would be a reasonable defense...if she didn't know she was perfectly fine.

The lawyer they found her had hinted at that. An insanity defense.

"So," she remembered saying, "It's better to be locked up in the looney bin for the rest of my life than the jail?"

He had seemed to think so. But she could not stand this confinement. She could feel that if she did not get out, somehow, she would go insane. And then she might become dangerous. Oh, who was she kidding? She was already dangerous. She was quite possibly already insane.

They were about to move her. That might be an opportunity. She could see all the precautions they were taking in her mind, could analyze them.

They really would win if she was shot while trying to escape. They would win if she never got out, and she was not going to let them win...except...

She sat, now, in a cell. At least she was on her own. No roommates for the patricide. No matter what happened, she was doomed. All she could do was...what? Survive as long as she could. Make each day a victory. Never let go of the remnants of her dreams, even if they were shards that threatened to cut her.

She certainly would not spend her life...what would be left of it...in a cell. A particularly unpleasant cell, no doubt. Assuming the government did not try something. Would she cut such a deal? She might. It would be better than a life in prison, better than death, yet she knew what they would use her for.

Or would they silence her? That the government knew there were people with unusual abilities, she was sure of. Was it magic? The way she could heal herself. Some of the things she had seen, had felt. Would they use her as an assassin? As a bringer of death.

She did not want to be such, but she did not want to be nothing, either.

She stared at her hands. At least now there were no cuffs encircling her wrists. They seemed slender, entirely normal. Anyone looking at her would see an innocent little girl, not a trained killer. She could use that...or could she?

The evidence against her was circumstantial, but possibly enough. Even her lawyer would paint a picture of her as insane. He insisted that was her only chance of avoiding Death Row.

She had never thought she would hope she was insane. If she was insane, her parents were alive. If she assumed she was insane, she would die.

So, for now, assume sanity. She turned her hands over. The worst part about being in prison was the time one had to think. Maybe that was the point. To make people who had done bad things think about what they had done. She had done bad things. She had to admit that, yet she had not done anything she had not needed to do to survive.

She needed to survive.

* * *

They shoved her into the windowless back of a van, still cuffed. Two men with guns got in there with her. Sun and air had been briefly experienced, and then become a memory. One she would value if she never got out.

If she could get one of those guns. She would not shoot a cop, but they did not know that. The van rolled away.

Laura wondered if she would get motion sick in such a confined space and tried to listen for cues to where they were taking her. All she could hear were the tires on the road. At first slow, with multiple turns, then she felt them build up speed. They were taking her along the freeway to a bigger town, probably to a bigger prison. This was her one chance, before she vanished into the system. Before she became a number, her hair cropped, her face scrubbed of makeup. She had seen pictures. Not that she had worn any makeup in a while.

She hoped they got the bike back to its owner. She would have to steal another one, though. Without access to her inheritance, she couldn't afford to buy legitimately...and they had taken her ID. She had to steal items or cash, once she was out.

The freeway roared past. They took her clothes, too, and put her in one of those hideous orange jumpsuits. So she could be seen and identified from a mile or more away.

Oddly, there was no shame or humiliation in her. Only smoldering anger. They had ruined her life and any chance she had of getting it back was just...flowing away from her. Fleeing into...and bang.

A gunshot, and the van careened. She felt it slowing. Had somebody shot out a tire? They were armored, surely? Certainly they would be if she had anything to do with it, but did these small town cops really have what it took?

Not from what she had seen. Another shot. She heard a yelp...that one had found flesh somewhere. It was probably the people who wanted her dead.

Arrested wasn't good enough for them. Then she was spun around, violently swung against the side of the van. For a moment, she thought she might pass out. Maybe she did, then everything was very quiet.

She blacked out for a moment. The van was on its side. Cuffed or not...she had to get out before they finished the job.

The two cops who had been in with her were worse off. Unconscious. She managed, barely, to get one of their sidearms into her pocket, along with their keys. If they had any sense, those keys wouldn't open the cuffs, but she had to try. Then the best thing to do occurred to her.

She got into position barely in time, slumped as awkwardly as she could manage where wall met floor.

Footsteps. "I think she's dead," came a voice.

"I doubt it. She's too tough to be killed by a crash. Put a few into her anyway, just to be sure."

The footsteps came over. She couldn't open her eyes...although it was obvious he wasn't convinced. Last possible moment. Last possible moment...and she twisted to thrust both feet up into his most sensitive area.

He screamed like a little girl. Playing dead had not worked. She had to fight them with both hands tied behind her back. She did not know whether to hope the cops woke up or hope they didn't.

They were probably better off unconscious. If only she was just a little stronger...no, no human could break out of handcuffs. No human...

...and the chain holding them together snapped. A gun was in her hand almost instantly, and the man actually stepped back. She shot him in the arm...there was no need to kill him.

No need, and then she was out into the sunlight. It dazzled her, and she ducked behind the van quickly, a shot streaking past her.

Well, no question...how many men did these people have? How many had they hired?

All these resources against her. The only thing she could think of was getting the hell out of there. Blood flowed from the cab of the van.

The cops in there were probably dead, and she felt no loyalty to those in the back. She knew they had a better chance of survival if she just booked it.

Unfortunately, they were in the middle of the highway. Traffic streamed past, some stopped to rubberneck. Those streaked away, with the exception of one car in the ditch, driver slumped over the steering wheel.

If she just ran, she endangered everyone. Same if she started shooting. What she needed was...

...well, she was no longer sure of the limits of her own capability. Higher than she had ever thought, of that she was sure. Who was she? What was she?

She'd worry about that later, because she saw an opportunity. A lumbering, crawling semi, and she leapt onto the side of it, firing carefully back at them.

She felt sorry for the driver...but she had no intention of involving him. Feeling strength flow through her, she pulled herself up onto the container roof, flattening herself to it. The truck hit the top of the hill and began to accelerate down the slope on the other side. She could hear the rumble of the engine braking, trying to keep it under control.

Barely, she clung on. She was alive, but she was not free. She would never actually be free again. But she could at least take those who had ended her life down with her.

With thoughts of revenge firing her brain and freezing her heart, she rode the truck west to Ohio.

9

She rapidly decided Ohio had been a mistake, but then, in some ways, she had been going with the flow. Nothing more, nothing less.

She had ditched the truck just over the state line, slipping off it in a truck park, vanishing into the trees. She hoped nobody had seen her, but there were no guarantees. This part of the state was fairly heavily wooded and it was not hunting season. Those were the things she had in her favor. Against her, how busy the road was.

Unfortunately, she was penniless and, as the adrenalin had long since worn off, desperately hungry. Wilderness survival was not something she had learned. She could not live off the land and with no ID, she could not work.

Great. Maybe she should have let them shoot her.

There was a farmhouse through the trees. Clothes hung on a line outside. Only in books did people steal from clotheslines, but she could not go further, dressed as she was.

In books, the place was not guarded by a black dog so large it could have played Cerberus, had it not been short a couple of heads. It was asleep, and remained so as she stole jeans and a shirt that looked like they might fit, but woke up and started barking as she fled. She ran into the trees.

A close one, that, the jumpsuit abandoned, wrapped into a ball and tucked between two roots. The handcuffs, eventually pried off. How strong was she?

She wondered where Simon was. She'd lay bets he knew how to get a woman a fake ID. She wondered, too, where Nancy was. She did not want to involve Simon any further. He had paid enough of a price for his connection to her. Yet, she needed help.

Laura found herself walking into a small town. It was larger than a village, at least. Strip mall and movie theater on the outskirts, a couple of diners. It felt like a good place, a homey place. A place she could stay for a while.

She could not stay anywhere. Truthfully, what she needed was food, a set of wheels, and to get her ass back to New York. If there were answers, they lay in Manhattan's canyons. She was sure of it. If there were answers. Most of them had died with Ella Miracle.

She would find none here. Food, though...well, there was one obvious option.

She walked into the smaller, shabbier diner, deliberately making her steps seem more shaken. She had a good bruise on her face, which would fit her story. She thought she might be bleeding from a scrape or two.

"What happened to you?" the waitress asked, her eyes brightening with concern.

"I got mugged. That's supposed to happen in cities, not..."

The woman looked her up and down. "You sure as heck look like you took a beating. Want me to call the cops?"

"No. I just need to sit down for a bit. I...know the guy. I can deal with it."

The waitress jumped to the same conclusion Laura herself might have. "Don't you be going back to him."

"He took my ID and credit cards. I don't have anything." She hated playing the victim, even as she felt the strength that flowed through her. She embraced it, appreciated it. It was a part of her, it was a part of the woman she was and could be. The question was how she could keep it from turning her into the killer she feared.

"I'll make you breakfast..." The offer was a little uncertain.

"I can work it off. Besides, he won't look for me in the kitchen." Fear was flowing through her, she could feel her heartbeat elevating again. As if she truly was running from some man, not simply afraid to be caught in a lie. Or afraid they would find her, even here. Could she change her appearance?

Again, the waitress studied her. "Let me just get you some food."

It was greasy diner food, but there was plenty of it. She ate without really tasting it. Guilt dominated her emotions. She was using this woman, although there were witnesses to her condition and her words. Still, that might protect her from the police.

Would she really have to kill all of them? No. She just had to find the person hiring them and kill him. Or her. Cold, those thoughts, a winter breeze through her. But she knew that she had no choice. Then what? Turn herself in and face, at best, life in jail?

Live on the run for the rest of her days? She should have been a boy. The words of people who underestimated females routinely.

She had no illusions. If her abilities came out, somebody would want her as an assassin. The mob, the government, a different government, somebody. Vanishing was her only good option, but she could not vanish until she had taken care of the person most determined to capture her. Even then, she might be forced to work for somebody. To choose a side, despite Nancy's words. To become some kind of agent. A hitman. She'd make a good hitman. No matter how much she wanted to be what she had been before, she could not.

"You look pretty grim," came a voice. "Planning on hitting him back?"

The diner was almost empty, and the waitress had come to sit next to her.

"If he doesn't give me my stuff back and let me go, I might." There was, she thought, just the right amount of disgust and displeasure in her tone. It was a role she could play.

"Just don't do anything stupid, like shooting him, okay?" Sympathetic, worried tone, the words of somebody who thought she might do just that.

If she really had an evil ex who took her money to keep her from leaving, she might get away with it. Or not. Women spent life in prison for killing their abusers all the time. "Oh no, I don't want to *kill* him."

"Don't knee cap him either," the waitress quipped.

"Heh." The laugh she managed was weak, but at least it would be expected. The woman seemed so ordinary. So distant from her, now. So fragile.

She finished her food, and then followed the waitress back into the kitchen.

It was the first time she'd ever been stuck washing dishes. Fortunately, nothing now seemed to be hard work to her. That meant, though, that it had the unpleasant side-effect of occupying her hands but not her mind.

She wanted this all to turn out to be a dream. A hallucination. Sure, she hated the trope in fiction, had ever since somebody had given her a book as a child which turned out to be a dream the main character had on the train, but this was reality. This was her life that had been taken away from her, and part of her blamed Ella Miracle. She did not want to, but she could not help it.

But had the woman not been a hooker, then Laura would not exist. No matter how much her life sucked...

She worked all day, building up enough 'credit' for lunch as well, then leaving in the evening. She had nowhere to sleep and did not feel she could demand that much charity.

Maybe a night trucker going east would be glad of some company. The air was clean and crisp in her nostrils. It rained earlier, she could smell it. Feel it. Hyperawareness drifting through her again. Her heart soared despite everything. She felt so alive, so real, so free right now that she could almost forget it all.

She felt as if she could take off into the night, as if she could grow wings and fly. Except that did not happen, no matter how much she might want it to. Her feet stayed firmly on the ground.

That would have solved her problems. As it was? She wished she could find Simon, but that wish was no more answered than the other. He'd probably take her to New York...

...and get shot. No. She needed to involve as few people as possible.

A bird flew overhead. She looked up. It was a red tail, circling on the air. She wished, once more, for wings.

* * *

Laura did not find wings. She did find a trucker heading east...a heavyset woman who saw her trying to hitch a ride in the truck stop and immediately called her over.

"Ya don't want to ride with any of those men. Not that crowd. They might not take advantage of you, but they might. You're safe with me. I'm Debbie."

Laura did feel safer with a woman, even if she was still built the way all truckers were. A body formed by greasy truck stop food and being on one's butt all day. But at least the woman smelled like she had showered recently.

"What's your name, girl?" Patronizing, that. Yet, it was not bad to be patronized. Debbie probably thought she was stupid, hitchhiking on her own.

"Laura." Again, she felt no reason to give a false name. Laura was too common. Heck, she might even have given her full name, except truckers were on CB. They heard APBs.

At this point the Feds would be involved. The trap closed around her again as the door did, sitting next to the driver. It was a relatively new cab. It even had seat belts, albeit somewhat rough and ready ones.

The view of the road was not like a car. It was still night, though, and she was tired. More tired than she realized, because the next thing she knew they were fifty miles down the road, the big tires rumbling on the tarmac. The mountains were climbing around them, closing in like skyscrapers. Under other circumstances, she would have appreciated their night clad beauty. As it was, she found herself looking for ambush points.

"You haven't had much sleep lately, have you?" the trucker commented. Her tone was amused, rather than concerned. By the time Laura found her, the bruise had faded, no longer needing an explanation.

"Pretty much none. I'm...not used to being on the road." That was an understatement. She had been pretty soft, she realized. She had never understood how homeless people could live, curled under bridges. On park benches. Now she envied them. They might have their shadows, they might occasionally have to move on. They were not caught between prey and predator, hunter and hunted.

"You aren't used to being anywhere but a comfortable bed." Debbie snorted a bit. "You've got a story, but I have a feeling you won't tell it just yet."

Laura's shoulders tensed up. "I'd rather not."

"Figured. You're running from the cops or your guy or both or...running away, anyway. You're better off finding something to run to."

That did strike Laura as at least some level of profound wisdom, but she shook her head. "If I come across such a thing, I will. Right now, I don't think it exists. Not for me."

"You aren't running towards death, are you?"

"No." She meant it, at least in that moment. Not her death, anyway. Perhaps somebody else's.

It came into her head that that might have been their intent. To create a killer?

'You should have been a boy'. That echoed through her, and she shivered.

"Be careful, kid. I can see it in your eyes. You don't have a damn thing left to lose, do you?"

Create a killer, then point and shoot her. "Life. Hope. They haven't taken those away from me yet."

"I'll get you to New York. As long..." Her voice trailed off. For a moment, there was a small hole in the woman's confidence.

"Anyone asks, you don't even exist," Laura promised. She wondered what was in Debbie's past, what haunted her blue-grey eyes. Something, she was sure. Maybe she was running too, eternally so. Living on the road because if she stopped, whatever it was would catch her.

That was how she would end up. She knew that now. Maybe Debbie could show her how to live that way.

The road flowed past. She felt more and more human as time went on, more relaxed and focused. Rested, even. Of course, she was not sure that she was human.

That, perhaps, was what all this was about. Heck, maybe it was the government trying to... And then she remembered stopped time and Nancy's disappearing house. There was no scientific explanation for those. She was not the debris of some semi-successful super soldier program.

Her hands fell into her lap. There was, for now, no conversation. Just the road and the radio playing country. Old country and western, not the modern stuff that hovered between that and pop music. Laura found she liked it. It had a rhythm to it that settled her.

The truck was pulling off at a small motel now. "I'm hitting my hours."

At least it wasn't Jane's. Debbie bought her dinner. Hamburger and fries, both made up more of grease than anything else. Coke. The caffeine didn't seem to affect her, but the air did. Still fresh and clear. She did not want to go back to New York with its smog and its lights and its crowds.

She had to. Without answers, there could be no solution. Without knowing why people were...and she saw three bikes pull up.

Laura tensed, then moved further away from the room. If they were going to shoot at her she'd rather Debbie was not in the line of fire. She'd ditched the police revolver, but she did know there was a shotgun in the cab of the truck. If she could get to it. It would probably be easier to take one of their weapons.

They cut the engines and got off. Their mirrored visors were a good enough disguise, but she had none. With a mental apology to Debbie, she broke for the edge of the parking lot. Maybe she could lead them further away from the civilians here.

All of it was cold analysis, her own life being in the equation not even lighting any kind of fire. She positioned herself behind a tree and waited.

Waited. She would look like a fool if they had nothing to do with her. As she watched, they headed for a room three doors down from Debbie's. She saw a gun silhouetted along the leg of one of them.

Nothing to do with her. And if she intervened, how would she know which side were the good guys? If she did not, there might be more deaths. She certainly did not want more deaths, on her conscience or anyone else's. It was a frown, thus, that crossed her features. What did she do? Then the light changed. She saw the uniforms they wore.

* * *

The next day, she curled on the seat next to Debbie.

"You see what all the shooting was about?"

"Sheriff," Laura said, as if she felt no other explanation was needed.

"Huh. Anyone actually get hit?" Amusement laced Debbie's tone.

"No. I'm not sure which side was the worse shot." In the dark, the sheriff trading shots with whoever had been in the room. The man coming out with his hands on his head.

She would have gotten away. That sure and certain knowledge, the feeling that...she always seemed to know exactly what to do. Well, except for the time in the diner. But then, anything she could have done would have gotten the place trashed and a bunch of people killed.

Why did she care? Because caring was the last remaining part of her humanity. Because she was damn well going to make her own side. She could be one of the good guys. The only question was how.

She realized Debbie had said something she hadn't quite heard. "What?"

"I asked if you were okay."

"I'm fine. I hid behind a tree." She tried to make light of it, to forget how fast her heart had beat for those moments.

"Trees are useful that way, at least where there are any of decent size left." A trace of bitterness marked the words.

Was the big trucker some kind of environmental activist? That made little sense. Maybe she just missed woods that had been bulldozed to build more houses. It did seem that some people were determined to pave the planet over. "I know what you mean."

Did she? How many trees had been bulldozed to make room for the childhood home that was now ash and rubble?

"Really? I thought you were from New York?"

She shook her head. "Not city. Long Island."

"Ah, that makes more sense. But your enemy is in New York?"

"The information I need is in New York, and it's not something I can get off the public internet." She could not just walk into a library, ask for thirty minutes computer time... No. First, she had to find that adoption agency. Which was in New York. Which claimed not to know who her father was.

It wasn't the adoption agency she needed to find. "I need to find a woman." No, she needed to find the memory of a woman.

Even hookers had friends. Or, heck, long-time customers, people who might know about the pregnancy. Who might know something. It was the only lead she had. She had lost the photograph, but Ella's face was still burned into her memory.

"Just don't hurt her."

"It's not like that." Laura fell silent, watching the road drift by. Hawks rode the thermals, looking for roadkill. Her life was roadkill. Her life was and meant nothing. Nothing except vengeance.

There was magic involved. The possibility that drifted back into her mind was that she was a half-vampire. If vampires even existed. She did not believe in vampires. But nor did she believe in vanishing houses and superpowers. She looked down at her hands. Slender, her manicure long since wrecked. Still not the hands of a killer.

Debbie's words interrupted, as if the woman had read her mind, "And don't get yourself killed, either. Whatever it is, it's not worth it."

"It's about not getting me killed," Laura admitted. "Somebody wants me dead." Great. Now Debbie would throw her out.

"And you're trying to get to them first?"

"Maybe. I think it's all a big misunderstanding and with the right information I can clear it up and go back to my life."

"Got it. Mistaken identity."

"Or they think I saw something I shouldn't have, but if I did, I don't remember it. More likely mistaken identity." Except she was growing more and more certain it was not that. That they knew exactly who her father was.

"Let's stop for lunch," Debbie suggested, pulling off at a rest stop.

Laura ate a wilted chicken sandwich and watched the road. No more undercover cops. It seemed very ordinary and normal and quiet, and then she saw a woman at the end of the parking lot.

A very familiar woman. "Oh for... Go away."

"Do you really want me to do that, Laura?" The woman strode towards her.

"Last time, you wanted me to leave a friend taking the rap, so yes." A pause. "I'd also like to know how you keep finding me."

The woman gave no answer to that. "A friend? A total stranger who should have meant nothing to you. The only thing you should be worrying about is staying alive and free."

Laura stepped over to meet the woman halfway, her head held high. "I'd rather care than turn into what people seem to be trying to turn me into. I'm not a killer."

"You are. That is what you were born to be. Woman or not, that is your destiny and purpose."

Nobody seemed to be in earshot, at least, Laura's eyes flicked around, then focused on the other. "Bullshit. I got a choice, as hard as everyone seems to be working on taking that away from me."

"Come on. Like you could be happy as a..." Contempt dripped on the next word. "...schoolteacher."

"It's called doing something positive. Fulfilling. You should try it sometime. What do you want from me? Who do you want me to kill...come on, admit it."

"Oh, it's nothing so precise. No specific individual."

"You're the bad guys." Why had she not realized before? "You're all the bad guys."

Both those trying to kill her and those trying to save her. Everything seemed to turn dark and grey, but she remembered Simon. The waitress. Debbie. Genuine human kindness. "Get out of my life. Now."

"But you will still seek your revenge. You can't help it. It's in your nature." Calm now, the tones of one who had absolute confidence in what she believed.

"Are you guys even on different sides?" Laura's voice sharpened, snapped at her. They were all...even Nancy...against her. Or against each other, with her caught in the middle. 'Nobody's side but your own'.

"Of course we are." She turned and walked away. "Go ahead, waste time riding with that...trucker...when I could get you there in an instant."

"You're a demon."

"That depends on one's definition of the word." And she was gone.

Laura trembled a little.. What if the people trying to kill her were actually the good guys? What if they had a good reason?

No. She had a choice. Nobody could take her free will away from her. Killing might come naturally to her, but she had already managed not to, more than once.

And Debbie was behind her. "Who was that?"

"Nobody important." Could she really stay with the woman now? Was she putting her in too much danger? "Look..."

"These people can't be worse than my ex."

"Sure they can."

"Come on." Debbie was making a beeline for the truck, opening the door. "Get your butt in."

As she hit the accelerator smoothly. "My ex was a hit man."

10

Laura must have slept, for she was only dimly aware of the rest of the afternoon. Perhaps the adrenalin of the confrontation placed her in that tired, uncertain state.

Either way, it was sundown before she regained full awareness. They were in the outskirts of New York. In a car she might have done it in one day. Debbie had not seemed in a hurry...and the full load had slowed them down.

There was Manhattan, and her heart ached. She wanted her life back so much it physically hurt.

She would be on the run forever now...but maybe she could cut it down to just the cops. Hide in some small town, waitress at the diner and write a book she could not publish. Or maybe she would find an idea for one she could. Historical fiction, a retreat into the past. But she could live and she would, if only to spite all of them. Or she could become what they wished of her, on her own terms.

Manhattan and the towers and the lights, but she no longer belonged. Not here, not anywhere.

She glanced at Debbie. "I owe you something I can't repay."

Debbie did not take her eyes off the road. "I told you about my ex, right?"

"One of the bad guys."

"By some measures. He was decent to me." One hand lifted from the wheel, fiddled with her somewhat short hair. "Until I wanted to leave him."

"Because of what he did?"

"Yes. I knew that sooner or later he would get arrested. I did not want children. He did. I did not want children who would see their father a few days a year in jail."

"I don't think I want children." Children struck her as a bad idea. When she did not know what it was she carried in her blood...demon, vampire, government super soldier...she did not know what, but something... Yes, definitely a bad idea.

"Children are a lot of work," Debbie opined. "And right now I'm not ready to settle down."

"He's still looking for you." A guess, likely to be dangerously close to the truth. Still looking for Debbie just as the men with guns were still looking for Laura. "How do you survive?"

"I keep moving. I let myself get fat...he doesn't like fat women, he wouldn't look twice at me now." She made a wry face. "It beats being his slave. Or being dead."

"Most things beat being dead. Me, I'm worried about staying out of the pen. Especially as I have a feeling they could find me in there."

"If it's the mob, they can. And it doesn't sound like you can trust the cops."

"I can't. There's at least one cop working with them." She paused. "I sound paranoid, don't I?"

"Not if they're really out to get you." Debbie changed lanes. "I know I could be humoring a paranoid, but I would rather do that than not help somebody who needs it. I'd suggest a dye job, for starters. It can make a huge difference."

Laura nodded. "I thought of that, but I'm broke. Plus, these people...they can find me anywhere. I suppose it might help with the cops."

"As a temporary measure, wear a hat," she suggested. "Shades. It won't disguise you close up, but it'll help against snipers."

Would it? It depended, Laura thought, on whether she was being tracked by some other means. She probably was. But it couldn't hurt. "Okay."

"Are you packing?"

"Not right now, and I probably shouldn't..." She tailed off. Having a gun made one tempted to use it, automatically. Not having one made one vulnerable. "But then, I'm already on the lam."

"Screw the cops," Debbie muttered. "They're never much help."

"Given what they think I did, I don't blame them. The bastards framed me." They had waited for her to show up before setting off the incendiaries. Their intent had been to get her fighting the cops.

It had worked.

"Are we sure this is not some kind of...no, now I'm the one paranoid."

"I don't think it's the government. There's enough strangeness going on, though, that I wouldn't be surprised if it was space aliens." Laura reached up to her temple. Space aliens. There was a possibility she had not considered. Maybe she was a space alien.

Debbie laughed sharply. "I don't believe in aliens. Not until I see one."

"Yeah, but when you see things, it's best to believe them, right?" All she had seen...a lot of it was not believable. Laura sighed. "Sometimes, I wonder if I'm going insane. Sometimes I think it would be better."

"Hang in there. Besides, if you're lucky, they will eventually forget about you." Words of quiet wisdom.

Laura looked out the window, ignoring that last statement. She wished this was all a dream. Or a movie. Movies had endings.

This was likely to end with death.

* * *

The closest Debbie's route took her to Manhattan was a truck stop close enough to a commuter rail station to walk.

On the train, there was nothing left to her except nerves. She had no ID. She owed Debbie a debt she had no clue how to repay, especially as she refused to take the woman's address. If she even had one. Debbie even bought the ticket for her, gave her a little bit of cash. It would not last long.

She refused to have any link to anyone. Nobody would be killed or arrested for her sake. Nobody.

The lives of the enemies, she valued less. She got off at Grand Central, caught in the press of people around her. Once, she could have lost herself in such a crowd. Now, everything she was rebelled against it. Too vulnerable. She forced reason on the matter. It was unlikely anyone would try to kill her here and she had nothing in her pocket to pick. There was no name attached to the rail ticket. She did wish for some kind of disguise, but then, she did not look that special. A hat and shades, Debbie had suggested as a temporary measure...but she had neither right now.

She feared she was glowing brighter than a star. The press of people ignored her. Down into the subway, which was even more crowded. She could barely get along the platform and it wasn't even rush hour. Most seemed to be tourists, cameras around their necks, struggling with the turnstiles. She did not bother even trying to find a seat on the train.

It swayed and rattled, and that rhythm found her heartbeat and settled her. Belong, no, but Manhattan was a good place to lose herself. A good place to be invisible. She felt the city close around her. As if it was a web of energy...supportive and angry at the same time. As if the city did not quite trust her.

That was fine. She did not trust herself. At least she was dressed plainly. Where she was going, that mattered a lot. The sun was setting as she climbed the escalator to the street. The neon was starting to brighten.

Ella Miracle had been no street girl. It seemed unlikely that the painted birds that emerged from various doorways would know anything about her, but she had no other place to start.

Rapidly, she discovered that these hard-faced women responded to only one language. The one she could not speak right now. She was about to give up when she heard a commotion. A commotion punctuated by a girl's high, thin scream.

Choose your own path, she told herself, as she set off towards the sound, into an alleyway, up a fire escape. The door was locked. That did not even slow her down.

A scarred man had a young woman... she couldn't have been more than fifteen...pinned.

"You will not even think of leaving, Janice. You are mine."

"Not anymore," Laura found herself saying.

"And you...oh, you would make a fine addition. A fine addition indeed." As his eyes focused on her, Janice squirmed away a little.

Laura laughed. "I'd like to see you try." He was scum, and every read she could make of him amplified that. Sure, he could take on the average woman. Against her?

He had a gun, but he didn't use it. His hand, in fact, went nowhere near the weapon. Instead, he launched himself at her.

She side-stepped. He flew out the door, became a crumpled heap, flat on his face on the fire escape landing. She was moving before he could pick himself up, kicking him in the midsection.

"You're scum," she informed him. "You're nothing." And then...she pushed him down the stairs. Several of the girls in the street turned.

Good. His humiliation had been witnessed. That hardness came around her again, that feeling as if she had every right to be doing this. This time it did not disturb her nearly as much.

She turned to Janice. "How hard did he hit you?"

"Not that hard. I'll be..." The girl swallowed. "...fine."

Laura saw the fear in her eyes. "I only beat on people who deserve it."

Janice swallowed again. "He was twice your size, though. But..."

"You want to go home, right?" She didn't have money to help the girl, she had to remind herself of that. But at least... No, wait.

Stepping out onto the landing, she came down the fire escape, head held high, and tugged the wallet out of the pimp's pockets. There was an entire gaggle of women watching now, none wearing more than they had to. Most were also wearing smirks.

"Looks like the Cap'n tried to recruit the wrong girl," one of them said, between puffs on a clove cigarette.

She flickered the woman a grin she could not resist, then went back inside. There was two hundred dollars in the pimp's wallet. She counted out half of it, offered it to Janice. "I have a feeling at least some of this is your money by rights."

The rest she pocketed. It would buy her some information, perhaps. Then she guided Janice down the stairs. "Can you get home?"

Janice nodded weakly. "I can."

"Take the subway. Stay in crowded places. And don't run away. Believe me, your parents are to be appreciated."

Laura started to walk away herself. For now, Janice followed her.

The woman who had made the comment about the Cap'n moved into her path, blowing smoke. "You a cop?"

"Nah. You see me cuffing and booking the guy? Call me a concerned citizen.

"Be careful. Cops around here don't take kindly to vigilantes. And we don't take kindly to people who ask too many questions." Her tone was harsh, but there was something in it. Something on the edge of respect.

"Ella Miracle was my mother." The name might achieve something. She was glad, suddenly, she had not disguised herself.

The hooker frowned at her. "Ya know, I almost believe you."

"I ain't here to get any of you arrested. I'm here to find who killed her."

Janice stepped behind her again, then abruptly she fled. Towards, Laura was relieved to see, the subway station. She made it, vanishing underground. Hopefully she would find her way home.

"Got it. Guess I can understand that one. I'm Tiff."

Laura nodded. "Know anyone who would have known her, who

might have a clue who'd want to take her out?" These people were a lower class than Ella had been, but...

A man pushed through the various women. "I knew Ella Miracle."

"Biblically," Tiff commented. "Maybe he's your dad."

Laura studied the stranger. "That would be kinda hard, wouldn't it," she quipped. The man had rich, deep, brown skin and tightly cropped black hair. She grinned, making a great show of looking at her own fair hands.

"Yeah, it would, wouldn't it?" Tiff grinned back, showing that she was teasing. "I mean, some mixed people come out pretty white, but..."

Laura made a great show of looking at her own rather pasty hands.

"Come on. And I promise not to try anything with you." The black man grinned. "I have a feeling you'd eat me for breakfast as thoroughly as you did the Cap'n."

"He deserved it."

"He sure did. Cops are useless," the man said as he moved up the street.

She did not follow him; she made damn sure she was next to him. She would not turn her back on him or expect him to do the same. "I noticed. Sometimes that's a good thing, though."

"Oh, half the time they don't bother even trying with the hookers and the pimps. And before you ask, I'm not a pimp." He flickered her a bit of a grin.

"Just a customer." She kept all judgment out of her tone. It was perhaps only chance that this man wasn't her father.

He stepped into a bar, one that was not too noisy. "Buy you a drink?"

"You can give me the money for one. I ain't letting anyone touch anything I drink." She knew that was rude, but...

"Only person who will touch it will be the bartender. I promise." There was a certain sincerity in his tone. He might be somebody who had to buy sex, but she did not sense anything dishonest about him.

She nodded. "Don't want to wake up robbed in an alleyway tomorrow, is all." She knew she had to keep her wits about her.

He bought them both beers, being careful not to touch hers. It was decent beer. She savored it, knowing she should not really have it. Fortunately, the bartender didn't card her. She hadn't looked at the rest of the contents of the Cap'n's wallet.

"So, I'm pretty sure you ain't working in the letter of the law." He was older, but not that old. Old enough, still, to be her father, had things gone a little differently. She could be certain he was not only because of his ethnicity.

"Cops are useless." She tucked the wallet more firmly inside her jacket for now. "Should have taken his gun, too."

"I suspect somebody will take care of that for you. I'm Branson."

"So. Ella Miracle." She turned towards him, looked at him through her eyelashes.

"High class woman. Independent...and you can imagine how hard it is to stay that way. Never worked the streets...never needed to. Expensive." A pause. "But she would sometimes take other girls under her wing. Sometimes she'd give a girl money if her pimp was putting the heat on her. She was decent. Not a hooker with a heart of gold, but decent."

"She dumped me." Laura let out a breath.

"No place for a kid in her lifestyle. You turned out better this way, trust me. But Ella served men who wanted something more...utter discretion and fine companionship." He kept his tone even, but there was the faintest echo of sorrow in it.

Laura nodded. "Congressmen?"

"UN officials. People who wanted that bit of class. She wasn't just about the sex, you know. You could take the woman anywhere, ask her anything." His face changed. "She was also my friend."

"With benefits?"

"Occasionally."

"Did she ever mention me?"

"Once. The...you'd be about the right age."

Laura nodded. "I know she's my mother. I know, too, that I have no chance of working out who my father was."

"Somebody rich." Branson's eyes met hers for a moment. "Rich and unsatisfied with his wife."

Laura sipped her beer. It tasted sharp, very much of hops and alcohol. "Well, duh. My concern is who killed her. Dissatisfied customer? Pimp finally caught up with her?"

"Wouldn't be the latter. You wouldn't destroy merchandise like that." Branson frowned a little bit. "Normally I charge for this, but I've been investigating myself."

"You're a detective." Not a question.

"Private investigator. That's how I became friends with Ella in the first place. She wasn't above selling information, although not about her customers. She helped me find several runaways who ended up on the streets. She thought women being forced into prostitution degraded the profession." He paused. "Like I said. Decent."

Laura digested that. "So, she wasn't a bad person. I wondered whether I cramped her style or..."

"Most likely she wanted you to have two parents, and given marriage was so not her style, I suspect she thought you'd be better off." Branson studied Laura again. "You're, what, eighteen?"

"You're corrupting a minor." She managed to find amusement somewhere, although she was not sure where.

"Eh. I always thought twenty-one was too old to drink, caused more problems. So, you dug into the records?"

"No." Laura breathed in, then out. "Whoever killed her, they're also after me."

"What?" His tone elevated to almost a squeak. "Does that put a different complexion on things." Not a question, that. A statement.

"I don't want to involve you, but I need a professional. I just..." She tailed off. She regarded him. He had slept with her mother. He *could* have been her father, but she was sure he wasn't even without a DNA test. There would have been some sign.

"I've been shot before." Branson dismissed the entire thing, curling a hand around his beer.

"But this is probably...almost certainly...the mob that is after me. I can't think of anyone else it could be." She did not want him involved, but she needed him. It tore through her a little, made her uncomfortable. A dilemma.

"I've dealt with them before too. If it is the mob, then there's ways and there's means. So...why do you think they're after you?"

If she told the truth, she would not be believed. It was all alien and real at the same time. Was this what a schizophrenic felt when they lost all touch with reality? So, she edited it.

"They seem to think that...it seems this is all some way of getting at an individual they believe may be my father. Of course..."

"No way of proving that without a paternity test." Branson frowned. "Well, we can narrow some things down. First of all, white."

She looked at her hands again. "Yeah, I think we can be sure of that. If I was a bit darker, then..."

"Well, no. Possibly Hispanic, although unlikely...Ella had very dark hair too. She was proud of it, never colored it or anything. You do look a lot like her."

Laura nodded. "Which is unfortunate. This would be a lot easier if I favored my father."

Which she did, but not in looks. In ways she could not, right now, reveal.

"Unfortunately, hair could be any color, dark hair tends to be dominant. Eyes...brown. Like Ella's. No help there." A bit of sarcasm tossed onto the end of the statement there.

She smiled at him. "You're the detective. I need a detective. I just don't want to end up getting you killed. Of course, if they would stop shooting at me, I'd cheerfully give a sample."

"I dodge well." He studied her. "Unless there's more going on than just a few bullets flying."

She looked away. "There's sure as heck weird stuff going on." Not able to meet his eyes, the tablecloth suddenly the most interesting thing in the room.

"I'm going to need to know everything." His tone was firm.

She did not look back. "You wouldn't believe everything. And don't say 'try me'...that's such a cliché."

He laughed. "I promise. I won't call any men in white coats. Or the police."

She glanced around. "I'm not comfortable telling the rest here."

They ended up in a hotel room. She felt safe from Branson, in no small part because if he tried to rape her, she would kick his ass. Detective or not. Of course, if he was, oh, fifteen years younger and not her mother's friend with benefits, it might not have been rape. He was far from the worst looking guy she had ever seen.

Her mother. That was just eww. But it meant something, too. Her adoptive father had never been that much of a father, emotionally. This man already seemed to be reaching across that gap.

"Okay. So. How about all of it? From the beginning?"

She told him. All of it. Even Nancy and the vanishing house. He sat back, half lying on the bed. It was a long time before he spoke. For that time, she curled her knees towards her chest, pulling herself into an insecure and yet demure position. She let her head sink onto her knees. Any moment now, he was going to call the police. Get her hauled off into secure mental. Maybe knock her on the head first. Yet, she also knew she had given him far more to digest than she should. She was not being fair on the man.

Finally, he broke the silence. "Girl. Not that long ago, I wouldn't have believed a word of it. But..."

"Have they been bothering you?" It was the obvious question. He was a friend of Ella's. They might have thought he knew something.

"Not exactly." He let his breath out slowly. "But it does seem as if things are getting stranger and stranger over the last few months. Odd stuff. The kind of stuff that makes you wonder if the people talking about the Age of Aquarius are really as full of it as they seem."

"Disappearing houses?" She had to ask.

"New statues in Battery Park that appear overnight then vanish as quickly. A client who insisted on only meeting in the hours of darkness."

Laura looked down at her hands again. "And now me."

"If it helps, I don't really think the guy was a vampire, just a nut. Or I didn't." He sighed. "I believe you. Because of the statues."

"What were the statues of?" she found herself asking.

"Gods."

11

Branson found her a lead. A woman, no longer young, greeted her at the entrance to the townhouse. Clearly, she had once been a looker, but now she had faded somewhat. Her hair was silver and her skin had a fine parchment tone to it. She was far older, Laura decided, than Ella had been. Old enough, easily, to be Laura's grandmother.

"You're Ella's daughter? Well, I don't think there's a question of that. Come in." The blue eyes pierced through her.

Laura stepped inside. Retired prostitutes, she noted, lived well. Then again, she was fully beginning to understand the difference between the cheap women who shook their tails on street corners and Ella's class of hooker.

This woman still had class. She might have lost her looks, but she still had her poise. Her confidence. She carried herself like a queen.

That was the real difference. Cheap hookers were controlled by their men. Expensive ones did all the controlling.

"You're Joanna." Not a working name, that. Presumably she had gone back to using her real name when she retired. Or, perhaps, never used the street name except with clients.

"Yes." Nothing more than that. "And you are Laura."

A parlor...an actual parlor. Did she still entertain men here? With something more sophisticated, more mature than sex? Laura thought so. Maybe even with sex. Old people had sex, too. Yet, this place did not make Laura think of sex. It made her think of refined conversation. There were several photographs on the wall. One of them showed a woman Laura knew, but took a moment to recognize. It was Ella.

"Please. Sit down." Joanna moved to do exactly that. Tea was set out on the table...a tea pot, cups. Cookies.

Laura reached for a cup without hesitation, curling her hand around the delicate porcelain carefully. She could shatter it easily, she knew that now. "I wish..."

"I don't know who killed her. I wish I did." Joanna's eyes went to the picture.

This place felt safe, which might have been what put Laura on her guard. "I know, but you might have heard something, seen something. Did she seem, like, worried?"

As Joanna opened her mouth to answer, the front window shattered inwards with a tremendous crashing of glass. The lace curtains were torn into shreds.

"Screw you," Laura voiced, turning towards the window. "Joanna..."

But the woman had already moved, with surprising speed, through the door and behind the wall. Smart, but Laura did not follow her. She moved forward, a roll that put her just inside the window, to the side of it. She was flat against the wall, expecting...

No, they had learned. A small object, spouting smoke...she smelled it, as clear and sharp as the edge of a blade. She momentarily mourned Joanna's lovely parlor, then did the only thing she could.

She threw herself out through the window, rolling to her feet as the explosion happened. It threw her forwards, almost to the ground again, disoriented her for a moment.

She was going to get shot again. She needed body armor or something. A crease of pain tore into her leg. It did not give way, so it wasn't bad.

Then she was moving, ignoring the twinge of pain in her leg. One was close, the one who had thrown the grenade. A flurry of blows took him down, hurt but not dead, and then his gun was in her hands.

She was neither trying to kill nor particularly trying not to. If there were witnesses, they were behind curtains, inside houses. Another gunshot, the weapon bucking in her hands, the man spun, going down. That one was dead, she was pretty sure of it.

Kill or be killed. She whirled, but the third man decided discretion was the better part. He was running, and no matter how tempting it was, she was not shooting him in the back. It hurt that she even considered it for a moment. Tucking the gun inside her jacket, she stepped back into the house.

"Joanna?"

"I'm guessing that was whoever killed Ella," came her voice, soft and small as she stepped out. Her eyes took in the damage and destruction, and she let out a soft sigh.

"I shouldn't have come here." She was tired of people getting hurt, their stuff wrecked, woken up in the middle of the night. "It's only a matter of time before I get somebody killed."

"You aren't responsible for the actions of your enemies." Joanna picked up part of the tea pot, the handle still attached to a fairly sizable shard. She frowned at it.

"I feel responsible," she admitted in tones no louder than the older woman's. "I know I didn't do anything, but..."

She would not be safe while whoever was behind this lived. Not while the police still hunted her, and the police would always hunt her. There was no statute of limitations on murder. A deal was her only escape, and that would not lead to a quiet life.

"You killed one of them," Joanna said. Not an accusation.

"Yeah. I'd better go. You can at least honestly say you don't really know me." She hadn't given Joanna her full name. But now she would get no information.

Joanna studied her for a long moment. "Try looking for Adam Fior. I don't know if it's the man's real name but try it. It's all I can give you."

She nodded and turned to walk up the street. The eyes of the buildings watched her.

* * *

Adam Fior. She felt vulnerable in the library. She would hate herself if somebody threw a grenade in here.

Adam Fior. Italian. Unfortunately, the only Adam Fior she could actually find was a painter living in Rome. He could not be the right Adam Fior, given he was twenty-three years old and, apparently, living with another man. Well, not that the latter meant that much, but the former certainly did.

So, not the guy's real name. 'Fire man'. Fireman. Fireman. She started to look up the various New York fire chiefs. Half too young, several female, but there were two or three possibilities. Of course, 'fireman' could also be some kind of mob term, or could mean he was a pyromaniac. Or, heck, had red hair...which would easily be hidden by Ella's natural black.

Laura tugged at a lock of her own.

"You look as if you're trying to solve a mystery." A male voice. A familiar voice, but one which she could not quite place.

She scowled at the voice, more angry at herself for being so obvious than the other. "Just research for school."

She would not involve anyone else. Annoyed, she closed the browser window and stood up. She had four or five possibilities. For now, it would have to do. She turned, and...how did he get here? Peter. Petey-boy.

Peter lifted his hands as she got up. "Whoa, just asking." His Adam's apple moved more than it should as he spoke.

She didn't like the fear in his face. Hated herself for a moment, but at least it would probably mean that he stayed away from her. "For..." she muttered.

She felt as if she needed a bell, to call 'Unclean' ahead of herself. Most of all this man, who fancied that he loved her. "How did you find me?" she said, hesitant there.

"Chance." He let out a breath. "Or destiny."

"Peter. Go home." Perhaps he sensed the difference within her, for he backed away, his hands lifted again.

He gave her the space to leave. She felt naked as she stepped back out, into clear sunlight, the buildings shadowing her. Half and half, light and darkness. Right now, she did not even know which was which. One side trying to kill her. The other to use her, to make her into...

She swore, stopping there in the street, somebody behind her almost walking into her.

She was trapped in her own mind, trapped with her own instincts. She was becoming what they intended, a honed weapon. Aimed at their heart. The question: Who was the target? Nancy? That woman who had never given a name? Adam Fior, who might or might not be her father? She shivered.

"You're blocking traffic," somebody snarled.

She moved, but her feet had no destination. She ended up in Central Park, heading out into the green. She had barely enough money for another day...should have robbed those men. What was she turning into?

She had abilities normal women did not. In comic books, that meant you put on a funky mask and fought bad guys. Or became a bad guy. She was becoming a bad guy.

She was also being followed. The hair on her trigger snapped as she whirled, seeking the shadow with her eyes. Let it not be some totally innocent person....woe betide anyone who tried to mug her right now.

Whoever it was stepped into the shadows. She let herself move at full speed, not really caring if anyone saw it. It was New York. People noticed nothing that didn't directly affect them.

"Eep!"

She slammed into the shadow and ended up on top of him. "Don't. Ever. Follow. Me."

It was Peter. His glasses had landed somewhere other than his face, making his eyes seem smaller than they had been even as they widened.

"You might have hurt me!" Anger and fear and concern, all wrapped up in that voice.

"I thought you were a mugger. Don't follow people in the shadows." Her tone was as sharp as a broken stick. She wanted him to go away. "Most especially don't follow me."

"Who do you think you are, Laura? Some kind of superhero?" He brushed himself off, regarding her, his eyes unreadable.

"No. I'm somebody who doesn't appreciate being followed." She let him up. "Who do you think you are? Jimmy Olsen?"

He looked hurt. Perhaps he at least imagined he was Clark Kent.

"I mean. Seriously. You're going to get yourself hurt." She was angry with him, but also deeply relieved. He wasn't somebody trying to kill her. Just a boy who thought he knew what he wanted. "Go home. Trust me and just...go home." She looked at him for a moment. Innocent. Ordinary.

He got up, started to run, then sort of sighed and collapsed. She hadn't heard the shot.

Silenced. And that was the point at which she lost it. Sometimes it is as hard a blow to see an enemy fall as a friend. He had been connected to her, bound to her, no matter how much she might wish things otherwise.

She was not about to tolerate this! She was not going to let this go...and she was on her feet, the gun in her hands, firing back where the shot had come from. The report seemed very loud. She felt time slow, the light brighten. This would be done and dealt with before the police stood a chance of getting here.

There was the shooter. She had missed him, of course, the lighting had been bad. But his own shot, too, went wide. It spun past her. She could almost see the bullet. The more she fought, the better she got.

She fired again. He went down this time. She did not check if he was dead. Briefly, she dropped down next to Peter's form, feeling for a pulse. Nothing. She stood, and turned to run, not towards the killer but away from him. Had she thought, she might have left the gun...except she needed it. She could not bear, either, to have Peter's parents think he was a killer.

It was getting to the point where only mortal danger made her feel truly alive. Yet, now she did feel guilt. A human emotion, breaking through the shell she had built. Petey-boy had, she realized, saved her.

* * *

Night, and she stood at the edge of the harbor, watching the orange bulk of the Staten Island Ferry glide across the waves. She had no place to go, and any place she went, danger followed her. Yet, she felt a sense of balance regained. Not worth it.

Not worth a life, even the life of a man she despised. Nothing was worth any of this. The only thing she could feel right now was pain.

It was easier not to be human. So much easier to just go with the flow and do what was necessary. Yet, she also saw what she had come so close to becoming. Somebody so focused on survival that she did not care who she hurt. Branson. Joanna. Using people. Except that if she was going to find out the truth, she would need help.

Statues of gods in Battery Park. She looked up at the sky, but saw nothing different. Whatever was going on was quiet for now, except for whisperings within her that became a roar as she turned...

...and saw Clark standing there.

"Go away." There was almost a growl in her voice. She did not want to see him.

"Have you learned yet that it's not safe to be on your own?" He sounded older than he looked, like a lecturing father.

"I don't particularly want to be turned into even more of a killer. And I don't trust you." Bitter words, yes, but she was fed up. "I don't trust anyone. People are dying and I want the truth, dammit." Clark might be on her side, roughly, loosely, and he had once saved her life. But no, she didn't trust him.

"A lot more people will die. That's inevitable. They don't have to include you." His tone was even, but there was something in his eyes, avoiding her gaze.

Did he care? She was certain he did not. No more than she did. He cared only about what she could do for him. Or did he? She was not sure about those eyes. She shook her head. "The truth. Either tell me the truth or walk away now before I lay one on that perfect nose of yours."

"The old gods are coming back. And they're going to be demanding all of the tribute they've missed. Much of it in blood."

"Doesn't have to work that way." She spoke only out of stubbornness. Statues of gods in Battery Park. It did fit, in some way, assuming she was sane.

"In the long run, things will be better. Look around you. So much hate and conflict, humanity making a mess of the planet. They need guidance."

"Oh, let's see. More medical discoveries, people living longer, we've touched the moon." Touched, and retreated. Perhaps they would go back, but her heart did not believe it.

"And killed children." Clark shook his head a little, his eyes seeking hers.

She did not let them meet. She did not want to deal with what might lie in his gaze. "Like the one who just got killed for the crime of being next to me?"

"He wasn't a child." Clark's words proved he knew about it. How, she did not know.

"That's not the point. This stops. Now."

"I'm sorry. I can't do that." His tone didn't sound very sorry. Then, he paused, his voice becoming more sympathetic. "I literally can't. I don't have the power to end it. No one person does."

"Oh, bull. You're not sorry at all. Except that I'm not under your thumb anymore." She shook her head. "It will stop. I will find a way to stop it. You just want me under your control."

"Safe. Out of the way. Where they can't find you to hurt you and anyone near you. Isn't that what you want?" He turned her own words and thoughts back on her.

Yes, she wanted to say. "No. Well, yes, but...with me out of the way, how much difference does that make?"

"It makes a difference to you. Heck, it makes a difference to me." This time, he caught her gaze. She could not, though, read the true depths within.

"Who is my father?" A change of subject, because she didn't like what she saw in his eyes.

He did not answer. The stars were suddenly very bright, and she realized she could not see the lights of New York. She realized that, much as in Nancy's house, she was no longer quite in this world.

"Dammit, let me go!" Reality snapped back together, as if by the force of her words alone. But Clark was gone. He had not answered her question.

"I'm going to kick his lousy butt six ways to Sunday." Old gods coming back? Where did one go for information about old gods? The library was obvious, but at this hour, it would be closed.

The woman, stopping time. Clark, apparently teleporting. Had she already been talking to gods? If so, she did not know which ones. She knew nothing. There were people who still worshipped those gods. A few, a handful here and there. Maybe they would know something. Or maybe she should go find a church.

Maybe it was the church trying to kill her. The tribute in blood...

"I won't let that happen. I will find another way." People had once placed gods in everything. Had she not seen what she had seen, she would believe they were no more real than fairies. Now, she was not so sure that fairies weren't real either. She would not be at all surprised if a pixie flew out of the bushes and threw dust at her. Possibly quite delighted, if pixies were as pretty as in legend.

Maybe Nancy was a fairy. Asian? Maybe she was an Asian vampire, who were supposedly quite different from the western kind. Maybe she was a Chinese god.

"I need to get un-confused as fast as possible," she told herself. But she could not do that in the middle of the night.

Sleep, she knew, had no chance of coming. She might as well save her money and stay awake...but not here. She walked the streets like a ghost, flowing through them without touching anything. She felt unreal.

Yet, she also thought of Petey. She would stay human. And she would work out what should happen. In the morning, she would...could she tell Branson this? He had believed her so far, but she was fairly sure he still thought something mundane and scientific was going on. Space aliens, maybe.

What am I? The silence in her head was the only answer to what she wanted to scream to the skies but did not.

The cop was half asleep, leaning against the wheel of the squad car, staring out of the windscreen. He saw her, though. She managed not to show any tension. Maybe he would not recognize her as somebody with an APB on her.

"Hey. Miss?"

She stopped, turned.

"Shouldn't be out alone at this time of night." His window was about half down, his tone more relaxed than concerned.

"Any guy who messes with me, I'll use my black belt on," she lied.

"Heh. What if he has a gun?"

"Then I'll just have to run quickly, won't I." Was he going to arrest her for streetwalking? She wasn't dressed like a prostitute. Yet she could not help the attitude that flowed from her.

"Attitude like yours'll get you killed."

She managed not to smile at him too much. "Don't worry. I really can take care of myself."

"You don't have anywhere to go, do you?" He studied her, his eyes running over her form in a totally non-sexual manner.

Any moment now he would realize there was an APB out on her and the jig would be up. She kept the tension out of herself with an effort, all the while praying that nobody would shoot him while he was talking to her. That did seem to be a pattern lately.

"Is there a problem, Officer?"

That voice was familiar, but instead of relief, for a moment, she felt fear. Branson. How had he found her? Coincidences, right now, were more disturbing than anything else.

"Just worried about the young lady."

"Well, she's with me." Branson reached for Laura's arm.

She let him take it, her eyes reaching his for a moment. It did indeed seem to be him, and she relaxed, her heart rate slowing again. He was still all but a stranger, but he was, right now, all she had. The one person who was neutral in all this, the one person who didn't want a piece of her. Or who did, but who just wanted her to be Jane's daughter.

"Well, okay then. Watch out, though. She's got enough attitude to go around."

"I noticed." Branson's tone wry, he took her hand to lead her away. Once out of the cop's earshot, he spoke again. "Why are you out here alone?"

"I had no chance of sleeping tonight and I knew it." It was a lame excuse. "No sense renting a hotel room to pace."

"Point, but with..."

"Like they wouldn't find me in a hotel room? I'm tired of this. People are dying." The worst part was how matter of fact her own voice sounded, as if she was talking about homework given her by a lousy teacher.

"Well, we need to make sure that doesn't end up including you." Branson let out a loud sigh, his hand going to his head.

"I'm starting to wonder why. All this would stop if I was out of the picture." Her eyes dropped closed for a moment. But still, no matter what, she did not want to die.

"There's a reason for that." Branson glanced back at the cop, who had returned to his own business.

"What if it's not a good one? What if they have a damn good reason for wanting me dead?" She shook her head.

"You haven't done anything." Branson spoke pure logic. One of his hands reached for her for a moment, then lowered.

"I'm not sure that means anything right now." She glanced up...the stars were clear again, as if the city lights did not exist. "The world's on the edge of falling apart and it might be that I'm contributing to that just by existing."

Branson nodded slowly. "If magic's coming back, then it's going to upset a lot of balances. I honestly wonder if it's the Catholic Church after you." From his tone he either believed her or was humoring her. He sounded as if he was capable, at least, of accepting this.

She shook her head. "I don't think so. I mean, not an unreasonable guess, but... I just don't think so." She had no reason not to, other than a hunch. The Catholic Church and old conspiracy theories "Maybe it's just too, ya know..."

"DaVinci Code?" The darkness closed around them, darker than it should have been, she could see the whites of his eyes against his skin. Yet, he still seemed calm. Almost fatherly.

She lifted a hand at him. "Yeah. Exactly. But I suppose just because something's in a book doesn't mean it can't happen in reality." She hesitated, then, quietly, "Somebody told me the old gods are coming back. And that they want blood."

"Some of them, maybe. All of them? Not likely. And it's not like there isn't enough blood being shed every day to satisfy a few gods." Wry, that.

"Point." Laura rolled her shoulders backwards. She thought of Peter, of the girl she had rescued from the pimp. Of every random death that happened. "Except that came from people I think want to see bloodshed. They want me to help them shed it."

"I would hope you aren't going to." His voice took on, for a moment, a schoolteacher-like quality.

She stopped, turned to look at him. "It's hard. I want to fight. I enjoy fighting. I can't help that. I... See, maybe things would be better if they got me."

"Oh, come on. Lots of guys enjoy fighting and never actually do more than dish out a set of lumps..."

She cut him off as sharp as a knife across a throat. "I've killed before. I doubt I'll come through this without killing again. It's hard not to when you're outnumbered by people trying to kill you."

"Afraid you're starting to like it?" No real change in his tone, as if he had dealt with this before. As if he understood, and as if he was determined to make of it no big deal.

"Yes." She looked down at her hands, fancied that they were shaded red. Except the only guilt she felt was for Peter. "I don't feel any remorse. I mean, it's all been self-defense. So far."

"And if you find your mother's killer?"

She said nothing.

* * *

Branson took her to a hotel room. A cheap one. Two beds, a nightstand, a television that did not work. She tried to sleep with no success, but as morning came she still, somehow, felt rested.

What was she? A creature of magic? Somebody who healed quickly, who could shatter chains. Like a super soldier, but if there were gods then there was magic. Those two things, surely, went together. Or, perhaps, she had read one fantasy novel too many. A gateway through which more could enter the world? Or was she intended to become a tool of the gods, shedding the blood they desired?

Not all of them. Maybe none of them. How did she know? She sat on the floor of the room, wishing she knew how to ask them. Ask the gods, directly, what was going on. Gods she didn't even know for sure she believed in.

Heh. The lawyer had suggested she plead insanity. It would likely be the truth, except that Branson believed her. Statues of gods.

Statues of gods. She stood up, checking her wallet. Not much money. Certainly not enough to... But then she had a better idea. Across from the hotel was a convenience store. She paid precious cash for a notebook and a pen, then took herself back to the cafe. Coffee revived her.

Okay. The first question was...which old gods? It wasn't like there weren't a lot of gods. Hundreds, in fact, if you counted all of the various pantheons...and Nancy was Asian, Clark Caucasian.

All of them? Was it that simple? She had to assume so, for now. So, which god did you ask for information? The gods that came to mind were those of Greece and Rome. Of Olympus. Hrm. Hermes.

Hermes, and the... She frowned and started to draw a winged sandal on the sketchpad. It was the best she could do...she was no great shakes as an artist, but did it have to be anything other than recognizable?

Time seemed to slow. It could be in her head, or it could be real. The people in the cafe were moving as through molasses. Those on the street slowed to the point of pausing mid-step.

"Who's there?" she asked softly.

Just a voice responded, "You call me and then ask who I am?"

She closed her eyes. "What do you want?" It came out as a plea, as a desperate search for answers. "What do any of you want?"

"What does anyone want? To be acknowledged, to be cared for."

It was a fairly high voice...definitely male, but not...she was hearing things. Except that everything else had been real, so this probably was, too. "I was told the old gods wanted blood."

"Some do. Some do not. You should know that."

"Who am I?"

There was a moment of hesitation. "Somebody born to darkness."

"Does that mean I have to walk in it?" It was a fight to keep her voice to a whisper, even if she was not sure anyone could hear. "Who is my father?"

"Ares."

She realized she was on her feet. That she had overturned the table. Catching her sketchbook and pen, she fled into the street.

Ares. The god of war. But that was not possible. Not...possible. She thought of her mother. A hooker. But of course. She'd been intended to grow up on the streets, become a tough kid who took no nonsense. A violent kid. Of course, she had been intended to be a boy. Had Ella known? Had that been why she had sent her away, after all? Had she hoped that in the bosom of a normal family she would grow up safe, secure, and never know who she was? She thought of the name Adam Fior...no wonder she had not been able to work out which one it was. A name put on for a night then set aside.

Somebody had uncovered her existence and set out to destroy her before she could become what she was likely to become. Nancy wanted to hone her...and she suddenly understood what the Asian woman most likely was. A demon. Or possibly an evil dragon, if such existed. She suddenly recalled reading that eastern dragons could supposedly appear entirely human.

Clark? Who knew. Demon, priest... But either way, they had sought to bring out the hidden, dangerous power within her. She was supposed to shed blood. For all the gods? Or just for one.

Her steps took her down the street. Then she noticed the library. Inside, she felt a certain calm come over her...at least as much as it was likely to. Her mind turned around and around. She did not want to believe it. Once more, she wished she was insane.

Mythology, mythology. She found it. Most of the books revolved around the Greek gods, a fair few the Norse. She hunted through the former. Taking a book down, flipping through it, returning it. She could not focus long enough to even know what she was looking for.

Dead, she could cause no more trouble. She had no more confusion. Those trying to kill her believed they were doing the right thing. Were they? She thought not, but this was her life they were talking about. She wanted to live. She wanted to be free of all this.

That, she realized, was what she was looking for. Any way she could escape, could go back to being ordinary Laura Maxwell. The old gods were coming back... No, they were already here. Probably always had been, just kinda sitting at the edges, waiting for this Christianity thing to weaken enough that they could break through.

They were real. She was real. As much as she felt sometimes as if she was becoming less so. Translucent, the darkness shining through her.

She had killed men. She had to find who wanted her dead, had to talk to him. Talk, now. Revenge only strengthened what was within her, what she wanted to get rid of. She had barely turned back from that path in time.

She flicked through, reading about Hercules and Helen. About Zeus's various kids...Hera must have wanted to kick his butt regularly. Hardly the best example of a husband, she thought wryly. But the myths only ascribed half-mortal children to Zeus. Not any of the others. Of course, from what she could read, Apollo didn't go after mortal women. He seemed to prefer boys.

Did the gods really have such human attributes? Or were they human modes of understanding, placed on the gods? She was confused. She set the books neatly back on the shelf and stepped out into the sunlight. Now she was looking for them, she saw subtle indications that reality was indeed becoming a little more flexible. A gargoyle on a building that had not been there a moment before. Somebody was selling flowers on the corner, and one of the blooms had the patterns of a butterfly's wings. She stopped by the convenience store again, looked at the paper. A plane had flown out of the Bermuda triangle, one that had vanished there in the 1950s...and that was not in a tabloid. It was documented. It was acknowledged. Magic was back.

Mystery was back. And people, Laura knew, would not well handle it. How could they? Science had taken over, and those who did not believe in one God believed in none.

How did she find people...other than children...who still believed in magic? She wondered if this Christmas, Santa really would come down chimneys and leave elf-crafted wooden toys. At an intersection she stopped and watched. Most people were not paying enough attention to notice anything unusual. They hurried through the street towards their appointments, looking more at their own feet than anything else. She felt both envy and pity for them.

She thought of Peter. Who had just wanted to ask her out again, because he thought she was pretty. Who died not even knowing why. But he had been killed by those who wanted her dead. Not intentional. It could not be intentional. But then, they also had not cared about Joanna.

So, they did not care who they hurt. They were not the good guys. She was going to stop them. She had no choice. Then she would talk to Nancy and Clark. Maybe tell them where to go. Maybe thank them. Maybe both. She was definitely grateful for the training Nancy had given her.

Then? She was going to find some way to sort this entire mess out. Or if she couldn't, at least to help those people she could help adjust. At least nobody had turned into an elf yet. Yet. She laughed dryly, reaching up to feel her own ears. Yeah, still rounded.

She hadn't seen anything that resembled a fairy, anyway. She did see what looked suspiciously like a rather small dragon poking its head around the corner of a building.

Somebody else did see it, a blonde head lifting and turning. Whoever it was probably wondered what was in their drink. Or the air.

Laura moved. She was blocking traffic again. She headed for a better spot. A sort of plaza outside one of the banks. It would do. Once there, she tried to really focus her attention on what had changed. On whether reality was just flexing or breaking.

Perhaps most people's lives would not change. At the same time, at least some worldviews were going to be shattered as much as hers had been. She had bent with it.

Many people would break. Perhaps that was the bloodshed they had meant. But no. She knew what she was now, what she was meant and intended to be. The difference was that she was not some woman of the ancient world, raised to believe in fate.

She knew she could make her own choices and find her own path. What would that path be? Maybe she would end up some kind of vigilante after all. There might be monsters.

12

That mental prediction came true very quickly. Quickly enough that Laura almost wondered if somebody or something had heard her thoughts. Not likely. But also not likely a coincidence. More that the thought had made logical sense and was bound to end up being true. Just bound to. Murphy's Law of the paranormal.

Unfortunately, the monster did not show up anywhere near her. She only became aware of it because the large news screen on the outside of the bank suddenly showed something in Central Park. Several somethings.

Large vultures with women's faces. Harpies. What did she know about harpies?

Nothing. Well, they ate human flesh, something like that. They were showing up on cameras. She felt fear flow through the crowd here. She felt panic. They didn't want to accept it, their minds on the verge of breaking. She hoped somebody noticed and turned the broadcast off. She needed to get to Central Park. Her feet took her to the edge of the crowd that had started to gather. She could see the whites of all of their eyes. Sheeple.

The edge of the road, and a cab with no fare. She would have just enough money...she needed a bike. She flagged him down New York fashion, by almost stepping in front of him.

"Central Park."

"You sure?" He was a black guy, with one earring and an uncertain expression to match the concern in his tone.

"I'll pay extra. Just get me to the edge of the park, okay." Obviously, she was not going to ask this man to go into danger. Even asking him to go closer to it made her faintly guilty and uncertain.

"What's going on? Do you know?"

Laura took a deep, slow breath. "The world's changing. Just got to ride with it. Let those of us who know what we're doing deal with the monsters." It sounded good, but did she really know what she was doing? She had...a gun. Against harpies.

Maybe they would recognize who she was or something. Or something would come to her. Harpies. She was trying to recall everything she knew about them.

"You get rid of those things..." He tailed off. "Please?"

"I intend to try. I can't make any promises." One of her, gods knew how many monsters. The report had said harpies, plural. It could be an entire flock.

He wasn't able to get her much closer to the edge of the park. People were running in a mass panic towards her. She wished for the ability to fly. Or alter time herself, but she didn't seem capable of doing that without help.

"Help me," she whispered, although she was not sure who to. Then she more or less charged against the flow of the crowd. They did not, of course part for her. That only happened in movies and comic books. She had to elbow quite a few sides before she got close enough to see what was going on.

The harpies were feeding. Fortunately, one doesn't have to be faster than the harpy...most of those still alive had a good chance of escaping. So, how did you kill a harpy? She had no clue. She pulled out her gun, shifted her stance, took aim.

There were seven of them. Three lifted their heads, turned and looked at her. Twisted vulture-things, no beauty to them at all, yet she saw them as something that needed to be.

Had to be. "You're in the wrong place," she told them. They were supposed to be in places of death, places of war. Places they could feed undisturbed.

And one of them spoke in a deep woman's voice, "So are you."

"The difference is you know where your place is. Go there." She did not raise her voice into a shout, but rather did her best to imitate a respected teacher.

For a moment, it seemed as if they might even obey her. Their wings rustled, seven sets of eyes on her.

"Go," she repeated, no doubt in her voice.

The report of a shot came a moment later, echoing from somewhere behind her. She could almost feel the bullet fly past her. The spell, the moment was broken. The harpy that had been shot hissed and leapt. It took three more bullets and kept coming.

"You can't kill them that way!" Laura found herself screaming. The idiot had ruined everything. Any chance she had had of ending this without bloodshed was gone.

The wounded harpy, dripping acidic blood, landed on him, tore through his uniform into his body. She knew that shooting it was a waste of time and bullets. The gun went back into her belt in one smooth motion as she charged.

"We're of the same being, on the same side," one of the harpies told her, hissing and spreading her wings.

"I'm on nobody's side except my own. I make my own choices." She did not say it to them. She said it to herself. She would protect these people.

It intercepted her. The force of its body slammed into her and she went down, talons raking her side. She could do nothing for the cop. Her fist flew into its face; she felt the skin on her knuckles tear as she made contact with it.

It dropped her. She realized she was moving quickly, in that hyperaware state. This time, though, she faced an opponent equally fast. "Go. Home." she told the harpy before it could get up.

"Or what? You'll tell your father?" Now it had the tone of a teenager, hinting that she would do no such thing.

"I don't need to." She had an audience. She could feel eyes on her, human and harpy. "I don't need anyone other than myself to deal with you."

The cop had stopped making any sound. He laid broken, acid burned through cloth and flesh, his body rended. She felt energy flow around and through her, and was pretty sure it was not entirely adrenalin. It was as if she stood on the cusp of something. As if her choice was being observed. "Leave."

And then there was nothing but a flutter of wings, the harpies lifting off into the air. Yet, what they left behind them was carnage.

* * *

Laura did not stick around. She departed as rapidly as possible, before anyone could stop staring.

Photos, though. There were photos, and they would be put together, and pretty soon people would know who she was. She had made her choice, and now she could never disappear again. What would the cops do?

Yet at the same time, she felt that power in her hands. Although, they had not been afraid of her. No, not exactly.

She was in the wrong place? She had free will, the same free will as any other human. Right?

She had found her way to a coffee shop, spending the last of her cash on coffee and a pastry. It tasted a little dry in her mouth, almost ashen. As if it could not compete as an experience with the fighting, with the power.

Now she was probably on national TV as...what? A vigilante, a hero, a monster? She did not know and she did not want to know.

She could still feel that transparency, although now it seemed more as if she was real and the world less so. As if she could walk through the cafe walls. She knew, of course, that she could not. That she was as real as they and vice versa.

She also felt, just a little, chilled. Cold. Probably the after-effect of the adrenalin.

Branson found her about ten minutes later.

"Okay. I've gone past freaked out," he said instead of a greeting.

"How did you find me so quickly?" This was New York, this was not a place where people ran into each other easily. He had to have had some means of locating her.

"Been trailing you all day, actually. I was hoping you'd accidentally stumble on a lead."

Her shoulders sank backwards. "I've given up on leads. All I'm worried about right now is trying to save what lives I can. You saw the harpies?"

"I did. You dealt well with that, especially..." He trailed off, slumping into the seat opposite her.

"Stupid cop," she pronounced. "But then, what other way do they know to deal with this stuff?"

"People are leaving the city in droves. Of course, they have nowhere to go. I was on the internet. Fairies in London. Dragons in Shanghai. Somebody or something opened all of the floodgates." The calm acceptance now covered something else. She heard the slight tremor in his voice, the uncertainty of it. His eyes did not, quite, meet hers.

"What if it was me?" She asked in a small voice. She hadn't done anything other than stay alive, but what if that was all she needed to do?

"I don't see how one person...no matter what...could have caused all of this. But if they thought you did..."

"Would explain why it seems to be the good guys who want me dead. Or maybe there just aren't any good guys." She let her head sank into her hands.

"Never are." His voice still held that unnatural calm. "There's better and worse, but I reckon good and evil don't really exist outside cheap fantasy novels."

Laura digested that. It tasted as poor as the pastry. "No. Some things are still right and wrong. They killed an innocent man. No matter what they intended, that was wrong."

"Right and wrong, yes. Good and evil people, not hardly."

She began to understand his point. "We're all mixed together, none of us all one or all the other."

Born of darkness? No. She had to think this through. War and slaughter. Violence without a rein on it. The Blitz, war crimes. Good war was Athena...right? Right.

And she thought of how the world had been of late. Athena had been somewhat ascendant. Until somebody had flown two planes into the World Trade Center.

Then Ares came back to the fore. Two forces that struggled with one another. Humans would fight war. It was their nature. The question was always how. Whether war could be limited, chained, placed within bounds of honor and acceptable behavior.

"You've got a lot on your mind." Gentle, now, his hand reaching across the table towards her.

She flinched away. "Too much. I can't keep up with my own thoughts."

"Been there." His tone now held genuine sympathy. "And whatever else is going on with you, you're still human. Don't forget that."

"I did for a while. I got reminded. I wish I could just be human, none of this other stuff. None of this..." What else could she say? She looked down at her hands. She wasn't human. That was the problem.

"You don't want to be hero or villain."

"Hell, Branson, I want to be a schoolteacher." The words came out with bitter sharpness and more than a little pain.

He laughed. "That would make you both."

She couldn't help but laugh. She hadn't really laughed in a while, but his comments were so true, so human...and she felt so much better for it.

"But I can't now. Heck, I'm probably going to end up rotting in jail." If she was unlucky. She would rather be dead. She would far rather be free.

"Cops would have a hard time arresting you after today."

"After today, I don't know that we'll have cops. Or anything else." Laura regarded him. "How long before things fall apart? Completely?"

"They won't." His tone was firm, confident. Who, though, was he trying to convince?

"They did when the gods left. They will again now that they're back. Humans can't handle the change. They need their laws, they need to know that when you do X you get Y."

"You're...right." His chest rose, then fell. "Maybe that's what they meant about bloodshed."

"Maybe, but in that case what do they need me for?" The bitterness was back, this time cynicism about humanity. They needed no help to kill each other.

"Given what we know...and assuming the truth is being spoken..." He looked tired. "You're an aspect of war."

"Who is absolutely refusing to be any such thing." Her voice sounded calmer than she felt. Except, she had to fight. They kept... "Both sides are forcing me to fight. The more I fight..." She tailed off, looking at the half-eaten pastry that was likely to remain so. She was not an aspect of war, she was a person. A person with free will and a side of her own. She would not let them force her into a mould.

"...the more that other side comes out. But when the alternative is to lie down and die." He was not looking at her at all now.

"Anyone would fight. Anyone. I can't be judged for that." No matter how 'right' it might seem to let herself get killed, she couldn't. Her drive, her need to survive, to stay alive and grow strong, was far too powerful.

"I know." Still not looking at her. At the table, as if counting the veins in the fake wood.

"What I can choose is what I fight for, and how much force I use. I cannot kill them...or try my best not to, anyway. I can find who's behind them and talk." She pushed at the pastry, knowing that was far easier said than done.

"You think whoever it is will listen?" Not quite skeptical, questioning.

"I have to try."

That line gave her the last word. Branson headed out, promising to keep looking for leads, although his success so far did not hearten her. He had found almost nothing.

Maybe he wasn't very good, but beggars couldn't be choosers. He wasn't charging her, and she was likely to be constantly broke for a while.

She had a guess as to who it might be behind her problems. What she was not sure of was what to do about it. Contacting Hermes had been one thing. The messenger, he stayed aloof of conflicts between the gods. This one should have played out, though, on Olympus.

Not on Earth. What had opened the door had nothing to do with her. Or had it? She might never know.

She did not care. She cared about making this all work out in a way that got as few people killed as possible. Slowly, she stepped out of the cafe. She had forced herself to finish the pastry. It was bad, but it was food. She needed food...fuel, anyway. When would she next be able to really enjoy something? She settled for trying to appreciate even the feeling of the breath in her nostrils.

The sky seemed clear, still, as if the changes had washed away all of New York's pollution. The cars still worked, though. She had read a book once where magic took over and technology stopped working. Where the planes had fallen out of the sky. A woman of great beauty moved down the sidewalk opposite and glanced over at her. Their eyes met.

It was not the woman who had hassled her, so Laura gave her a smile. That one, she would just as soon slap.

Of course, whoever it was was not human. Hrm. What could she be? Demon, she kept coming back to demon. The woman across the street could be something like that. Or some kind of nymph. Not a dryad, not in the middle of a city.

Yet, at least, it reminded her that beauty was coming of this, not just monstrosities. She was a monster herself, but she glanced at her own reflection in a store window. She did not look like one, but neither did she look normal, not any more. Something about her carriage. She stopped, turned to face herself. Something about her eyes.

She hated all of it, but at the same time, could not help but try to embrace it. What kind of woman was she? A torn one, divided between two worlds, two paths. No, far more than two. Her life was a labyrinth.

She reacted without thought, rolling to the side before the bullet hit the window behind her. Fragments of glass showered down upon her, clinging to her clothing, scraping at her skin.

She would not kill them. Broad daylight, crowded street, she would let them hang themselves. The lovely woman was gone. Laura might never find out who or what she was. So was the shooter. Or was he? She was not hurt.

She had been sniped at, she realized, probably from an upper story window. Like that would get her! She told that cockiness to go away, but it didn't seem to want to. She felt indestructible.

People had scattered at the sound of the shot. With another not forthcoming, they started to move again. There were fewer on the streets than there should be. People were fleeing the city...but there was nowhere to go. Nowhere to run to.

She had no clue where to run to herself. There was no way of knowing which window he was behind, how long it would take to reload. The subway? She had no money, but hiding amongst the people appealed.

Then it occurred to her there were monsters down there too. Possibly even including alligators, even though she had never believed that legend. If other legends were coming true?

Something moved in the corner of her eye. Yes, that was definitely a small dragon. Shoulder-sized, green with a yellow belly. She moved more quickly, determined to get out of the kill zone one way or another. Around a corner, down a block.

There. Well, except that the dragon was following her, watching her with beady little eyes. A tiny bit of smoke came from its nostrils. "Oh, go away," she told it.

It gave her a look that was pure puppy dog, then lifted off and flew above the street. She felt almost guilty, but come on, it was a dragon. It might be a small dragon now, but what size dragon would it be tomorrow? Blotting out the sun, maybe?

What sort of allies might she have?

* * *

Downtown was definitely quieter. Her feet ached, and she had considered more than once stealing another bike. Most of the office buildings had few lights in them. Anyone who could get away with it had to be working from home.

Anyone who could get away with it was hiding. Even the number of yellow cabs on the street was diminished, and anything that could scare a New York cabbie? That was something she didn't want to meet. Let alone, possibly, be.

No. Not here. Blast it. She did not have the energy to keep walking. She slumped against the outside wall of the United Nations building, exhaustion a wave that almost swept her into sleep, right there. If she collapsed in public, she was dead.

She forced herself back to her feet, but she knew she needed to find a bed or a couch for a few hours. Superpowers or not, she needed some sleep. The world blurred through her eyelids. She was not going to make it much further, let alone to anyone who might be able to help her.

"Dammit," she cursed. Where could she go? A homeless shelter seemed the only answer. Heck, a few square feet of floor would do her right now. Swaying like a drunk, she forced herself to keep moving.

"Are you alright?"

Most times in her life, those words at such a time would have elicited gratitude. Instead, she snapped, "I'm fine."

"You're not fine. Something nail you?"

She turned. The man was maybe fifty, and he kept looking at the sky. "No. I've just been on my feet all day." Any moment now he might recognize her as the freak girl. Or perhaps not.

He had not yet, but that meant nothing. Or it meant she was lucky, her appearance not yet circulating. "Then maybe you should sit down for a bit."

Maybe she should, but she knew that if she did she would fall asleep. "I'm fine."

"Suit yourself." He turned to walk away.

Maybe that was where she would end up, sleeping on a park bench like a bum. She did not go after the man, though.

Somehow, the encounter gave her a bit more energy. She made it to a small plaza and sat down on a bench, her head falling into her hands.

She must have slept after all, for the sun was lower when she was next aware of her surroundings. However, she had not been mugged...and anyone who wanted to rob her was welcome. She had nothing to steal. Her sight was clearer, though.

The world, however, was not. There was absolutely nobody in the plaza. She did see the rear of a business suit vanishing into one of the buildings. Maybe that dragon really had turned into one that blotted out the sun.

She looked up. The sun was setting, flowing down through the clouds. It had mostly vanished behind the skyscrapers, touching them with fire.

The night would be a long one. Balance. She did not even know, consciously, what she sought, but it was not here.

Then a man stepped out of one of the buildings, lifting a gun.

"Truce," she called. "Nobody shoots anyone."

He hesitated. His finger twitched towards the trigger. Her vision tunneled in on her opponent. Time began to shift and flow, but she fought it back. Maybe, for once, she could avoid violence.

"Come on. Even if you have people covering me from the windows, you can't take me down now. You missed your chances."

"Your existence will bring..."

"I'm as capable of choosing what I will bring as you are." She cut him off, not letting him finish that sentence. She knew the end of it, knew what he believed. What might even be true. "Truth is, what I want is everything back in balance...not to make things worse."

"The only way you can do that is to die." He still had the gun trained on her, but he remained hesitant. Perhaps he could not look in her eyes and shoot her.

"I know who sent you. Who really sent you." She was bluffing. "I want to talk to her."

The bluff hit home to some degree...the look of surprise that flickered when she used the female gender. "There's nothing to talk about." His voice, though, had a bit of a shake to it.

"Sure there is. Like how we can fix all of this." She flicked her fingers to indicate the empty plaza. "Humanity can't handle this."

"They don't have the choice. All we can do..."

"Bull. You expect me to put my head on the block, but you're as defeatist as the other side. I'm tired of this. Either try to kill me...knowing you'll fail...or go tell her I want to talk. Or just run away." She knew there might be others. He was probably not alone, but she could not back down. Not now.

He still had the gun out, but she could see the barrel dip a little. Wavering. Perhaps they were dredging the barrel for guys. Perhaps he was hoping a sniper in the window would do his job for him.

Then the small dragon stooped on him. It slammed into him, winged upwards, something in its talons. All that came from the man was a squeaking sound that did not quite manage to be a word.

The little so and so had grabbed his gun! Laura could not help but laugh. "I hope it doesn't know how to use that thing."

"You called it." The man was starting to get freaked out now. Professional or not, he seemed no more capable of handling dragons in New York City than the average person.

"Not consciously. I keep worrying one of its bigger cousins will show up." The entire thing had turned into a farce, thanks to the creature. A farce that suddenly shifted everything. "So. Do you really want to kill me?"

"I don't have any choice." But he was shaking. It was clear he had never wanted to do it, and now it was beyond him. She had touched him, had made herself human to him.

Where was the sniper? There had to be at least one. Where would she be if she was going to...and she rolled to the side as the bullet snapped past her. The gunman was not ready for that, quite, rolling to hit the deck.

Rookie...but then, so was she. Or was she born for this? Made for this? That did not mean she had to be a force of destruction. A second bullet, and this one hit the dragon in the wing. It spiraled into a tree, clinging to it, a hole in one membrane. She divined that it would be fine.

The gun had fallen to the ground. She rolled forward, took it before the other had even moved. "You can't beat me. We're better off on the same side." She wanted peace with these people, darn it.

"We can't be."

"I haven't shot *you*. Come on, get real." The air was feeling clear again, almost too much so. That feeling that they were not quite in normal time. Maybe they weren't. Maybe in the end, everything would go back to the edges of sight, where only those who could see would know it existed.

If she could manage that, then she would have won. And she herself would walk those edges...there were no two ways about that. If she lived.

"Why not?"

"Because I'm not the monster you've been told I am. I don't want to hurt anyone, I most certainly don't want to kill anyone. I will if I have to, but I don't want to. Sure, I'm a fighter. That doesn't make me an out of control monstrosity, or a sociopath, or anything else you might think I am. I am not just my father's daughter."

"You can't avoid being that." He was still shaking.

"Tell your mistress I want to talk." She turned to walk away. The sniper did not fire again...perhaps those uber-accurate rifles took forever to load. Out of the plaza, she saw only a few people on the street. A lot of closed doors. This had to change. The fear had to be taken away. Whether they told their mistress she wanted a truce or not... If she had to do it on her own.

What if they were right? What if her death was needed to put things back the way they were supposed to be? As little as she liked the idea, she could not help but contemplate it.

She should have mugged that guy for his wallet. Instead, she ducked into a cafe. Of course there, in the city, she could not work off a meal. Take it and not pay for it? She found her wallet, opened it, eyed the contents. Bank cards she dared not use and lint. Dammit.

Branson was nowhere to be found, and she certainly could not seek the help of anyone else. Then the woman who had once stopped time stepped into the cafe.

"Buy you a sandwich?" she offered.

"I don't trust you." Laura knew that the expression on her face would say it all; she could feel her own lips tug downwards.

"And you'll starve without food...even you can't go forever."

Laura scowled at her. She knew she was right, but did not want to admit it. "I refuse to be in debt to you. I know you work for my father."

"And what is wrong with that?"

"People are dying. For no damn good reason. And don't give me crap about tribute, or worse, crap about human nature. What's going on is more than most people can handle, and it has to stop." Laura flicked a finger towards the windows. A couple of men ran past, as if something chased them, although she did not see what.

"Too late for that now. It was too late a while ago, before you even knew what was going on. And can you really say that humanity couldn't use some culling?" The woman's spread hands encompassed Manhattan, the world.

"It's not our place to decide that." Or was it?

"Oh, but it is. That's what gods exist for, after all." Her voice was so soft, as if she was speaking of perfumes and fragrances.

"Then maybe they shouldn't exist anymore." Humanity did not need gods. Humanity certainly did not want gods. Perhaps a few did, those who would rather have guidance than make their own decisions.

"Careful. You want to cease to exist?" Now her tone was amused, regarding Laura with laughing eyes.

"No, but I don't want any of this, either." The waitress ignored them, her eyes sliding off them. She realized she was just a bit out of time again. Out of sync. Of course, she also knew she could just walk away. "I want none of this to have happened." Under other circumstances Laura could like this woman.

"That can't be. Even Chronos can't change the past once it's this set."

"Or his daughters." Laura eyed her. "You control time."

"To a point. And you fight. Accept it. It's who you are." Gentle, now. Something in her tone made Laura's impression mutual. They could perhaps have been friends, had they not been enemies. Perhaps it was, even now, not too late.

"The only thing I'm accepting is that this is real. Beyond that..." Laura shook her head. "Beyond that, I'm still keeping an open mind."

"You are chaos and war."

"Only if I let myself be." Time snapped back to normal in rhythm with her words. "And you can't really touch me."

"I could..."

"You need me alive and intact for your little plans. I'm not going to play ball." Chronos' daughter could kill her. She could also, Laura thought, possibly trap her outside of time. Possibly, too, she could not do so. She had escaped from one of these timestops before, she could do it again.

"But you could still use a sandwich."

"Maybe there's some humanity in you after all." Although Laura doubted that. She doubted this stranger understood humanity at all. She certainly didn't understand her.

"Who wants to be human?" Again, the light tone, the wryness. Yes, this could be a likeable woman.

"I do."

* * *

The sandwich was not drugged or poisoned, and it hit the spot. "I don't know that I want anything from you," she told the woman finally. "I thought it was the mob after me or...something."

"Of course you did. You were kept so sheltered you had no chance to find out who you were. You should have, you know, years ago." The woman half-smiled. "I'm...actually sorry about your friend."

"He wasn't my friend." She somehow knew the woman meant Petey. "He was my enemy."

"Sometimes..."

Laura finished her sandwich. "Are you going to stop me from leaving?"

"No. At least, not this time."

She walked away, out onto the street again. The dragon flitted overhead, its wing already healed. It was definitely following her. It liked her, she realized. Or perhaps it just knew she wouldn't try to shoot it out of the sky. How many bullets had it dodged today?

Chronos' daughter had not tried to hold her.

People had drifted back out onto the streets, at least. Starting to adapt, a little. She, though, could still feel how stretched reality had become. How thin it was, how little it would take for another incident. She stretched it herself, she could feel that now.

Okay. Was there any way she could not stretch it as much? Was that a phoenix perched on that statue? She was not sure, but she sort of focused, and she felt things become more solid. Had she made things better or worse? Was her existence really such a bad thing?

Was the magic a bad thing? No, in moderation. It was not the magic she feared, it was the response to it. Or was it? Things could easily go so far out of control that cause and effect faded away.

Reality rippled again. She felt anchored, but for a moment, the buildings were arching trees, the cars great beasts. "Oh no you don't."

She would not let a change that big happen, but could she prevent it? She found her gun in her hands...the one she had taken from the man trying to kill her. It felt solid.

New York. New York. She was not going to let this happen...and reality snapped back into place with an audible crack.

"Whoa, girl, point that someplace else." She had not even noticed there was anyone there.

She stuck it back in her belt. "Wasn't aiming at you."

"I think that somebody put freaking LSD in the water." The man addressing her lowered his hands as she put the gun away.

Not a bad explanation. Heck, maybe it was even the real explanation. Maybe she was on acid. "Bad trip if so. Long trip, too."

" I admit I haven't ever had one last this long."

He looked old enough to have experimented in the 1960s. "I haven't ever had one, but I figured." She glanced up. The dragon was gone. "But I don't think it's a trip."

"I don't either. Wishful thinking. I thought for a moment that we were all being swept into fairyland." He glanced around, then stepped over to a building. He rested his hand against it as if to make sure it was real.

"We were." She adjusted the way the gun felt against her side. It weighed a lot. Or was that the weight of guilt, forming into that relatively small object.

"I think I'm getting out of the city."

"That won't help. You want your world back, then you have to really want it." It might help. It might not help. It was all she could think of as she turned to walk away.

What did he think of her? He probably thought she was completely insane. Heck, she was completely insane. Just that right now, being insane was a good thing. Those in the asylums might well inherit the Earth if this went on. Those who had always questioned reality, always believed in fairies. Held a lingering wistful desire for Santa to be real.

They would be the ones who stayed sane, if anyone could. Yet, she had prevented things from getting worse. Had she? Or had that been a coincidence?

She walked towards Central Park. The harpies had run from her, but that was probably as much because they didn't want to get shot at as anything else. If she shot them, it would probably hurt. She was a part of their reality, and her actions affected it.

Destroy and kill. Was that all...and then she stepped into the park.

What was left of it? This particular area seemed to have been trashed in what, as far as she could tell, was a running battle between people on foot and...cavalry?

She frowned, glancing around, and then followed the hoof prints northwards. About ten horses, at a guess, and not small ones either. She doubted very much that they were the park police or the carriage horses. Apart from anything else, they did not seem to be shod. She'd tried riding once, but her mother had decided it wasn't safe after another kid got hurt.

There were some trees to the north, these were undamaged, and she saw a dappled form move within them.

"Ho!" she called.

It was not a horse that stepped out, regarding her warily with a bow and arrow in his hands. It was a centaur. Dapple grey fur covered his equine parts and a long, white tail reached the ground. His human torso was shirtless. He wore only the quiver that held his arrows. White hair flowed over pointed ears all the way down to his withers. She could not help but stare. His human half was stunningly handsome, and his equine half well proportioned. A scar ran down his shoulder from some old injury.

"So. Not the one that opened the door after all." His voice was deeper than any human's and rich. Of the creatures she had seen, he was the most beautiful.

"Not that I know of. I think the door was opened a crack a good while ago." The centaur's presence was oddly relaxing. She noticed how his hair flowed down his back and over his withers, how the breeze caught his tail and swished it against his hind legs.

"It was. Humans are not ready for our return."

"Hence why you got shot at." Not a surprise. It was probable humans had driven them to whatever part of fairyland or neverland or wherever they had been hiding in the first place.

"With the door as wide open as it is, they will hunt us even to the Otherworld."

"Okay. So. Any bright ideas on how we close it?" Maybe he would know, possessing some understanding beyond anything human.

The centaur lowered his bow. "I do not know. You smell of war, of violence."

"Sorry. I don't think I can help that." She managed a lighter tone for a moment but could not make it last. "But if we leave it open...there's going to be a lot of bloodshed."

"Which you should be seeking to cause, not prevent."

"What can I say? I'm a stubborn bitch." She liked this guy. Guy? He was more than that. Of course, he was not human. How long did a centaur live? How long, she wondered, would she live? Probably not very. But this being she spoke with could easily be centuries old.

"Good. Or I would probably have to try and kill you."

"And I would not want to have to try and kill *you*. So..." Not just because she thought she would probably lose. To destroy such beauty would be a crime worse even than murder.

"I don't think the door can be slammed shut again," the centaur mused. "But I think it can be closed part of the way. Enough to be open to those who seek it, without causing this."

"I'm willing to help with that."

"Even if you, by your nature, have to cross to the other side of it?"

That did elicit a hesitation. She sighed and her shoulders slumped. "No matter what happens...I am bred for war. I can never be an ordinary person. I can't have my life back." He, at least, did not want her dead. "I'm so dangerous people are trying to kill me left, right, and center because of what I might do."

"I do not blame them. But there may be a better way. Come. I am Ilorin."

This time, when reality began to shift, she did not fight it.

* * *

The herd of centaurs numbered close to fifteen. Unlike horses, they did not seem to group as one stallion and a harem. She saw about an equal number of adult males and females and three youngsters that she guessed were the equivalent of ten or so. They came in all the colors horses did. No foals, though. Perhaps they had left the foals somewhere safe...for she also saw no old centaurs. Or at least, none that looked old.

She felt as if she walked in a dream next to the grey one. She would not have dared ask if she could ride, although she suspected he would not be above carrying somebody in an emergency.

One of the women offered her a bowl of porridge. She was not about to turn it down, even if it might not be as satisfying to humans as it was to centaurs.

"It feels good to be around people who...get it." She sat down, resting the bowl in her lap, but was not comfortable.

"Get it?" Ilorin asked.

She forced herself back to her feet. Talking to the centaur from a sitting position was going to give her a crick in her neck. "Understand."

"I cannot say I do understand. However, I would dismiss no life, regardless of her origins. And certainly none that seems so determined to follow her own path." Seeing her stand, he slowly lowered himself, lying down.

Relieved, she sat down again, although she was still afraid to touch such an elegant creature. "I'm not an extension of him. I refuse to be."

"He may not be happy about that."

"Then so be it. As long as he smites me, not anyone else. Right now, I think he's still hoping I'll come 'round." Or was he? Maybe she needed to talk to him...although she was not sure how. She had managed to talk to one god. So, it was quite possible.

"You are still his daughter. I doubt he would actually smite you. Making your life difficult, however…"

She noticed that at the word daughter, Ilorin glanced over at one of the youngsters. She too was dapple grey, but far darker, the color of steel. She wondered if he knew entirely too much about rebellious offspring. "I don't know. I've even had people try to convince me to kill myself."

"Not a smart solution. But perhaps..."

"I think they either work for Athena or think they do." She frowned a bit. "No. I need to stop making assumptions. My assumptions and guesses are getting people killed."

"Could be the church," the centaur mused.

She shook her head. "No. I don't think so. I suspect all the Christians are hiding *in* their churches right now."

The centaur's laugh was deep. "Depends. There are more who would accept the return of magic than you think."

"Judging by the general population...no, I'm not being fair." She could not judge all humans by the actions of those shooting first. Nor could she even blame them. It was fear that guided them now.

"Fairer than most. You care enough for them to want to save them."

But she still hoped to avoid ending up dead. Even if that wouldn't be the end, she still wanted to live. What if she did have to leave? Bridge, cross, come to. It would be a life of sorts.

A plane screamed overhead and she glanced up. For a moment, she was worried somebody had called down an air strike.

"Great. They might start shooting at us."

"We are not entirely in their world," Ilorin reminded her. "Do not worry."

He was right, of course. She knew she was somewhere on the edge of...Faerie, maybe? Were centaurs a kind of fairy? "I have to come out sooner or later." What if they decided to keep her here? "I'm no use to anyone hiding."

"You're less use without food and sleep. Rest...please. If need be, we'll shoot them for you." He put a bit of amusement into that tone.

With... No, they probably had magic as well. She let herself slump down to the ground.

It was dawn when she awoke...and it had been mid-afternoon. She had not quite slept the clock around, but it was close. From the way her head felt, she had badly needed to. Clarity flowed into her as she sat up.

The centaur youngling watched her. The one she suspected was Ilorin's daughter.

She saw that it was a girl now...barely budded breasts concealed beneath a simple halter, the only clothing the centaur wore.

"I've never seen a human before." Her voice was deeper than a ten-year-old girl's should have been, yet managed a distinct feminine quality.

Laura smiled. "Hey, you are one of the first centaurs I've ever seen."

"Don't you get tired with only two feet?" The girl looked down at her almost primly.

She could not help it. She laughed...the best laugh she had had in a long time. "You know, I never thought about that. I've always only had two, so..."

"They have to work twice as hard, though," the centaur girl pointed out, seriously.

"Not really. I weigh a lot less than you do." Ilorin had to weigh about fifteen hundred pounds. Even the girl...eight hundred, maybe? Maybe she was gauging that wrong.

"Oh. Yeah. You can't see over things either."

"Depends on the thing, I suppose." She wasn't sure exactly how to assess the centaur girl's age. She had guessed ten, but she sounded more like seven or eight.

Were they stuck between the worlds? No, she realized. They did not want to risk leading humans back to their world. To wherever it was that centaurs ran.

Was there room for them here? Not likely. Humans pushed everything out. She saw something of the point of view of Chronos' daughter. Balance might well require a few less humans. However, did that mean bloodshed? No, it meant understanding.

"I guess. And I guess you're used to being smaller than a foal."

"You're not much more than a foal." Which was harsh, but likely accurate.

Ilorin's daughter actually blushed, and then Laura heard heavy hoofbeats as her father came up behind her. "No, and a foal who asks too many questions."

"It's okay. I always wanted to be a teacher." She liked children. The fact that this one had hooves did not make her any less a child.

"Perhaps you still can be."

She doubted it. She stood, slowly. "I have to leave."

"Breakfast, first. Please."

She did not linger much longer with the centaurs. As she stepped out into the real world, the harsh scent of traffic hit her. Maybe it would not be so bad to leave, to fade away into the mists.

The sun shone down, touching the trees, sending sharp light bouncing off the windows. A few people ventured out into the park. They seemed dazed and confused. Like as not they would forget if things returned to normal. If. She felt reality tug around her, and she knew it could go many ways.

She also knew she could do nothing about it. Nothing except refuse to submit to any of them. That was the only power she had. To insist that she was still Laura Maxwell.

She saw nothing dangerous in the park. A dryad leaned against one of the trees, trying to come hither a young man in a truly spectacular red and blue mohawk. He was, for right now, resisting her charms. She sensed that she would not harm him. He would probably enjoy the experience if he did succumb.

Something that looked suspiciously like a wolf poked a nose out from one copse, but it promptly vanished. She supposed it could have been a German Shepherd.

She walked out onto the Great Lawn. There, she could see anything coming. No cover for gunmen or anything else. There was no sign of the dragon. Or of the centaurs. In fact, the lawn seemed completely empty.

This was a good place, she thought. She sat down on the grass, cross-legged, feeling the dew against her ankles. Feeling the morning chill. She closed her eyes and the wind became softer, cooler. She focused on the wind.

It brought with it the smell of blood, of fire, of war. Instead of quailing from that, she followed it. Embraced it for a moment, knowing she now had the strength to come back. She needed to understand.

She saw men fighting on a battlefield with sword and shield. Then she saw planes dropping bombs on cities. She saw the blitz. She saw nothing but death.

It was good. It was bad. She could feel the two sides of her tugging at one another. Pulling, threatening her careful equilibrium. How did she find her own balance, let alone that for the world?

Maybe she should only worry about herself. If everyone did that, then the balance might take care of itself. Might.

She forced her eyes open. She was attuned to conflict. Did that mean she had to perpetuate it? She needed to talk to a general or similar. To somebody who understood. Maybe somebody who had been a Ranger or a SEAL. Somebody trained to combat until they became part of it. It had taken very little to trigger that in her, but she was born to be that way.

How did somebody like that learn to walk on civvie streets again? Did they? Maybe she should have joined the army herself.

She opened her eyes and stood up. There was a shadow above her, and she looked up. Not a dragon, no, just clouds. They seemed to her like the clouds of war.

She stood. Sitting there taught her nothing...although she did feel more confident. Stronger. She needed to accept that side of herself if she was to command it. She could not simply walk away, no matter how much she might want to. She could not be ordinary, but she could learn to fake it.

Better yet to use what she had in some way that was positive. She laughed inwardly. Maybe she would end up a superhero. Except there were no such things outside of colored panels and the occasional movie. If there were, the cops would try to arrest them and the National Guard would go after them. They would not be allowed to disturb the order of the world.

There was no order of the world any more. Whatever things settled down into, there might be space for such a thing. A little space, carved out of the edge of reality and...no, this was not fantasy. This was another kind of reality, another level to it. Hence why she, who existed in both, might have to leave. A memory, a memory of something from when she was a child. The little patch of woods outside the development. A repressed memory, forgotten until this moment, of when the woods had gone from day to night. Of things moving through the trees. Leave or die. Or perhaps death was the method by which she would cross into that other world. It was possible. It was even probable. There was no need to fear it, if so. She still did not want to die.

She did not want anyone to die. She worried about Ilorin's young daughter, who looked so like him. Who had never seen a human before. Just a cute kid. Just like any human kid in the same situation.

Children. What about the kids? They would remember this even if the adults didn't. Of course, they would stop believing. Was Santa real? She wondered...the tooth fairy she was pretty sure was not. Santa, though, might have a reality that came out of the beliefs and hopes of all of those children. Out of the spirit of giving. Maybe Santa was a god of generosity?

She was not a god. From what she recalled, Zeus' various children had been heroes, had been superhuman, but had not been gods, not from what she had read. Her teacher had explained what a demigod was. Not immortal, no

She was a being of conflict, and she seemed to affect reality more than those ancient legends would indicate. Of course, maybe they were wrong. Or maybe Perseus and Theseus had not actually been like her.

More likely, she thought, there was more to this demigod thing than was generally written or known. There, she had admitted what she was. What difference did it make?

It might mean her soul belonged to Ares, but that might not be too bad a thing. It did mean nobody else would dare to mess with it. She laughed inwardly. She felt better for being rested and fed, but she still was nowhere near a solution for her problems.

Perhaps she could still teach. What had Ilorin meant by that? Did centaurs...adult ones anyway...always speak a little cryptically?

She saw another dryad. This one tried to give her a come hither. She laughed again, calling over, "Sorry, you aren't quite my type."

The response from the fae creature was ringing laugher. "I could fix that."

"Thanks, but no thanks." The proposition lightened her mood, lifted her. She walked on on the strength of her own amusement.

13

She found more food for herself at the edge of the park. A vendor willing to give her a hot dog at a steep discount. Seeing how empty the area was, she could not blame him. Yet another reason to fix things.

But she promised him nothing as she walked away. She had nothing she could promise or offer. She was amazed he was still there.

She heard the roar of a motorbike. No, of several motorbikes. She wanted one, she wanted the wind in her hair and the freedom of the open road. That was something she would hold within her and cherish, that ride out into the mountains. Something she might never do again.

They swung around the block, along the street. She thought of Simon, and wondered if she would ever see him again. Likely not. They had been ships passing, and as long as he was alive and free, she would have to be content.

She felt empty. She hadn't managed a sardonic comment, even to herself, in...how long? Too long. Was she Laura Maxwell anymore?

She was nothing and nobody. Well, maybe it was time to change that. "Hola!" she called to the bikers.

One of them slowed, then turned the bike into a quick halt. "Well, hey there, hot stuff."

Oh great. He thought he was God's gift to women. Yet, that she could handle, she felt something well up within her. It was probably annoyance, but she wanted annoyance. Needed a human emotion. "Watch out, I tend to burn people who get too close."

He laughed, tugging off his helmet. "You got guts even to be out. 'Course, you know what the government's saying."

"LSD in the drinking water." She didn't know. She guessed. It was the only scientific explanation anyone was likely to be able to come up with.

"Yeah. Which given I haven't drunk the tap water in weeks..." The biker glanced at his two companions, who had stopped a bit behind him. A man and a woman.

"They need to say something, or the ordinary people..."

"They're already panicking. Hasn't helped, has it?"

"Eh," Laura said. "When it's over, that explanation will work. People will need one."

The question was when...whether...it would be over. She glanced up again. The harpies were back, but now they circled high above the city. She could tell that they were not birds. The shape was wrong, the pattern of their movement not any she had ever seen. Besides, she could almost smell them from here. Vultures. The archetype, the ultimate vulture. Centaurs, the ultimate horseman.

"I dunno. I think this may be the new reality." That came from one of the other bikers, a tone of cynicism laced with fear.

"Not if I have anything to do with it." She could be confident. She had to be, to try and instill some certainty into these people.

"You act like you have the power to change it." The one who had called her hot stuff. He seemed the most talkative.

Her lips twitched. "We have the power to change it."

He shook his head. "All we have the power to do is kill monsters. I'm going to go hunt me some." He whirled the bike around and gunned it. The others followed him.

She wondered now if he had been the one who had shot up the centaurs. She idly contemplated trying to find Ilorin. Maybe he could help her more. Or she could lead those hunters straight to him. If they knew, they would hunt her.

But then, she had to get used to being hunted. It was her future and her destiny, the way things were going. Until she was finally brought down. Or she found another solution. She told herself that, firmly.

She turned and walked in the opposite direction from that in which the bikers had left. At least they were dealing with things, coping, albeit in a violent sense. It was better than hiding or fleeing. Or was it? She did not want any more bloodshed.

We have the power to change it. Why had she said that? Because it sounded good. No, because she wanted to believe it. She had said it before, it kept coming out. Maybe she did believe it, at some level below the conscious. The street was empty when it should have been full. A newspaper blew down it, landed at her feet.

Just like the biker said. Drinking water contamination. That would not wash for long. People would realize it was not local, that the entire planet was affected. They would grasp that and they would lose their grip. Was reality more than a consensus?

She closed her eyes, there on the sidewalk. The wind rushed around her, and she saw the flickering of sword play out of the corner of her eyes. "I know you're here. I know you're listening. Is this really what you want, Father?"

No answer, at least none in words, none in any form she could understand. Just a sense of a presence. Strong, solid, but somehow unsure. Could a god doubt? Perhaps he had underestimated humanity. Perhaps he had misjudged modern culture. If he wanted a war, he had not gotten one. Or had he...what had he wanted? She might be his daughter, but she did not know his mind. If the gods were merely sentient beings, then they were capable of making mistakes. Capable of having emotions. Capable of loving? Did he love her? Maybe, maybe not. He had not loved her mother, but then he had chosen a woman used to not being loved.

Carefully chosen. She pulled her mind back onto the humans. Onto the people of the city, the way they were acting. The way they were likely acting in other cities, other places.

"They're mostly cowards, aren't they," she murmured to herself. Or to Ares, if he was still listening.

Why did she care to save them? For the ten brave men in Sodom? For Peter.

Except he hadn't been brave. He had been ordinary. The wind became warm, very warm. For him?

She realized that the god was there, was touching her. Embracing her for a moment. Did he want war and bloodshed?

It was in his nature to do so. But she had free will. She had her nature but also her choice. He did not speak to her in words, it was just a reminder of that. Did he have...he had freedom within the limits of what he was. Mortals had more freedom than the gods.

"You're telling me to do what I want?" She spoke out loud now, not caring who might hear.

Finally, a voice, "No. What you need to do." His voice sounded rough, fierce. Did it sound that way because that was how she imagined it, or was that how it was? A bit of both, perhaps. He was speaking to her heart and soul, not to her ears.

"So you think I'll do what you want anyway?" She was defiant, she could not help it. She did not fear him, and she knew that he did, in his own way, love her. Perhaps in her own way she loved him, as best she could when she did not know him. Was that a good thing or a bad?

"There are choices." The wind returned to its normal temperature.

He had acknowledged her stubbornness. But he was still sure she would end up doing what he wanted. "What do you want?"

But the sense of his presence was gone. She was standing in the street, talking to thin air. She wished there was somebody around to hear her, to think her crazy. It felt as if time had stopped again. There was nobody there, the street empty except for pieces of paper and a stray cat who padded up the sidewalk, unconcerned. Cats had always had their own view of reality.

Chronos. Ares. Who was on whose side? Nobody's side but her own. Nobody was on anyone else's side here. All selfish, the entire lot of them.

Including her. Didn't she have her own agenda? It might be favorable to humankind, but who was she to decide that? "All of you. For crying out loud just stop and think about what you're doing," she said to the air.

This time she was heard. A girl of about fifteen had come out of one of the buildings. Was she afraid to go to school, or had it been closed? More likely the latter, Laura decided. She didn't seem afraid.

"All of who?" She glanced around. "I don't see any monsters."

"You can't always see them. Or distinguish them from men." That sounded good, Laura decided. There were plenty of human monsters out there, after all.

"True. My uncle's a monster. He hit me."

"I hope you told the police."

"I did. Now he stays away from me. Are you a monster?"

Laura revised the kid's age downwards. Thirteen, but a big thirteen. "I try not to be."

"But you know what's going on." The girl reminded her of Ilorin's daughter. Children, not so different. Older, though. But afraid in a way the centaur foal had not been.

"Some of it," Laura admitted. She still had not placed Nancy, had not established her identity, her nature. Maybe she was a dragon after all...the other kind. What was her agenda?

"Who's behind it?" The girl had her eyes on her, desperate for somebody to talk to, somebody to trust.

"All the old powers of the world, tired of being shut away." It did seem to be all of them. About the only thing she had not seen was an angel and, if she was an angel, she would probably be protecting a church.

"Maybe somebody needs to talk to them."

"What do you think I was trying to do?" Laura glanced around. She hadn't been shot at in a while, but she still did not want to stay close to this kid any longer. "But I need to go."

She walked away. Not asking for a name. Not doing anything that would make the girl want to come after her. Or make her stand out as anything, as anyone important. Distance. She needed distance.

She had choices. One choice, obviously, was to step aside and let all of this happen, see how it shook out. Another was to let her nature win out and go around killing people. A third was to do that but kill only bad people. Of course, how many people on death row were exonerated each year? How could she be...she could never be sure. The fourth was to try and close the door. The fifth...was to close it halfway.

One, was not in her nature. Not in any part of her nature. Two was the easy route. Let the monster out. Three just tried to justify that.

The monster had to be controlled. Between four and five? It was not for her to decide. She understood that now. She would not be a god. She would not...but how did she get hold of people to ask?

A knot of men passed her on the sidewalk, men in fatigues. The government had called out the National Guard, for the good it would do.

Her steps took her to the library. Maybe there would be people in there. The climate control enveloped her. Technology was not affected. Yet, anyway. There were people in here, sitting in huddled groups in the reading room. Trying to hide from the irrationality amongst the very symbols of human intelligence and control.

It did feel like a safe place.

"Is it still insane out there?" an old woman asked, softly.

"I'm afraid so." She looked up and down the stacks, then walked over to an unoccupied computer. If the librarian was around, she did not care enough to sign her in.

Where did you find people in this day and age? You found them on the internet. She pulled up a search, found bulletin boards.

She read, and what she read both troubled and excited her. Some people were welcoming what was going on, but they were in the minority. There was a large segment who were expecting the Rapture to rescue them any minute. And quite a few bought the LSD in the water explanation. Most of those, though, thought the government had put it there. The rest blamed terrorists.

But could she navigate a consensus amongst this? And did she...she was overstepping. Choices.

She could choose what she wanted, but she knew she could not create it.

The snatches of conversation, though, were telling. *I tell you, it's aliens.*

That wouldn't be that unreasonable an explanation. Heck, maybe it was. Maybe that was what they were, the old powers, something from another world. She'd read books with that premise, multiple times. The gods nothing more than beings with power and knowledge mankind did not possess. Except, she knew that was wrong. Nothing of this world, surely, could bend apart the very laws of physics. Could any advanced technology stop time?

No. It did not quite fit. Not gel with the reality she was experiencing. With the myriad of creatures. She could buy that Ilorin was a representative of some other civilization. That centaurs walked among the stars. Yet, that could not be the explanation. She read on.

'It's the Greek gods and they're pissed off that nobody worships them anymore.' To which somebody else had responded, 'I do'.

She wondered if she could find that person. Heck, maybe all it would take would be a bunch of people making libation to Zeus. It could not be that simple. She made a login quickly, signed on and responded to the thread.

'It is. Anyone got any clue how to get them un-pissed?' she typed, and then refreshed.

Somebody was leaning over her shoulder. "You really think so?"

She turned. It was probably the librarian. No, that was stereotyping, but the thin man did have the wire rimmed half spectacles and lack of a tan that she associated with librarians.

"Yeah, actually, I do."

"So, do you think that if we did something in their honor, they'd go away? It's a shame the Olympics only just happened." His tone seemed thoughtful.

The Olympics. Wasn't that plenty of honor? No, because nobody really believed it anymore. They didn't even honor the Olympic truce. Didn't even honor... War. Oh no, it couldn't... "I know this sounds stupid, but maybe that's part of the problem."

"The fact that we keep doing the Olympics and forgetting to mention the gods?"

"No. I was reading up...hold on." She typed in another URL. "In the old days, no warfare was allowed while the Olympics were going on. They had a truce. Last year, it was suggested the truce be honored. Nobody listened."

"Which ticked off the gods."

"Probably not the only thing that did. And now they want appeasement. Possibly in blood."

"They probably want the heads of the people who broke the truce."

That...she knew she could not achieve. "Probably. I wonder if they would settle for a sincere apology accompanied by some kind of offering." She looked at the librarian. "You believe me."

"Odd as it might seem, my mind is finding angry gods more reasonable than acid in the water." He shook his head, producing an amused laugh...half a laugh, anyway. There was some humor in it, but it was not of the most pleasant kind.

She laughed. "I haven't been drinking the tap water."

"I'm going to try something."

Her sketchbook. She pulled it out, quick pen notes. There had been people around before, so that part did not bother her. Her attention was entirely on what she was doing.

But she was interrupted. Clark, walking easily across the library floor.

"Look what the cat dragged in." No, Laura did not care if the librarian realized that this person was not much of a friend to her.

"You should come home, Laura."

"Is this about the truce?" She stood, turning to face Clark.

"Screw the truce."

"I don't think that's what he wants you to say." She did not specify which he she spoke of, she knew she did not need to.

"I'm not exactly working for him. And he was probably whispering in their ears." Clark smirked a little bit, regarding her. He did not seem to care what any of the civilians heard at this point.

When had she started thinking of people like that? Separating herself off from them?

"What do you think you're getting out of this?" She moved between him and the librarian...who was finding the stacks interesting. Good. If this turned into a game of fisticuffs, she wanted nobody in the way. It might. She was not sure whether or not she could beat Clark. She was still not sure who he was. Maybe nobody important. Maybe the latest of Zeus' byblows. Not like there had not been enough of them.

"Hrm. Well, I was hoping for you." His eyes rested on her.

She stopped dead. "What?" He was attracted to her. She knew that, probably had always known it. Now, he was making it obvious.

"I...was hoping when we had everything dealt with that I could ask you out."

She couldn't help it. She laughed. It was a good laugh, a ringing laugh. "So, your entire involvement in this is because you think I'm hot?" Could she return it? She considered it for a moment, weighed it in her mind. She found the idea of such a relationship wanting. She had other things to do, more important than any romance.

"Not all of it. The human population needs to drop. War is the best way to manage that." He sounded like he meant it. The librarian edged further away.

She shook her head. "There are always choices. Unleashing war, uncontrolled?" She sketched the image of a mushroom cloud in the air. "With the weapons we have now?"

"Would it..."

She cut him off. "It would be a holocaust. Genocide multiple times. You know that. And the reason everything is stirring is not to cause that. It's to stop it."

"There's not really that much chance of it without appropriate...encouragement." Clark glanced at the librarian, who was now scurrying into the stacks rather like a mouse into a hole.

"Without sneaking a satchel bomb to the right terrorists. Was that what I was supposed to do? Somebody more inclined towards combat than anyone else you could find? I worked it out, Clark. The good guys are the ones trying to kill me. They're just a little bit confused. Well, and poor shots."

People were staring now, as if the altercation's sphere of influence had spread outwards, encompassing everyone in the library. Heads turned in their direction. "It's over, Clark," she concluded.

"No, it will never be over." His stance shifted. "Especially not for you." There was something close to pain in his eyes.

She shrugged. "I'm not what's important. They are. There will be no holocaust."

"You really think you can stop it?" Now he was angry with her. No, not angry. Disappointed.

She was hurting him. At the same time, his words triggered

something. Whispers of fire, of swords through the air. She nodded. "Yes."

She half expected him to attack. Instead, he laughed and walked away, not at all the nice young man who had rescued her. He was upset with her. Because she would not play ball and because she would not give him a chance romantically. Perhaps more the latter. She shook her head.

Had he even rescued her? Had that entire thing been some kind of setup? That would not surprise her. It was the way of things, she decided. Everyone was after something, everyone had an agenda. Everyone manipulated, even those who thought they were the good guys. They all thought they were the good guys. The worst evils were committed by people who believed they were right.

She felt her breath in her nostrils. In, then out. She was alive, but she did not feel it. She had divined an unpleasant truth about reality.

Nancy was right. Nobody was on any side but his or her own.

14

She slept that night in an office that had been left unlocked. She wondered how many other squatters had done the same thing, in small walkups at the edge of the city. In buildings that did not have massive security. In the low rent district. It was better than the streets, even if all she had was the floor and her clothes. No blanket, a jacket for a pillow. Somehow, she managed to sleep anyway. That spoke to how tired she was.

When she stepped out the next day, she saw a grimness, a grit that had not been there before. People were trying to go about their normal lives, even in the face of chaos. She felt her respect for humanity grow. Perhaps they could even force the magic back by the force of their wills. More likely, though, it would fight. Some of them would die or be consumed. Some, she knew, would embrace it. Would willingly step into the shadows.

Some always had. The word that came to her mind, of course, was witch. Could a witch help her? She didn't know enough about witchcraft to answer that question.

The air had a chill to it that promised fall, although the leaves were not yet turning. Persephone was still with her mother. The earth was moving away...no, it was axial tilt. Yet, she could not help but lean towards the more poetic explanation. The goddess of flowers would soon descend into the Underworld.

Seeing people out and about, though, she felt an energy that had not been there before. Hope glinted in the windows. No, hope was the reflection of humans walking...even if she was pretty sure she saw a naiad amongst them. Was that a faun, sitting on that low wall, raising his flute to his lips?

She stopped to listen to the soft woodland melody echoing across the street. So did others, and perhaps they caught a glimpse of possibility amongst the horror. One even tossed a bill...she could not see the denomination...towards the forest creature. He did not take it, but he did bow slightly towards them. The money was useless to him, but the appreciation still mattered.

Could there be a balance? A moment later, it was upset, three youths stalking towards the faun. "Get out of our city," one said.

"No, we don't want them to *leave*," the other one said.

She was on the side of humanity, wasn't she? On the other hand, they were drawing knives on an intelligent being that was doing nobody any harm. It wasn't as easy as that, was it. Nobody's side but her own. She could do whatever she wanted, she was not bound by human morality or by any rules other than her own.

"Leave him alone," she found herself saying. It came out almost without thought.

"Oh, what have we here? Another one?" They turned towards her.

Run, she thought to the faun. He didn't. He got up and decorously walked to a different location, but not without winking at her. Quite willing to let her fight his battles for him, it seemed. Coward, she thought wryly. Then again, he was not armed and she was, the gun coming out of her pocket, although it was inside her arm. Not obvious.

"She's prettier than the other freak," the one who had told the faun to get out said.

She kept much of her attention on the one that wasn't talking. They were generally the most dangerous. Whatever danger she faced, though, she could handle. "You can't actually hurt me. There's answers to this but beating on fauns sure isn't one of them."

"The freaks are taking over," the one who had said he didn't want the faun to leave said as he walked towards her. He was a big white man, wearing a heavy gold chain around his neck and short cropped hair. He looked like a skinhead.

"There's a reason for it. It's going to take everyone to solve it, and the more you resort to violence, the longer it's going to take." She kept her tone reasonable.

He tried to punch her in the nose. He ended up hitting the space where her nose had been a moment before. To her, he moved as if he was in molasses.

She did not hit him back. She did not need to. The other one tried to trip her. He was just as slow. "I already said you can't hurt me."

The third one finally spoke. "Guys. Stop tangling with Wonder Woman there and let's go get something to drink."

Maybe not the dangerous one after all. Or maybe he was. Maybe he would come back later, with a gun. She stayed in a relaxed stance, waiting for them to try and hit her again. She had a feeling they would not. Then, they ran. Relief flowed through her. She had been worried she might have to hurt them.

"Not bad," said a voice from behind her.

"Not bad?" She turned. "Hello, Nancy." She should have known she would bump into her again before the end of this.

"Would have been better if you had killed them." Nancy's tone carried mild disapproval.

"That would have been rather wasteful," Laura pointed out. Part of her wanted to drift back into the role of student.Those two weeks had been oddly comfortable, which was why she hadn't left sooner..

"You fight your nature so."

"I thought your kind were ancient and wise beings." She circled Nancy a little, warily. "Peaceful."

"And what did it get us? To be forgotten until it suits the world to trot us out as tourist attractions?" Bitterness flowed from the woman. Something like lightning glinted in her eyes.

"You just want respect, then?" Did she respect Nancy? Yes and no. Now she knew for sure what Nancy was, she had to respect what power she possessed."Do you really think all of this is the way to get it?"

"No, but what better opportunity can any of us have?" she asked, softly. "What do you seek, Laura?"

"Peace." One word, one concept, but something so hard to reach. So hard to understand.

"Given who you are, that seems unlikely."

"Maybe I'm just a rebellious kid," she quipped, feeling herself relax. "I won't cause...or if I can prevent it...allow mass bloodshed. Not for anyone or any reason. I know that's not what you want, but that's my choice."

"Good luck keeping to it," was all Nancy said. Then she faded away, leaving behind her the faintest hint of wind.

"Talking of freaks," Laura muttered. Of course, how long had she spent in the dragon's lair unharmed? Nancy had not touched her.

How much did time matter? It might not matter at all. Or it might. It certainly mattered to the mortals...surprisingly few of whom had glanced over at the confrontation.

Could they actually adapt? No. Definitely not. They would hate and they would fear, because they had too much knowledge to fully respect. To fully accept magic required ignorance...willful or otherwise. Except...she was having no problems.

She had, she realized, always wanted there to be magic. She had given up believing in Santa a lot later than most children. This Christmas, he probably would ride in his reindeer sleigh. Maybe she could leave that much of a door open. Yet, if anything could come through, then so could bad things. There could be no discrimination of that kind. The monster under the bed might also become real, to be chased away only by a parent's strong arms. Did that make her willfully ignorant? No, it simply made her a dreamer.

She realized she was staring at the space where Nancy had been. There was magic, it was real, and she had accepted it easily because she was magic. No need to psychoanalyze herself. She would have been a schoolteacher, had she been left alone. Perhaps that had been the intent. To leave her alone, to let her be. If the door had not opened. How many others had there been? Not many, for if they were out there they would have come to help. Could she really have lived in obscurity, or would she have been inexorably propelled to some kind of greatness? She thought of Mahatma Gandhi and Florence Nightingale. And Hitler. Great does not mean good, and what does good mean?

The faun waved to her, then went back to playing his flute. She didn't have cash to leave, so instead she stepped over and bowed once before walking away.

His face showed only surprise.

* * *

It was the faun, of course, who gave her the idea. Not a good idea, but the only one she had. She went back to Central Park.

She went back to where the centaurs had been attacked. The grass was starting to grow back, slowly, but there was still much damage to the ground, to the trees.

She could not repair it. There was nothing she could do to heal the damaged earth, but it would heal itself. That was a promise, she thought. So far, those promises had been kept. The sun had risen on schedule, the air was starting to cool as the seasons progressed. The stars had moved only as much as they usually did. There was, Laura thought, some stability.

She stood there, though, looking at the destruction. Somebody should at least come here with grass seed. That would send a message of determination. Yet, it would not be her.

That was not why she was here. The centaurs, she divined quickly, had moved on. Perhaps now they walked in the Appalachians, or even further west, in the Rockies. There was room for them there. She even entertained the image of them helping with a cattle drive, cowboy hats and all.

She tugged out her sketchbook, marking down the lines of such a picture. She was no great artist, but she didn't want to lose the image now she had it. Ilorin, wearing a cowboy hat, a lasso around his shoulder. Pure fantasy, of course. She doubted the ranchers would accept such company, even if all they needed was grain and water.

She wished that what she envisioned could come to pass, but as it was...the door had to be slid back. Not all the way. And there was still a door here.

She walked over to it. Would she, after all, have to close it from the other side? There were worse fates. Nobody else would have known it was there. Most would have walked past that threshold and on, still within this world. Perhaps it had even been here before Manhattan was Manhattan. Before the skyscrapers had been built. Before the white man's eyes had rested here, but what came through the door were white man's gods. She wondered what the original inhabitants of the continent thought. Did their gods, too, walk? That, perhaps, might give Nancy the war she wanted.

She felt the gunmen rather than saw them. Too many of them, moving to surround her. She heard weapons being cocked. She sprinted for the door. She did not want another battle right now, even as her blood called for it, sang for it. Her will overcame, finally, and there was a certain joy in that. She could control it; she did not have to be this thing.

They did not try to follow her. She was in the mists between this world and the other. She was where she had talked to Ilorin's young daughter. There were still some signs of the centaurs' encampment...hoof prints and the like. A dropped arrow. She picked it up, then glanced towards the door. There was another exit from this place, if she could find it. One that would drop her somewhere other than amongst the gunmen. There had to be, because the hoofprints led away from the park.

She followed them. Centaurs were easy to track, she discovered.

They were more careful than horses about certain things...she saw no droppings in the trail itself, and presumed that they were moving to one side when nature called so nobody would step in it. Too late, she realized that she might well be simply moving deeper in. She might end up in Narnia.

Then again, that would be fun. Talking animals and divine lions and, of course, fauns. And grumpy dwarves. She hadn't seen any dwarves.

Then one of the trees moved. "Are you lost?" A beautiful, female voice.

Laura knew instantly what it was that spoke. "I'm looking for a way back to the world of men other than the one back there."

The dryad sounded amused. "Some problem with that one?"

"About six men with guns I'd rather not be dealing with right now." She managed to make her own tone wry, matching the tree spirit's.

The tree nymph looked her up and down. "Not like you couldn't."

"I'm just not in the mood." Part of her was, but another big part was not.

"I think there is one if you go left and into the cave, but it comes out in the basement of a building." Presumably, the dryad had already investigated it.

"Honestly, that works for me." They would not look for her there. "If they manage to find their way this way, just stay out of the way. I don't think they're above shooting at you."

The dryad laughed. "I will vanish if I see them. They are welcome here only as long as they don't use their weapons. If they do, I will cause them to become so lost they have no chance of returning to the world of the living."

"Fair enough." Laura hoped they would not meet such a fate. She also resolved not to touch her gun until she was out of here. The place seemed almost like...she supposed, once, Manhattan had been a wooded isle. That thought, returning. Gods of this land...but they were not here. Too many white people, perhaps.

"You are not what I would have expected." The dryad, turning back towards her.

"I'm just too stubborn to follow the obvious paths." She was in no hurry to move on. More lighthearted than Ilorin, this being, but still surprisingly human. Or perhaps simply close enough to understand, or faking it. Could she really understand a being bound to her tree, to live as long yet never to travel far from it? One so...well. Her mother had lived from seducing men. Dryads did it because there were no male dryads. She must have read that somewhere, or did she simply know it?

The dryad stepped towards her, rested a hand on her shoulder. No heat came from her. "Good. We could use more of that in the world. This world and that one."

She felt welcomed for a moment, although her nature...no. This could not be a place for her to stay. There were places for her, but this was not one of them. "I can't stay," she told the dryad softly. "I would bring death here." She would bring fire, she would burn these forests. If not of her own actions then of those of her enemies. Would there be rest for her? Not likely.

"You would," the tree woman agreed. "But at least you have the strength to make your own choices and are not merely an axe in the woodsman's hand."

Laura smiled at her, then took the left-hand path, stepped into the cave...

...and into a basement full of crates. It looked like it was mostly old office equipment. Obsolete stuff they did not want to throw away in case they needed it, she supposed. She wove through it, looking for a way out. It seemed so much dimmer than the woods. As if that was the reality and this the echo.

Neither was. They were simply layers...and there was the door. It was locked, but that would not stop her. She was strong enough to break it, feeling almost bad about it. Some poor person would have to replace it. Up a set of stairs and into an empty lobby. Apparently, everyone had stayed home or gone home. There was not even a security guard to be seen. The main doors were locked too, but these opened easily from the inside, clicking shut behind her.

She made a mental note of which building it was, but kept moving. The truce, it seemed, was over. She was, too, blocks from anywhere at all useful to her. The dryad had directed her to the nearest door, not the best one.

Well, too late for that now. She glanced up. There was a great clock on the side of one of the smaller buildings. It had clearly stopped, reading about one o'clock. She frowned and glanced at her watch.

Blast it. It had stopped too, albeit not at the same time. About, she realized, when she had gone through the centaur clearing. She banged it against something and it started again, but she had no way to set it to the correct time.

Dammit. She did not even want to ask a passer-by. Besides, it was entirely possible Chronos' daughter was wandering around again and messing with things. Or something else that affected time.

Time, something she wanted to rely on. The sun was moving towards setting. What if it was setting early. What if... Okay. She had developed a headache. A bad one. One that would not go away. The few people on the street hurried. She guessed the actual time at about six. Her stomach informed her in no uncertain terms that it was at least close to dinner time. She would have to find food, even if she had to steal it. The dryad, of course, would have had none. Laura was pretty sure she lived off of photosynthesis, like a plant. She saw another knot of guardsmen on the corner.

Young men, uncertain faces. No better equipped than those they were supposed to be protecting, fingers itching towards triggers. They would likely make things worse.

She turned the corner, and stepped into Times Square. That clock showed a more reasonable time, and she felt relief flow into her. Just a mechanical failure. Or some kind of mischievous creature going around stopping clocks for the heck of it. She would not be at all surprised by that. Times Square was, to her surprise, not empty. Far from it, in fact. It seemed that people had gathered there. She frowned.

Right at the center of it was Chronos' daughter. She was speaking in clear tones, her voice carrying, "Only blood will appease the old gods. There is no other way."

"Bullcrap!" Laura yelled. The word caused a few heads near her to turn. Good. She had their attention, or some of it. Attention torn away from Chronos' daughter. Who was apparently trying to start a small war of her own. Or a riot. Or something. She pushed closer, towards her, the crowd parting reluctantly in front of her.

"Bull. It was bloodshed that started this. Hell, it might have started during the blitz." She wasn't above swearing. "The door is open between this world and the other world. Closing it is going to take all of us, and even then, it can't be closed all the way. Magic is here, and it's here to stay."

"She says different," a large man said, dark eyes on her. Challenging. Challenging her to counter the other's words.

Not easily done. "She lies. Or more accurately, she tells only those parts of the truth that suit her."

"And she is a murderer," Chronos' daughter accused.

"I only hurt people who try to hurt me." She had expected that and responded to it quickly. With the truth, instead of trying to claim she had never caused harm, never taken a life. She had been given, after all, no choice. None. Now, though, she had become more skilled, good enough to be able to avoid fatalities.

"So, what, you admit you've killed people?" The woman's lips quirked, something that came about halfway to a smile. Not a very nice smile.

"When somebody's shooting at you and you shoot back, it happens. I try to avoid it." She regarded the woman who claimed to be the daughter of Chronos. She saw something which heartened her and caused her to pity, all at once.

The other woman was clearly, visibly, exhausted. "Come on," she said as she approached. "How about we stop the rabble rousing and come up with a good way to handle things?"

She snorted. "If you won't do it, I have to. You have a responsibility, Laura."

"Again. Bullshit. I have it straight from the horse's mouth that there are always choices. Blood is only *one* way to appease them." It might work, but it was not the way towards peace and understanding. Certainly not the way to get respect.

"You're a stubborn fool," Chronos' daughter pronounced.

"Takes one to know one." Laura shifted her stance. The people there did not know who or what to believe. They were those, she suspected, who had most accepted what was going on. Many had embraced the return of magic, had dreamed of it their entire lives, but now it was here? Now, they wanted some control back. The ones who could not accept it would have run.

Was that a smile? "Maybe so. But we certainly don't have to be enemies." Yes, a smile, but a tired one.

"That comes from your choices just as much as from mine. And don't give me any crap about not having any..." Laura tailed off.

"Just because you think you have freedom, means nothing. Some of us have accepted our fate."

"I talked to him. He trusts me." That, she realized, was what the god had been trying to say to her. That it was up to her to judge the best course of action. Perhaps, after all, he had not sired her on purpose. Heck, it didn't seem like he knew quite what to do with her, perhaps because she had not turned out a boy. Great heroes were still supposed to be male. People had forgotten about the Amazons. Great heroes also tended to end up dead.

She stepped forward, offered her hand to her rival. "Look. You're exhausted. You're over-straining your power doing fancy tricks. You look almost as bad as I feel. How about we go somewhere, get some food, talk about this?"

She expected a no. Her matter of fact tones, though, seemed to get through to the other woman, who took her hand...and then they were somewhere else.

Teleportation. Of course, another way of bending time.

"What's your name?" She had never found it out, and she felt she needed that connection right now.

"Lucia," Chronos' daughter said, after a long moment.

Roman, not Greek. Laura tried to envision Lucia in Roman dress, and found it an interesting image. "How old are you?"

"Old enough. Sometimes, the children of gods age, but I don't."

"Probably this power over time thing you have going on." Would Laura age? If she stayed in the world of men, then yes, instinct told her. If she went to the other side, then perhaps not.

"Oh, not probably. Certainly. It has its uses. So. You claim that he offered you choices?" Her tone was somewhat skeptical.

"He doesn't seem interested in telling me what to do." She had got the impression he cared, though, which had surprised her. Given all the legends, all the stories, that implied he was a cold and ruthless god. Still capable of love.

"He's a somewhat chaotic god. But believe me. The only way to end this..."

Laura cut her off. "The gods are angry. They are also frustrated about not having many worshippers any more. So, they did this. I'm only tangentially connected...probably the result of Ares getting bored and horny."

Lucia frowned a bit. "This started when..."

"It didn't start on my birthday or anything else significant. It was around when people started trying to kill me, but that's more likely an effect of the same cause. I didn't do this, consciously or otherwise." She kept her words clear, her voice sharp but firm. She was determined to convince Lucia of certain basic, to her, facts.

Lucia was still frowning. "We can't be sure of that. And you..."

"How many children of gods are walking? You, me, Clark?"

"To my knowledge. And Clark is not even our cousin. I think he's one of Thor's." She pauses. "Our kind tend to be rare, we tend to hide when we can, and few of us stay on Earth long once we find out who we are."

Laura considered that for a moment. "Yeah. I think I can see that. He's so fair. As for the other...I guess it's down to us then. I'm not surprised we're rare, especially as not every god..." She tailed off, the thought about not every god being straight bringing up a specific name. "Apollo."

"What?"

"Is there still, anywhere, in this day and age, an Oracle?"

* * *

The silence had lasted a while. In fact, Lucia had stepped into a diner and ordered food. Laura wondered if she even intended to pay for it. Right now, she did not really care. The growling of her stomach overcame any moral objections to stealing. They sat there, awkwardly picking at sandwiches until Lucia spoke again.

"If there was, do you think we wouldn't have consulted her?"

"I don't know. People do miss the obvious, sometimes. And if I can, you can." Her way of saying that she was pretty sure demi-gods were not immune.

"Definitely true. But no, I don't think any of the women calling themselves priestesses of Apollo these days have any trace of actual foresight."

"They might now. If the door is as wide open as it seems, then..." Laura tailed off. "It's worth a thought, at least."

Lucia eyed her sandwich, then bit it almost angrily, as if as a substitute for snapping at Laura. "Okay. You have a point."

"An oracle would tell us more of what we really need to do. Apollo has no specific interest in blowing up a ton of people. That was what you wanted me to do, right?"

"Something like that. But can you really say we don't have too many humans on the planet?" Lucia sighed. "I remember when things were..."

"I'm not denying the problem, Lucia. I'm denying the solution." The civil conversation, without threats or cryptic actions, affected her oddly. She felt almost as if she had slipped into an alternate reality. One in which Lucia was a nice person, maybe? She was nice, though. She just was...hard and cold. Laura hoped never to become like that.

"You're too close." Lucia's words almost echoed her thoughts. "You haven't developed a proper perspective, yet."

"Maybe I am, but I'd rather be too close than have no heart left." She wanted to bite that back the moment she had said it. It was cold, it was insulting, it was accurate.

"You'd give everything for these...people." Lucia said 'people' with utter disgust.

"What are they to you? Mayflies? If they aren't important, why bother?" Laura shook her head.

"I'm trying to save them."

Laura could hear and see the sincerity in her. She truly believed that she was saving humanity, in the long run. The worst part was that Laura was not even entirely sure Lucia was wrong. The state of the earth, the starving people in India and Africa. AIDS. There were too many humans, but then she saw the image of destruction in her mind. Of a winter both literal and metaphorical. Of starving children poking through the ruins.

"Yes, but you won't succeed. What you want to set in motion is something you can't control. And you don't care. You've forgotten how to care."

"You can. Control it, that is."

Laura studied her for a moment. "There are choices. What you plan is not the only way. And for right now, don't you think we have more important worries?"

"It won't hurt them to be reminded of who's in charge."

"Maybe not, but it's gone on for long enough. How do we close the door?"

A long moment of silence, a pause before Lucia admitted, softly, "I have absolutely no idea."

15

An uneasy truce formed between the two, but Laura did not want to actually hang out with the raven-haired woman. She had lost perspective rather than gaining it.

She had also walked away, leaving Laura back in Times Square. This seemed to have become sort of a center of human resistance. Was that a good thing or a bad? It depended on how far they could close the door.

If Lucia, though, who might be thousands of years old, truly had no idea? She could, of course, be lying. Everyone could be lying. Her own mind might yet be lying to her. The only way to stay sane was to assume sanity.

Times Square, then, and she walked to where they dropped the great ball on New Years' Eve. If there was any place of purely human power...this could well be it. Not a church, not a place where people called on gods old or new, singular or plural. Simply a place where the passage of time was marked. She stood in the center of a clock.

Chronos' daughter. Time.

No, not time. The one thing life and technology fought. Entropy. War was...not a factor of entropy after all.

War led to development. War led to invention. War led to stark necessity. The deaths, the price, were part of it. That was why there were two war deities...the dark and the light. Why Athena was also the goddess of progress.

"We're not on the same side after all." Lucia did think, most likely, that she was doing humanity a favor by tearing down what they had built. But the truth was, it had to balance. War was a key part of that. War was part of how humanity moved forward, became more than it had been. It was also...there was another thought, an important one, but she could not yet formulate it into something useful.

For the moment, war had to be held back, or the war that would happen, red and raw, would be between humanity and the supernatural.

That was the bloodshed she had seen. That was the conflict. It had to be prevented, because it would end only in destruction. Sooner or later, it would occur to somebody that weapons of mass destruction were the answer to this invasion. Sooner or later, things would fall completely apart.

As if in answer to her thoughts, she heard a shot, then a high-pitched yelp. Not a human voice, that, and she started to move towards it, then felt a hot breeze flow over her.

"What have you done?" she asked as she moved through the crowd.

"Killed a freak," said a dark-skinned man. He had a gun, and he did not holster it.

"Idiot. Do you have any clue what you might have started?" What lay on the ground appeared to be some kind of demon or imp. She was not sure exactly what. Might be a gremlin. It did not matter. Then there was another rush of hot air, and the body was gone.

"What? It's dead." His tones were flat, as if untouched by the body that had, for a moment, lain at his feet.

"Not entirely. And it probably had friends." The war was about to start, and she knew that the best she could do was try to contain this one incident. She moved to face the man. "Friends who might not care that they get the right humans."

He pointed the gun at her. "If you're sympathizing with them, you have to be one."

"Oh for crying out loud. Grow up." That came from a blonde woman in the crowd. She stepped out next to what Laura suspected was her man. "I think she was trying to hint that you can't just shoot these things."

"Depends. Some of them you can. That, I think, fell into the category of can't. The solution is to send them home, not kill them." It might have done something to warrant being shot, but whatever it was was not worth starting a war.

"And how, exactly, do you plan on doing that?" Skepticism laced with distrust laced with fear.

"I don't. I'm working on the plan, but I know I'm going to need help. A lot of help." She was bluffing and she knew it, but she forced confidence into her tones.

"You're all talk. And I'm still not convinced you aren't a freak." His eyes fixed on her, looking at her not as a man looked at a woman, but in a distinctly darker manner.

"She doesn't look like one. Please, Barry." The blonde was shaking her head, clearly more than a little frustrated with her lover.

"She's trying to talk us out of killing them all." His face was set. "Either she is one of them or she is responsible for this mess. Or both."

"They'd win." She did not say that softly, she raised her voice. "Or, worse, humanity would win at the cost of many lives and many souls." War could destroy a man's soul, his heart, his capability for love. She could do that.

Could she also give it back? She was fairly sure she could not this time. No...it was beyond her. On the other hand, she thought she might have got through to Lucia. Have given her something to think about, at the least. This man did not seem about to start thinking.

"That's not worse." His tone was absolutely flat.

"You haven't seen what I've seen, you don't know what I know." She had a keen awareness of limited time. What decisions were being made, now, in command centers and silos? There were already Guardsmen in the city, trying to work out what to do. Trying to come up with a feasible plan. They might be there right now, unseen on the far side of the crowd. "We start this war, and we won't gain anything."

"They'll be gone. We'll have the world back."

She shook her head. There was clearly no talking to him. She started to turn away. The man would have to hang alone, with the possible exception of his girlfriend. People had listened, people were weighing what they had both said. Who was she? They were asking that, when she did not know herself. What kept war in line? People's ability to choose, to refuse to fight. What protected that? Was she somehow coming to represent freedom? No, she knew with an odd certainty. Not that, not for her.

He tried to shoot her in the back. Instead of hitting her square on, though, the bullet grazed her shoulder. She whirled, her own gun out. "I said I wasn't going to kill anyone else unless I can avoid it. You're heading towards being an exception."

He held the gun steady towards her. "Nothing human moves that fast."

"Leave it. Leave it before the police get here." The blonde was almost begging now.

"I'm leaving. If you don't let me leave, I'll hurt you. I don't want to, but I have the right to defend myself." Laura kept her words even. She would not kill him, even as much of a jerk as he was. She would simply make him wish she had for a little while. Somebody had to, before he got other people killed. The blonde woman being the most likely candidate, although she was now moving away, giving up on her attempt to control him with words.

At this point, a sort of circle formed around them, but people were nervous. She felt it, sensed it, their fear of the guns and their wielders flowing through them. Time slowed once more, but she was aware, too, that it was a moment of balance. If he fired again, then that balance could tilt. She might have a problem getting out of there.

"Please." She did not beg for her own life, but for his. She did not want...

The moment passed, the gun lowered. "I ever see you again," the man growled, "I'm going to kill you."

The balance shifted. As she walked away, she became aware that a couple of people followed her. One of them was the blonde.

"There's a way to fix this?" she asked, softly.

"I can't promise. I'm looking for one." They were looking to her. Because she hadn't fought back? She kept her gun out until she was sure she had some distance between her and the man.

"I don't even understand what's going on. Are we being invaded?" It was a male voice, a somewhat whiny one. Its owner looked like a clerk, even down to the bad polka dot tie.

"Sort of. The door they're coming through...doors, rather...can be closed." That was a promise. "Mostly closed." Mostly. There would be a little bit more magic in the world, but that was probably not a bad thing.

"But how?"

"That's the hard part. The only way I've been told isn't acceptable, so I'm looking for another one." Or was it? A small voice. What if the sacrifice was that of soldiers, of cops, of guardsmen, of people trained and prepared for it?

No, that was the war, that was the route that led to a wasteland. Besides, if this started with somebody breaking a truce...? One way to close the door might be for everyone to stop fighting, everywhere, for a period of time. If that was actually possible.

The other way would, of course, be an apology. An apology, except that it would mean nothing when, in four years' time, the truce was broken again. It would be. So, what if there was somebody who had the power to enforce that truce? The power to remind, the power to... But that would take one of the gods, and they were not willing to do it. The spark of the idea flowed through her, then faded away. It was worthless and pointless. Humanity had to want to abide by the truce. And the thought that she might be wrong remained with her. She could only guess, only think, only try to work things out.

At the same time...then an idea hit her. She knew what she needed. "I have an idea." She turned to the clerk looking guy. "Don't suppose you have any friends in the media?"

"No..."

"I do." It was the blonde. "And I'm sorry...did he hurt you bad?"

"I heal well." It was already beginning to. She could feel her flesh knitting together.

"I know somebody who works for one of the local radio stations. Will that do?" The blonde's voice was a little breathy from worry.

"It's good enough. We are, likely to get in trouble with the government." That would be the fair warning. The government would want their own story to be believed. To keep control, if control could even be kept.

"Acid in the drinking water..." That was the blonde again, making a wry face. She clearly did not believe it.

"Totally not true, although I half hope that's what people will remember as true in a few months or years. But they're going to want to sit on the truth and, for right now, we need people to believe it. Even if they forget later." Especially if they forgot later. It was for the best if they did, for the best if they went back to their normal lives. Leaving the few who could not forget to hold the torch. Heh. She was thinking about the Olympics again. Perhaps enough. Perhaps enough honor for the old gods, or for those particular old gods. What about the rest? Those who were not of Olympus. Clark... What of him? Clark and Nancy, neither of them were Olympian. It was as if all the gods had allied together, even the ones that normally did not like each other.

Then again, had they not all been pushed to the side, first by Christianity, then by atheism? They did have reason to make common cause. Reason to walk the earth and look for new followers. She would have been willing...maybe...to be one, but her destiny was tied. Chosen for her on that front. She could make her own path and her own side, but... Could she? Nancy seemed to think so. Even Ares seemed to think so.

Except she could not change what she was, or at least she, herself, did not have the power to do so. Did anything have the power to, say, make her human? The worst part was, she was not sure she would accept such an offer. She had been... Until she faced violence, she had not known, had not felt the power that flowed through her. Once she had, she could not go back, and she did not want to. Or did she? She was torn between the desire for a normal life, and the siren call of power. Anyone would have been. Perhaps it was even the human part of her that sought it. If she had a human part, if things could be so split up. It was not that simple. Not that easy, not for her and not for anyone. Nobody had parts.

"So they'll be willing to do what they need to do?" the blonde asked, breaking into her thoughts.

"And what they need to do isn't even that hard," Laura admitted. "The hard part is simply the acknowledgment." Which was also part of it. People believing it.

"Most people are going to find it hard to acknowledge that the pagan gods exist," the blonde pointed out.

"Hopefully, all they need to do is open their minds just a little. That's not really the important part." Open their minds to peace, to harmony? No, just to reality. To the fact that things existed that they had not thought of before. For her, it had been easy, but it was inside her. In her blood. She had, at some level, always known.

"What is?" The blonde had fallen in next to her, leaving the clerk looking guy mostly behind. She seemed ordinary and fragile, brushing back her very fine hair.

Laura envied her and pitied her, all at the same time and for the same reason. "The reason these creatures are being unleashed on the world, dark and light alike, is because the gods are tired of people ignoring them, breaking promises. It might be the Olympic truce. They want an apology and they want people to at least try to stop all the fighting. They are fed up with not having many worshippers."

"We'd never actually..." She tailed off.

"I know. Not without humanity growing up some more. But I'm hoping effort counts for something." The idea of humanity stopping war for even a day, even an hour, was beyond anything she could imagine. They were not capable, not yet. The only thing they were capable of was limiting war, restricting it.

"The good things have to go too." The blonde turned towards her. "Some of these things are beautiful. And..."

Laura considered that. "Not entirely, not necessarily. It depends on how many people want it to stay open a crack."

"And you?" The blonde was still looking at her, walking partly backwards so she could do so. Awkward. Especially with all the likely extra obstacles, with all the things smaller than humans and larger.

"I don't know," Laura admitted. Then she paused. "I suppose I do want it to stay open. I'm sort of caught between the two. But not this open, not so that people don't know how reality works anymore." If it closed completely, she would have to choose. There had to be enough of a connection for her. Or did there? If she had to leave, even if she had to die, she would. Her own preferences mattered little. Yet she still had them, and she would not entirely set them aside.

"So, you admit it. You're not human." The blonde looked her up and down, as if hunting for some giveaway feature. Some clue. Some indication as to what Laura was.

"Not...entirely. That's not important right now, though. Right now, only one thing matters, and that's fixing the problem as quickly and easily as possible. Which means we need to contact as many people as we can. Radio is the quickest way."

The blond nodded. "If we can get something out through the radios in the hot dog stands."

"I had utterly forgotten about those." She thought of radio as a third class means of doing what she wanted, but she had been wrong. It was the best way.

"It's okay. I can get us in the studio. The question is..."

"...our chances of being believed. I expect to be called a total nutjob in about five seconds flat. However, I have to try." She let a breath out. People would think she was psycho. People already did. She thought so herself. Although, she was not a psychopath. She felt emotions, she felt empathy. She felt what she had felt when Peter had died. So quickly, almost so easily. Where was his soul now? Somewhere good, she hoped. Even if he had been an ass, he did not deserve to be consigned to some Hell.

"And if they lock you up?" A logical question, one that followed on from her own thoughts. One she herself would have asked. The blonde's eyes were somewhat wide, somewhat uncertain. Her skin was very pale, but it seemed to be naturally that way.

"They can't hold me." Laura felt confidence flow through her. "You've seen me move." Why was she risking this woman? Because she had no choice, because she needed what this one had to offer right now, whether she liked to admit it or not.

She did not want to admit it.

"They might use a tranq gun or something." Worry, still, and it was almost worse that the worry was for her.

"Maybe. I have no clue how much something like that would work on me." That was a nasty thought, though. It might well be a good way to capture her. What then?

She could probably not be held for long. She felt fire and war within her. They could not contain her, not any more. They had succeeded once, but she was stronger now. "I'd rather not find out. But you need to worry about yourself."

"Dodge well, then. Okay." Maybe too much confidence, now. "I..."

"You might get shot at. You need to be aware of that. I should probably go alone." She did not want to think of this woman collapsing, silenced.

"You'd never be let in without me." The blonde chewed her lower lip. "I'm willing to risk it. If this doesn't stop, I'm likely to get eaten by a grue." She paused. "We need transport."

"Bikes would be best. Cars in Manhattan are insanity. Failing that, we'll need a cab." It was obvious that nothing Laura could do or say would dissuade this woman, and she needed her. She decided that it was only her responsibility to a point.

"And I bet you have no cash," the blonde said, wryly. "Do they even use money where you come from?"

Laura laughed, "I was born in Brooklyn."

"Oops." The blonde's laughter also sounded, a lighter, higher tone. "I'm Carrie, by the way."

"Laura." That had to sound like too ordinary a name, and she was...not exactly afraid to tell Carrie who she actually was. She was...embarrassed, she realized. It felt like throwing her weight around. "I'm surprised you believe me."

"I think I've always wanted to. Believe in gods, that is. I hated church, as a kid. Always thought there had to be something more, something different. Something that made more sense." Carrie brushed back her hair, again. "Something powerful."

"This makes more sense?" Laura could not keep amusement out of her tone, flicking her fingers to indicate the entire mess. Some kind of pixie flitted overhead, circling around a lamp post like a moth.

"Than an omnipotent, all-loving God who lets cancer happen? Heck, yes." Her eyes fixed on Laura, dared her to disagree.

Put that way... "So. Transport."

"Cab," Carrie decided, moving to the edge of the street. Even with fewer people around, it took her a moment to get hold of one.

"If you tell me to follow any cars, the answer is no," the cab driver quipped as the two got in. He seemed almost familiar, but then, perhaps, they were simply all the same at this point. Blurring together.

"Sixth and Elwood," was Carrie's only response. "Try not to run anything over."

"Don't even go there. I just almost hit a unicorn." His tone was that of a man trying to lighten the situation with humor.

Laura flinched. "That would have been bad. Unicorns are pretty big." And Murphy's law being what it was, the horn would probably have gone right through the windshield and skewered him.

"World's gone insane." A practical mind this one, his tone showing nothing but stoic acceptance.

Laura leaned forward. "Gonna ask you something."

"What?"

"If it was possible to have world peace, would you want it?" He was just a cab driver. It made him a perfect random person to ask. Maybe she should take a poll, she thought wryly. For what it would be worth. The knowledge was of little use without the plan for what to do with it. That she did not have.

No plan, not yet. Nor any clear way to develop one. On the other hand, she was closer than she was. She felt as if she was on the right track, a sense that things were unfolding, if not as they should, then at least in something resembling the correct direction.

"Heck yes. Shame it's not possible."

"Oh, I wasn't saying it was. Just...being wistful, I suppose."

"Odd topic, given the world's being invaded by aliens or whatever these things are."

Laura shrugged and sat back. It was a short trip, even if they did have to stop while a pack of wolves padded across the street. That or they were wolf-like stray dogs. There might have been nothing supernatural at all about them, but she would not have bet on it. Certainly, the small person sitting on a lamp post wasn't human. Looked suspiciously like a leprechaun, in fact.

She watched the reactions of the people. Some had weapons, openly. Others were studiously, pointedly ignoring anything strange, as if by that means they could make it go away. A few watched with wild eyed wonder...and not all of those, she was pleased to see, were children. One was in her seventies, easily, and looked as if a long-held dream had come true.

If possible, she would leave the way open for them. If possible, she would give them something to remember. Something to cling to when and if the world became dull again.

Chapter

Then they were at the studio. One of the nearby buildings was being taken over by some kind of vine or ivy. She frowned. "Hold up."

"What is that stuff?" That came from Carrie, peering across the cab towards it.

"I don't know, but I have a feeling it's nothing good." She stepped out, regarding it, as Carrie paid the cab driver. Another debt. Then, she would have to hide after this was over. To vanish until the police forgot she existed. Except they wouldn't. There was no statute of limitations on murder. So, perhaps, it would be a new identity, perhaps...

She felt an odd sense of foreboding as she stepped towards the vine. A sense that she stood on a knife's edge. A warning. She walked over to the building...and leaves and stems reached out for her. She leapt back.

"Looks like you were right. Anything we can do?" Carrie stepped towards her but went no closer to the vine.

"Burning it out would work, but that would probably end up gutting the building, too."

"Giant can of weed killer?" Carrie was almost joking, staying well back with her arms folded.

"Would have to be pretty potent stuff. Besides, I think it's intelligent. Not to mention carnivorous." Laura indicated the skeleton at its base. Fortunately, it seemed to be a dog, not a human.

"Ugh. That would be cool...in a horror flick. Let's go." Carrie was backing away, further.

"Hold on. Please." Laura contemplated. Some way to contain it, or cordon it off, or something. Then she saw the guardsmen. "Hola!"

The lead one stopped. There was a squad of them, keen eyed men and women. Well, except for one at the back, who actually looked a little green.

She wondered what they had seen. "Dog eating vine, guys."

The one that looked a little bit green now looked a lot green. "Dog eating..."

The leader, who had officers' stripes, stepped towards it, then saw the skeleton. "For...okay."

If there was still an APB out on her, these guys didn't have it. She noticed that Carrie was outside the studio. Well, best to let her go on ahead. "Dunno what can be done about it, but we can at least keep people from walking into it."

It had a rather sweet smell, too. Quite pleasant. Probably part of its lure.

"At least it doesn't hypnotize people," the guardsman mused.

"Don't give it ideas."

He scowled at her. "I doubt it's that smart. But then, you never know."

Laura saw wings out of the corner of her eye. Oh please, not now. It was, indeed, the small dragon, and this time it dropped to land on her shoulder. The guardsmen stared, all of them falling silent.

Then one broke the tension with, "Who are you, Kitty Pryde?"

She couldn't help but laugh at the reference. "No. I don't know quite why it's taken a liking to me. I didn't even feed it my lunch. Besides...it's the wrong color." She wondered if it was the right gender. How did one sex a dragon?

She was pleased to notice that, at least, its wing was fully healed. It tugged on her hair affectionately for a moment.

"I think you're about to feed it your hair." The man was obviously trying to reduce the tension.

"Shoo," she told the dragon. It dug its talons in. "Shoo. I have to go inside and I doubt you'd like that." No...it wasn't going to move.

Great. Maybe it was a spy for daddy dearest. She shook her head. "It doesn't seem to want to leave." As she turned to walk away, the guardsmen started to carefully and cautiously study the vine. She hoped they came up with something. Dragon still on her shoulder, she stepped into the studio.

"I don't know whether that is cute or disturbing," Carrie commented as she turned to face her. She was talking to a man in worn jeans and a sweater, and he stared as much as the guardsmen had.

"How about both?" Laura suggested. "I can't get rid of him." Maybe it was a good job this was a radio studio after all.

"Does he...bite?"

"Not as far as I know, but I wouldn't put your fingers too close, just in case." He would not bite her...but she was not sure about others. Of course, as she said that, he dug his talons in and hissed a little.

"I think you offended him," Carrie mused, regarding the dragon.

He hissed again, as if in agreement, but did not stir from Laura's shoulder.

"I think...I was wondering if you knew what you were doing, but you're one of them, aren't you," the man said, quietly.

"Not exactly. I'm connected, but I'm still human." Not exactly a lie. She still thought of herself as human, even as she acknowledged that she was not entirely so. "I'm not a dryad or anything like that."

"A dryad would be green, anyway, right?"

She nodded. "Yes, a similar shade to her tree. And I suppose naiads are blue, but I haven't seen any of those."

"I hope they're not swimming in the harbor. It would probably make them sick." The man made a face at that, but he also relaxed, visibly, his shoulders lowering.

"Anyway. The issue we have is convincing people of exactly what is going on." She frowned a little bit. "I have things I can say, but I am not sure any of it will be believed."

"And not just a few people..." He tailed off. "I don't know. I wouldn't have believed any of this myself. They want peace?"

"They want respect. They might or might not want peace. They might not care, although they do care about the survival of humanity. But they want people to quit the half measures...to quit acknowledging them out of one side of the mouth and calling them myths out of the other." Laura shook her head. "Either they're real or they aren't. So they decided to prove it. If we can at least show some people took their point..."

She actually reached up to touch the dragon. He was warm, she noticed, without surprise. If he could breathe fire, of course he would be warm, and a flying creature would almost certainly be warm blooded. His skin was rough with small scales.

"Got it. I can see where you're heading."

"And we need to do it in a way that will appease them enough that they won't demand any more lives." Again, that sense of foreboding flowed through her. "Enough people have died."

"But will things ever return to normal?"

"Sure they will. People have short memories, especially for things they don't really want to believe in. Some will continue to believe, of course..."

Laura had quite a bit more to say. She didn't say any of it, because she heard a loud kaboom at that point, followed by a shuddering crash.

"Sounds like they blew up the man-eating vine," Carrie noted.

Her train of thought was completely derailed. "Anyway."

A second kaboom took her right out of it again, and she could not help but run for the door, stepping out into the street.

They had indeed blown up the man-eating vine, but that was not all. About two blocks away there had been another explosion. The dragon on her shoulder hissed again. "Not happy, are you."

She almost wished he or it could talk, then she might get an answer. But it had shown no sign of being able to as yet. Or perhaps she didn't know what language it used, perhaps there was meaning in its sounds. She could tell only that it was not happy. "Who sent you, anyway?"

It's only answer was to tickle her with its tail. Apparently, she was not supposed to ask that question. "Stop that!" She was trying not to laugh. Laughter would have been inappropriate.

Carrie frowned. "I want them to stop, too."

"No, I mean Puff here." He dug his talons in again. "Okay, okay, I won't call you Puff."

* * *

The red light above the studio door was visible from the inside as well as the outside. Laura noted this and other details. She had never been in a radio studio before. She might never be in one again. It was an interesting experience, but not as nerve wracking as she would have thought. It was easier to talk to people who were not right there in front of her.

The dragon perched on one of the chairs. He seemed to be growing just a little bit bigger. Perhaps his size was related to magic or something. He could be feeding off of her aura, somehow. That would certainly explain exactly why he had picked her to hang out with. His gender in her mind kept oscillating between he and it. She would be embarrassed if the dragon turned out to be female, but she still knew no way to tell. Her instincts leaned towards male.

"And we have somebody who might have an answer for us. She calls herself Laura. Honestly, I'm putting her on because I'm all out of ideas." He sounded like a man doing his best to sound calm, trying not to project any aura of fear or uncertainty.

How many people would hear her? Her throat felt dry. Not so easy, now she was 'on'. "I know what has caused what is going on. And it's not acid in the drinking water or space aliens. I'm also fairly sure we're not all in virtual reality." That would have been a great logical explanation, had her mind worked that way. For some people, it undoubtedly was the thought they had had. "What is happening is real. Every bit of it. It's happening because we have lost balance. It's happening because we forgot the gods and stopped respecting the Earth." For you, Lucia, for your concern for the planet, she thought.

Her words seemed to drift away from her, as if consumed by the microphone. "All the gods want is a bit of respect, a bit of acknowledgment that they're out there."

Some might give them more, but then, some had stayed loyal to them all along. Was there a woman out there who would let Apollo speak through her? She had no idea where to look. Would some people remember a few drops of wine as a libation? She would, if she lived through this.

She would do more than that. If she lived through this. She was questioning the likelihood of that again. "They are angry because we said there should be an Olympic truce, then we didn't follow through." She knew she was assuming again, but this time it felt right. She couldn't prove it. Gods, what if she was wrong? "I know we can't manage world peace, but we could at least do our best. At least try. I'm offering them an apology, right here, right now. If enough people do the same, then life might just return to normal."

She lifted her hand in a cutting gesture, to indicate that she was done. Nothing happened, but the dragon flew back to her shoulder as she stood. Yes, it was slightly heavier. "You keep growing and you'll end up carrying me."

She thought about that for a moment. Riding a dragon? Not, she decided, without some kind of harness to keep her on board. She was pretty sure she could not survive such a fall, and the dragon might apologize to her squashed body, but that would not be very helpful.

The dragon's only reaction, though, was to tickle her with its tail again. "Now I know you're doing that on purpose," she mock-grumbled.

"I don't think it will work. Actually, you should go before the men in white coats show up." His lips quirked in amusement as he started to fiddle with the equipment.

"Right now? They're probably too busy with the people who have been reduced to quivering jelly by this." She was probably right there. The cops would not bother with her right now, they would bother with the people shooting at random in the streets. With the people who were breaking, shattering into pieces. She thought of Joanna's parlor. Too much of beauty had been broken.

"Good point. I've come close myself." He turned towards her. "Turned us back to music for now. You want a drink?"

She considered the matter. "Yes and no. I want one, I'm not sure I should indulge, though." She paused. "Okay. I'll have *one* drink."

He took down a bottle of bourbon and two glasses, pouring the shots quickly. "I wonder how many people are hiding from it all in the bottom of a bottle."

"Or worse. This is New York." She wondered how many people were trying, say, pot, who would never have considered doing so before. She wondered how many suicides there had been. She also wondered how many babies would be born in approximately nine months, as people hid from reality by another means. A means that tempted her, but so far she had managed to restrain herself. Selecting a random partner right now was foolish, and selecting a well-chosen one even more so.

" People here do tend to graduate from alcohol to other stuff." He set the bottle down on a small table.

"Heck, I could use a joint myself. Could use the calm down." There was not much else that would help, in any case. Other than a break from it all. Not happening.

"I don't have any of that." He downed his bourbon. "We'll have to settle for alcohol."

It wasn't very good bourbon, but it heated her stomach, resting there as a core of warmth. She felt a little strengthened by it, and the temptation to ask for another grew.

No. She needed her head to be clear. One drink would not muddy it. More than one definitely would. Besides, it really wasn't very good bourbon. "Thank you," she said anyway. "I need to work out what to do and try next."

"Yeah. Can't assume people will get with the program." He said it as if they were talking about some kind of addiction response thing.

"Or that I'm right. Or that it will be enough." Foreboding, flowing through her again. Had she made the right choice? In a way, she would never know, for this had been the choice she had made. She could not unmake it and try another. Maybe Chronos' daughter could see possibilities. No, she thought not. She could see only what was happening, or she would have suggested alternatives. Laura was sure of that, anyway. They had touched each other, they had made a connection. A connection Laura herself would value for the indefinite future. But the choice had been made.

She had chosen humanity, and perhaps that was the reason for her foreboding. Perhaps she would lose something by it.

The dragon was now trying to drink out of the bourbon bottle. She laughed and poured about half a shot for him...a full one and he probably wouldn't be able to fly in a straight line. "You're not purple enough to be Lockheed. I dunno. You should tell me your name, or I *will* start calling you Puff."

He glared at her. His eyes narrowed, and she thought she even saw a tiny bit of flame inside his nostrils.

"I think he wants a more dignified name," the radio guy pointed out.

"Talking of names..."

"It's John. Sorry, boring, I know."

"You could turn it into Jack. That would be more interesting." He was interesting. It might have been the bourbon, but she was suddenly finding him very interesting indeed. Would it hurt anything if she acted on that?

It would hurt him. Firmly, she set the thought aside. "However, I probably should go. There's people who don't much like me, don't want them coming here." She had to get out of there.

"Oh, they will. Don't worry about me. I know all the back doors. Figured somebody would pull something. Heck, I can leave the broadcast on auto and go." He was already standing, reaching for his coat.

"Just don't choose the same direction as me." As she stepped outside, the dragon flew off of her shoulder, and spiraled up into the air. As if he had only been there to make sure she did what she said she would. Or maybe he was that upset about being called Puff.

She did not leave by the front door. Carrie was long gone, much to her relief. She had spent too much time with her as it was. Anyone she was seen with could be in danger, anyone she cared for.

She idly wondered what happened to Simon. He was fine, she was sure of that. A guy like that wouldn't get killed easily. Or go insane.

It was shading towards night, the street lamps popping on one by one. A couple seemed to be odd colors, as if shaded...or as if the bulbs had been replaced by sprites of some kind. She shook her head. That could be a trick of the light. She was glad, at least, that it was summer. And had, so far, stayed summer, the nights relatively warm, the days heated. Fall was approaching, yet not here. Add a snowfall to this, and things would be worse, if they could get worse. Could they get worse? Odd colored lights. Statues of gods. Gargoyles. No, they could not get any worse.

The dragon, she realized, had gone to roost. Dragons were diurnal creatures. Now the creatures of the night would come out.

Perched on one lamp post, she saw something with the wings of a moth, but which she instinctively knew would consume her flesh if she let it.

Shuddering, she gave it a wide berth, going as far as to cross to the other side of the street. She could kick its butt, but she did not want to get munched on. The energy seemed to change as the city went from night to day, in a way it hadn't before. The city that never sleeps was dozing.

People were getting off the street more rapidly than normal. Most seemed to be heading to establishments that served alcohol. She was tempted to follow, then thought again. Her head needed to be clear. One drink, more than enough. She felt, at the same time, no desire to sleep.

Stay up, then, walk the streets. She had her gun, although that would serve better against human predators than the supernatural variety. Yet, she needed to see the full spectrum. She also felt confident, secure. Nothing, though, had changed. Had anyone even listened to the broadcast?

A growing sensation that it was not, remotely, enough flowed through her. How could it be? There still had to be sacrifice.

Changing her course, she headed for one of those liquor selling establishments. Not a bar. A liquor store. Hesitating at the doorway. Once more, she had no money. So, no, she could not buy wine, even cheap wine. And cheap wine would be an insult. Not wine, then. She should have taken some of the bourbon, except that had been cheap, too.

She had nothing to offer. Nothing except her own acknowledgment and belief, and that probably counted for less, rather than more, than most people's. She was part of this, the energy that flowed through her came from them. For her, there could be no faith.

Or perhaps there could. She had faith that she was not, after all, going insane. She had faith that reality was reality, no matter how twisted...that this was not a hallucination or a virtual reality simulation. Unless the entire universe was one and always had been.

She had a vision of programmers in Greek togas and laughed. It seemed that laughter changed the energy. Laughter is the opposite of fear. No, laughter is what drives fear away.

Was she afraid? Yes. But she was not afraid for herself. More street lamps came on, more people vanished into bars.

She leaned against the bars that protected the liquor store window. The radio studio had not been in the best part of town, she realized. The bars were grungy, the office buildings the kind of walk ups occupied by private investigators and cheap lawyers. Branson might well have an office here.

Somehow, it felt like a good place to be right now. A real place, a place that was New York far more than Midtown.

Then she found herself moving without any volition. Represented New York, was the city, was what everyone thought of when they heard the words. There was one symbol that did just that, but she could not see it from here. And she would not, could not, call a cab. Yet, she felt even more energized. As if the patterns of power were flowing towards her. Perhaps it was because she had acted.

She had called for peace. The half-mortal daughter of a war god. That was one heck of a piece of irony, but she saw Peter's dead face. Remembered what it felt like to kill. Remembered, worse, what it felt like to kill and enjoy it.

She would not go down that path. She wanted to, but she would not. She saw, suddenly, that future. She saw the streets piled with dead bodies, the few living picking among them...perhaps taking their watches. She could not prevent it. She might, however, be able to cause it.

Or could she prevent it? The energy that flowed through her was of war, plain and simple. She was divided against herself, and she knew full well what they said about divided houses.

The night seemed very long as she walked through the city, in no hurry. That first flush of the idea had faded a little. She would not go there alone, not now. As she walked, she saw more and more creatures that seemed to crawl out from behind lamp posts. From between a window and its shades. As if every possible portal was now in use. As morning began to shade between the skyscrapers, she looked for Branson.

She found him well into the morning, at the small cafe outside the hotel. He had mentioned he frequented it.

"I think you just muddied the waters with your broadcast." He came out with those words as she sat down, no hello, no greeting.

"I know what will happen if this goes unchecked. Trust me. We don't want that." She was asking a lot of him.

"We don't need panic either." He was not exactly judging her, though. He was unsure whether she had done any kind of right thing or not, and it showed.

She did not press it. "What I need right now is more answers. I'm out of places to look. I know exactly what I need to know."

"If you're the one with the direct line to the gods..." He tailed off. There was belief and skepticism warring in his tone and his eyes.

"I wish it worked like that. It doesn't. I have my insights and sometimes I can make contact, but it's not like this reliable thing. Plus, I don't think they're entirely in agreement."

"Okay. Maybe what we need to do is find people who actually reconstruct the old rituals."

"I've looked. It's hardly a crowd I've ever hung out with." She had never felt any interest in or desire for religion, of any kind. Her mother had hauled her to church a few times, but it had achieved nothing. The mass was an empty ritual. Perhaps she would have had more luck with, say, Wicca. With something that, she now knew, flowed closer to the truth. Or did it? If all gods were real...then perhaps the emptiness had come from that god's rejection of her. The Carpenter of Nazareth could have no interest in the daughter of Ares.

"Leave it with me. I'll try and call you." He regarded her, his eyes concerned, but he was treating her as an adult. Sort of. Trusting her, offering her help, but not trying to do everything for her.

She appreciated it. "Might be best to arrange a rendezvous. I don't want to use my cell."

And the lights in the building went out.

"I really hope that was just the fuse box," Branson said, standing up.

The person behind the counter produced a flashlight, but it was hardly enough. Laura stepped out into the street carefully, then promptly back into the building as a bullet zipped past her.

"I was really hoping all those guys had been eaten by grues." Her tone was wry as she reached for her gun.

"What is a grue, anyway?"

"I have no clue. It's something a friend used to say. I think it's some kind of gaming reference. Somebody else said it too, so...it's obviously a reference to something." She had never managed to get into that either. Now she was living it, out of some dark irony.

Branson pulled out a piece. "Let's use the back door?"

"They'll have somebody there too, but...probably better cover back there." She moved ahead of him, quickly. She noticed he wasn't arguing with her. "Maybe you should stay here. They're only interested in me."

"You need somebody to watch your back." His tone was firm, he was not about to let her go anywhere.

"Branson. Please." She knew she could not stop him. But she could feel that he was the one in real danger. Danger she had caused by seeking him out.

And then she was out into the alleyway behind the store, diving and rolling to come up behind a dumpster. Another bullet zwipped past. She'd hung left when she should have hung right, and she whirled to return fire. Branson was on it, though, and she ducked around the solid object, hearing the sharp retort of his gun. She csmelled the gun smoke, faint as it was with modern weapons. She felt alive again.

She fired at a moving shape. She didn't have chance to call the shot. If he died, he died. It was self-defense, the oldest justification, but she would not try to kill them. That was the only balance she could find, and then she was running. She could hear Branson's footsteps behind her, then he yelped. He was hit. She turned for a moment.

He was still running. Either it wasn't bad, or the adrenalin was so firmly in charge he did not know it was bad yet. If they stopped to find out which, they would be caught for sure. So, she kept running, out into the street. Lots of people, she saw to her relief, even if they seemed wary. Thin and drawn, too. Some had clearly not slept in days. Her resolve to fix this quickly grew as she saw them.

The gunmen did not follow into the crowd, although she did hear one last report.

"What the hell are you doing?" came a stranger's voice. She ignored it, tucking the gun back into her belt, pushing through the crowd.

They eventually ducked into a store. Branson was bleeding profusely from his shoulder. She wrapped it, feeling his flesh under her hands.

The store was empty, the clerk hiding behind the lottery terminal.

There was a pause, then Branson let out a breath. " I need to get to the hospital."

"The bullet's not still in there, at least." He was right, though. He needed stitches. "I'd take you, but I think..."

"You're a target. I'm probably safer on my own. Assuming..." He paused. "You still need somebody to watch your back. And they might know I'm with you."

If they had tied the two together, he was in real trouble. "Just don't look into the eyes of anyone, especially if they look odd. I think there are some real nasties around now." She paused. "And my back will be okay."

Awkwardly, he stood and left, leaving her alone in the store.

She felt bereft, empty. She wanted to follow him. He was, perhaps, becoming her one friend. At least she hoped so, when all of this was done. She wished he had turned out to be her father.

Instead, she watched him go, then left in the opposite direction. Nobody bothered to call the police. Or, perhaps, the police were too busy to deal with everything going on. Then again, it was entirely probable crime was down. She could do nothing for the clerk but saw him start to come out of hiding as she left.

No cops anywhere. Maybe they were all at the donut shop. She laughed bitterly at that old joke. The streets were starting to empty again, and she realized that the sun was shadowed, as if seen through a bluish mist. That was enough to make her want, for a moment, to get inside herself. She felt as if things were about to get far worse.

She wondered where Lucia was. She would probably know what was shading the sky as if a net had been drawn over it. The clouds were turning green...and at that point she did duck into a building.

She had a feeling that there was about to be something bad, and moments after she made it inside...the heavens opened with lightning and thunder. A storm, but not a natural one. The building she had ducked into suddenly had a lobby full of people.

"For crying out loud. I'm starting to wonder if the world's about to end."

She glanced over at the person who had spoken, an ordinary man in a business suit. "I don't think it is."

He gave her a scathing, what would you know look. Of course, she rather looked...well.

She looked like a bum. When had she last showered, let alone changed her clothes? She supposed she should try and sneak into a homeless shelter to shower. She had her pride, but at this point... She probably stank, and she was surprised she wasn't being given a very wide berth indeed. Nothing she could do about it right now...she wasn't going to go stand out in the sheets of rain. If it was only rain, maybe, but forks of evil colored lightning flickered from building to building. Rain would get her clean, but the lightning might well kill her. Or it might not. It might depend on whether it was Zeus or Thor, and how either of them felt about her.

A moment later, the lights went out in the lobby. Enough light filtered in from outside to keep it from being pitch dark, but she heard somebody scream nonetheless. Wait it out, she thought. Wait it out. The storm could not last that long. Or could it? The way things were going it could last forty days and nights and wash Manhattan into the sea.

This is enough, she thought. Or was it? They would probably not think it was enough until people were begging for it to stop. Well, some already were.

Whoever had screamed was now sobbing in frustration. She wanted to go slap her. It would do no good to be reduced to that state. At the same time, how could she expect somebody to handle this? The city had reached a breaking point, and it was not just here. The news had tried to hide that, but she could feel it, like a wave across the face of the planet. She wondered if the Earth even still orbited the sun. No, the Greeks had known better. It was people in Medieval times who got it wrong.

She wondered if the entire wider universe was not all just illusion, if the stars really were just pinpricks in the heavens. If the sun was a chariot drawn by horses. Maybe both things were true at the same time.

Outside, the rain still fell, turning the sidewalks and gutters into one large puddle. A single yellow cab crawled along the road, windshield wipers vainly struggling against the fall of water.

She hoped it stopped soon. She felt trapped, encased in the glass of the rain.

She wanted to fight something. But she forced herself to breathe, to stay calm until eventually the rain eased off.

It was still falling when she stepped out, but slowly. The blue haze, however, did not appear to have departed. Even the supernatural creatures hid from it. She saw a faun hiding under a pile of newspaper and wondered if it was the same one from earlier. Afraid to enter a building full of humans? He looked like a drowned rat. The dragon was nowhere to be seen. She hoped the centaurs had not been caught out in it. Horses were large creatures to dry.

The blue haze. She peered up at the sky. Was it just an after effect of the storm, or was it something else? Was reality starting to bend even more?

Reality was something on which she could no longer rely. She was certain of that, as certain as her own name. Not a very divine name, she thought, wryly. Laura Maxwell. So ordinary.

She would always be Laura in the depths of her own mind, even if she changed her name to avoid consequences or to hide who she was. Lucia, centuries old, no doubt still used her birth name. Laura would not live that long, or would she?

It might be up to her father. Most likely she would not survive this, and her soul would cross into the otherworld. To become what? Some kind of lost spirit?

Or would she simply die and go to the afterlife, like anyone else? She might be less afraid if she knew the answer to that. She had forgotten what she intended to do, and why she had sought out Branson. Now she remembered, but she still did not want to do it alone. Nor could she trust anyone to go with her. She hesitated, thus, on a crux of action.

She had to do it sooner or later, but she could delay, there was time. There were things she needed to do first, she was sure of that. She walked the streets, thus, tired but energized.

16

She found some lingering human decency a few hours later. She showered at the greyhound station. Nobody seemed to care that much about who went where. There were no buses going out of town. In fact, the station seemed empty, as if everyone who could leave by this route already had.

A bus rumbled in, but there was nobody on it. She shook her head and started to leave. An old woman moved to sort of fall in next to her.

"Don't have any money?" The voice was gentle, concerned and, yes, motherly.

"Right now, no," Laura admitted. Money was a small worry, but it was a worry. One could starve in New York without money. The reminder of her adoptive mother, the similarity in tone stung, but she kept that down. Kept that to one side. She was not going to reveal her pain to a stranger, even a friendly one. Yet, she could not turn down charity. She could not afford to.

"Let me make you a sandwich. The cafes are all closed.

She looked like a church elder. "I'd...appreciate that."

The woman nodded, taking her down a street to a small church, which had its own cafe. It was a little dingy and, to Laura's surprise, there was nobody there.

"I know you have your pride," the woman said, "But..." She moved to the counter, smoothly.

"I'll get through. If anyone does." Why had she said that? Maybe because this place seemed so desultory, so abandoned, as if an echo of the final end of humanity. Which was not about to happen. She just felt as if it might, felt as if the end was truly nigh, even if there was nobody wearing a sandwich board in sight. Just desultory sandwiches, a little wilted.

"We'll get through. The Lord will protect us."

She bit back something. But she was not about to turn down somebody actually being nice to her, even if everything that was going on spoke against that person's beliefs. Even if she knew she was, at some level, wrong. Wrong that there was only one God. Probably not wrong about the existence of her deity and his desire to have followers. Possibly not wrong about what he wanted. At the very least, she was walking her talk.

Besides, maybe the Christian God could help. She wasn't about to turn down assistance from any source, even if by their standards she was pretty much damned from the start. In fact, by their standards she probably counted as a demon. The thought amused her. She bit back a laugh.

"You don't think He will?" An expression of concern again. Concern for her soul as well as her body.

Her thoughts must have been obvious on her face. "I honestly don't know. I don't think this is the last days or anything. I just..." Denting this woman's faith struck her as cruel.

"Obviously, some forces are on the move. Equally obviously the way to escape them is through Him." From the woman's tone, this was an absolute fact. Not even a matter of faith, but beyond that.

The sandwich was dry cheese and too much butter. She did not care, munching on it rather mechanically. If faith in another God could protect this woman, then it had to be left intact. If she could still believe through all of this...then she was either very strong or in some serious denial. Laura felt the latter more likely, but even so... Even so it could provide her with some protection. "Thank you," she said between mouthfuls.

"Pay it forward." A smile crinkled the woman's face. "I'm Sharon."

Laura smiled. "Don't worry. I am." She left once she had eaten, though, not entirely comfortable in the woman's company. Sharon made her almost question her own reality. But if it was not real, then she was insane. Or everyone was.

Part of her still wished she was. It would be better if she was hallucinating. That way, only she was lost in the maze. She had to believe it was real, though. Questioning it led to madness of a different kind. She was doomed no matter what. Doomed to fight against her own nature...whether it was truly the nature of a demi-god or just that of a madwoman.

Laura recalled the thought she had the previous night. She began to make her way south to the very tip of Manhattan. The sun was still veiled in blue, as if to threaten another storm. A shiver ran through her. It was not the end game yet, but it was rapidly approaching. Nothing she had done made any difference. Or had it? She could not see the big picture, only the streets she moved through. Her body ached...she was pushing her limits again. They might be greater than most people's, but they were there.

The harbor. She thought she saw something with a silver tail larger than any fish dive into it, but she could not be sure. If there were mermaids out there...no, she could not see any self-respecting mermaid swimming in New York Harbor. Far too dirty. They would be further out to sea, where the water was still somewhat clear. Maybe they would clean some of the mess up.

The ferry was still running, but nobody was taking it. She sat by the rail alone, watching as Liberty came closer and closer. If there was a true symbol of New York, she was it. Not just a symbol of New York, but potentially of a goddess of sorts. An archetype...like Justice. Nothing seemed to have yet touched the statue. She was not even sure what she would do when she got there, only that she needed to check on it.

She stepped ashore and noticed only one other person there. Cold ran through her.

It was Nancy. The dragoness stood on the shore, regarding her as she stepped onto solid ground.

"I might have known you would come here. You can't use the power of this place, Laura." Her tone sounded almost disappointed, certainly disapproving. As if she could yet be the sensei, yet dictate what Laura did and how she felt.

"They can." She flicked a finger back to the city. Dismissing her, even though it took an effort to do so.

"I won't let that happen." Nancy shifted her stance. "And if you won't join us...you know I'm better than you."

She was going to have to fight her, Laura realized. "I appreciate everything you've done for me. But I won't do as you ask. I'm not the person you hoped I'd be."

"You're weak," Nancy pronounced, starting to circle towards her.

"Because I won't be a good little girl and do as I'm told?" She was tempted to pull out the gun, but she had a feeling, almost a knowledge, that it would not work. The battle between them had to be fought and won the old-fashioned way. Just her and the other. No modern weapons. No interference. No audience except, far above, Liberty's impassive face. Her crown glinted in the sunlight, the blue haze beginning to fade away.

A sign that Laura made the right decision? She was not going to strike the first blow, as inevitable as combat was. Perhaps it was one last attempt to maintain the...

...and Nancy was moving. Full speed. She felt her awareness speed up to match her opponent. Had the storm been caused not, after all, by Zeus, but by the Asian woman? The haze gathered around them. It became a fog, marking out the area of their conflict. Laura lifted her hands, shifting into defensive patterns then striking back.

Everything was happening so fast. She felt alive, she felt real. They were closely matched, blows exchanged, but most of them blocked or dodged. It felt like a video game...real and unreal at the same time. She was in mortal danger, but that did not seem to matter. All that mattered was the moves. She realized she was driving Nancy up into the base of the statue. If there was anyone else on the island, they would never see through the fog. If either died, then it would be forgotten, another New York statistic.

If New York itself survived. *You can't use the power of this place.* She knew that to be true. She could sense it, but it flowed around her. Around Nancy, too. It sought somebody who believed in it.

It sought a mortal, and she knew that all she needed was those who believed. She believed, but she was bound to her path, to her destiny. Her belief was bound into that, the power that might have otherwise come out of faith was the power she used now.

"See. You can't use it." Nancy was calm, not even yet, out of breath. Was she playing with Laura, extending the fight?

"Neither can you!" Laura's voice echoed off of the fog. She was neither winning nor losing, and she knew it would be down to who tired first. She also knew Nancy would kill her. It had gone beyond any chance of either of them yielding. She aimed a flurry of blows at the other's head. Some of them landed, and the dragoness staggered back. Everything she had learned from Nancy was not enough. The dragon had experience, experience that more than overcame Laura's power. It was that power she needed, to let it flow through her, to let herself... She let it happen, finally, surrendered to the battle awareness. Felt the world slow down and speed up all at once.

"Better. But not good enough!" As if this was a lesson, despite how serious it was. As if Nancy felt that even if Laura died, she could learn from this.

Laura saw the kick coming for her face, ducked under it and swept Nancy's other leg out from under her. "Good enough?"

She had to finish her. She knew it. She knew that if she did not, she would be looking over her shoulder for the rest of her life.

She also knew that if she did... Nancy was on the ground, under her, and then their eyes met. "Go," Laura said.

"You can't finish what you've started." An accusation, the dark eyes looking up at her. Expecting death, perhaps even seeking it.

"I choose my own path, Nancy. Go. Before I change my mind."

She stood up. The woman faded off into the fog. Laura braced herself for her return, but apparently she was too exhausted to fight on. Her shoulders slumped as she left. But, for a moment, she looked back. Laura saw something in her eyes...approval mingled with the sense of defeat. The approval of a teacher who had seen what she wanted to see in her student.

Laura sank against the wall at the base of the statue as the fog began to clear. She was bruised in easily a dozen places, and she wasn't entirely sure Nancy hadn't cracked one of her ribs. It would heal. It would all heal because that was the way she worked. She would not, she thought, die easily when and if the time came.

Would she grow old?

Her breathing slowed, her heartbeat returning to its normal pattern. Thump-thump, thump-thump. She felt it, still, in the way it flowed through her. Her blood, her life. She felt alive. She wanted to prove it to somebody, but there was nobody there.

Nobody except the statue. They closed the entrance that would have allowed her to climb up inside, up and up to the crown. She contemplated breaking in. Would that be disturbing a shrine? A shrine to something people believed in. What was the difference between that and a god? Were the two the same thing?

Then she realized she was no longer alone.

* * *

"I had this feeling I'd find you here." Branson, walking across the lawn. One arm was in a sling, but he seemed otherwise well. His free hand hung near a gun clipped to his belt.

"You put a tracer on me," she accused. At least he hadn't arrived five minutes sooner. He'd probably have shot Nancy. Would have interfered, thinking she needed his help.

"Guilty. Who's the sour looking Asian chick?" He flicked his free fingers after where Nancy had vanished.

"Old 'friend'." She air quoted friend. "And before you ask, what hit her was me."

"Any particular reason?" His tone sounded almost amused. A little relieved, presumably because she had won the fight.

"She felt like a fight. I obliged her." Laura knew exactly how she sounded. Belligerent. Well, she felt she had a good reason to be. Besides, it matched his tone. Making light of the situation, creating a relief from tension.

"Good enough reason, I suppose. It occurs to me that if there is a place where we can push back the tide, this might be it." His eyes flicked up to the statue. "I'd have suggested a church, but those don't seem to be protecting anyone but their own."

"You're thinking." Somebody was, possibly more than she was. She was running on some kind of instinct at this point. On feelings.

"It's painful, but I managed it." Again, the amused tone, the faint deprecation of himself.

Again, she felt drawn to him, felt that deep attraction. It was not an attraction that made any damn sense. It had to be her desire, her need to reaffirm life in the midst of all that was going on. If he returned her feelings, it was even more that. Him loving her could be nothing but wish fulfillment.

"But I can't use the power here." She still felt it, but it shied away from her. No, that was the wrong word. It was a different power. They simply could not affect one another. She told herself she was not a god. Just a god's child, who would eventually age and die like any other mortal.

It did not like her, but it had liked Nancy even less. No, it did not trust her. She was war, she was chaos, and those things could both further liberty and lessen it. An image of Nazi soldiers goose stepping drifted into her mind.

"Then who can?" Branson's words broke through those images.

She almost forgot he was there. She was almost dizzy for a moment from the simple shock of him speaking. "The people can. If enough of them listened...and if we could get them here. You can. I can't." Her breath came far more evenly now, the sore rib already less sore.

Dang it, she thought, not wanting all of those reminders. She questioned, for a moment, whether she had a soul. Whether that was why she could not use the power building and building. No. It was because it was the power of a different entity. An entity born of of America. Of that land. Not the same pantheon, not the same power, but real nonetheless.

"She's challenging them. She's real...she's..." Laura tailed off. She did not how to describe it.

"She's just a symbol. What's challenging them is America itself." Branson studied her for a moment. "I should go. Start looking for people who can help."

She did not disagree, but did not want to leave that place. Did not want to move, her feet rooted to the ground. Perhaps it touched her after all. Or perhaps she simply desired, its trust. Its honor. She told herself that she did not care, but did not believe herself. She did not believe him. Liberty was real. America itself could not challenge, not without some force to center on. Or perhaps it was denial, for if it was America, then America rejected her.

She shook her head. America was not rejecting her. Liberty was not rejecting her, simply not accepting her. Fearing what she might bring. "I mean you no harm," she said to that power.

She stepped away from the statue, backing until she could see its bronze skirts. From here, that was as much as she could expect. It was simply too big. Too big to be taken in, all at once. Like the concept it represented, the concept the power here was fighting for.

Liberty. Peace. War. And she felt the anger of the gods build again, leaning over her. The sky began to cloud, and she knew the storm was returning. At the same time, she knew she was in the place safest from them. Here, it might not even rain.

She could not stay. If she did, she would draw attack on something not ready to be attacked; she sensed that at least some of that anger was directed at her. For not playing ball?

For trying to find a solution? No...for not killing Nancy. Was that it?

"Sorry," she told the air, for Branson had walked away. "But I'm not taking a life in cold blood."

The air shifted. It cooled a little. A test, and she realized she had passed. At least to a point. She walked towards the ferry, her idea of breaking into the statue forgotten.

She did not want to be on the same boat as Branson, did not want them both in the same place. So, she waited, on the edge of the shore, watching the boat pull away. She could barely see Manhattan proper, the mists still visible there.

Then she realized she had been stupid. Branson and Nancy were on the same boat. She did not want them together, not without her to keep the peace. Something akin to panic flowed over her. She stripped off her jacket, abandoning it on the shore, and dived into the waters of New York Harbor. No matter how strong a swimmer, she would not even have considered this bare days before. The water was not clean, and she definitely saw no mermaids or sirens in it. They had to breathe the stuff, and she knew they would stay well away. But she had to get to that boat. Before Nancy did something they would both regret. She was confident that even if she did swallow something toxic, it would do her no real harm.

Would she be rewarded for letting her live by such a result? She wished it would surprise her. Strong strokes. The current, though, tried to carry her away from it, tried to alter her course. As strong as she was, it was an exhausting struggle, and then there was a matter of getting on board. It wasn't a small boat, the sides were high and as she finally reached it, she saw no helpful, dangling ropes. She wished for Spider-Man's powers for a moment, to climb right up the side of the thing. Lacking those, she frowned, and then leapt. She slid down the side, and nobody seemed to have noticed her. She heard sounds from the deck that indicated her worst fears had come true.

She should have killed her. She should have...she had shown the better part of human nature, and now...

Then Branson, pushed to the edge of the rail. "Ahoy!" she called, but thought her voice lost in the noise of the water and the engines.

Perhaps it wasn't, for he turned...and then vaulted over the rail. He landed in the water near her, the splash hitting her in the face. Her eyes closed barely in time.

"That woman's nuts!"

She offered her hand. "I can get us ashore. She won't come after us."

How did she know that? But she was as certain of it as she was...no, she was no longer certain the sun would rise tomorrow. Not certain at all. The waters threatened to overwhelm both of them, but she would not allow that. Branson was not going to die today.

"I need help. I still can't use my arm properly." The sling had come off at some point in the struggle, but it was clear he did not yet have full use of the limb.

"The bitch meant to kill you to teach me a lesson." A bad lesson. The island was closer, so it was that way she went, half towing the injured man. By the time she reached the shore, it was all she could do not to pass out. Branson almost did for a moment, then he sort of laid on the grass. His breathing came hard and uneven, not yet settling into a pattern.

"I need to get to a hospital." He managed that between gasps. "I think she re-opened that wound."

"We have to wait for a ferry she isn't on." The practical truth. And would Nancy wait on the dock? She did not seem to care who saw her.

"What if she comes back?" Branson voiced her fears.

"I'll kick her butt, don't worry. I already did once. I let her live..." And she regretted that. Except, it had been the correct thing to do. The ethical thing...

"...and she promptly went after revenge. Just shoot her next time." Branson made a face. "I'd say I'm sorry, but I'm not. She's far too much trouble."

"It's tempting. I'm trying to keep to the moral high ground, but..." It was tempting. She had been honorable and she had been ethical, and the bitch had tried to kill Branson. Her friend. Nancy wanted her to cross the line. She wanted to force her into an action she would regret.

"Sometimes they won't let you." Words of wisdom from the injured man. At least his breathing sounded better. She wished she could lend him some of her healing ability.

As she could not, she rolled onto her back, stared at the sky. "They're making me hate them. And they're doing it deliberately, to turn me into them. I can't stop them. I just...I can't do this."

He did not move. "Who says you can't?"

"I do. I can't handle it any more. I should just leave, except wherever I go they'll follow me, and all of this..." She could not escape it, and she needed to be a child again, almost. Protected. Safe.

The mist cleared, and she saw green vines climbing the skyscrapers. Permanent damage would be done if it went on any longer. They would lose everything. Or would they? How real was it?

She already had lost everything. She had nothing to lose, nothing to gain. Win or lose, she could not...and the tears abruptly started to flow. Her exhaustion, her frustration, she let all of it out in choking sobs. For what seemed like a small eternity, she could do nothing else.

Branson could not or would not even move to comfort her. She could almost feel his pain. Her fault. Yet, if she had killed Nancy...or Nancy her...then things would be worse, one way or another. She just lay there, staring at the heavens. Her eyes felt empty.

They'd put their gods on Olympus. Then mortals climbed it, and then put them in the heavens. In Olympia. She fancied for a moment that she could see it, a floating cloud kingdom, all spires and towers of crystal glass. Yet, this time, she knew it was her imagination. She knew she still had one, at least, and she closed her eyes. She could still see it, in her inner vision. Surely, that would not be the truth? The image was too Disney, and she laughed, sharp and bitter. Then she closed her eyes more firmly.

She must have slept, for when she opened her eyes again, the sun had set, but she felt much better. Branson was still there...she still needed to get him to a hospital. Carefully, she helped him to his feet.

He leaned on her as on a crutch, but seemed to weigh nothing. Perhaps her strength was increasing to match the task. More likely, she had not noticed how strong she was before.

The sun set further, and the sky turned green and purple, lightning in its upper reaches.

"I don't like the look of that." The first words Branson had spoken. Saving his energy, perhaps.

"Neither do I," Laura said simply. "Zeus is playing with thunderbolts again."

"Or Thor. He likes thunderbolts too." Branson made a good point. "Or...some other thunder god."

"Maybe. I think it's Zeus." There was one last ferry, waiting on the shore. They were the only people on it, and the driver regarded them with something akin to fear and suspicion. Probably because they had obviously been in some kind of fight.

Branson mollified him with extra money, and Laura frowned. She had to repay him...he'd had his butt kicked for her and he had given her so much.

She shook her head, leaning on the rail. Something dolphin-sized but not dolphin-shaped leapt in the harbor.

She felt a sense of threat and foreboding again. As if reality itself was stressed, strained. Had even the gods pushed too far?

No, they were pushing against human disbelief. And which force would prove stronger had yet to be determined. She had perhaps given them an advantage.

The sky was still deep purple, although she saw no more lightning. It did not seem to be getting any darker, either, as if lit from above, evenly.

As if the sun's setting had revealed other light that now filtered down on them. As if there were no more stars. Not that one saw stars in Manhattan, but...

She shivered again. This time, she truly hoped it was an illusion. She helped Branson ashore.

He was pointedly not looking up. Eventually, he murmured, "I almost hope I'm dying and this is all a hallucination."

"I don't want you to die. Come on. Let's get to the hospital."

* * *

The hospital was crowded with minor injuries. Some of them were things people would not bother coming to an ER for normally. It was as if it was an excuse to huddle together. Laura stood outside. The sky still had not fully darkened, and the street lamps seemed to light only a small sphere around them.

Could she do anything about it? Not her sphere, but even so... "You're freaking people out," she murmured.

The only impression she got was that that was the point. "You don't get it. There's going to be nothing left."

Did they care? They had to, to a point. Would they continue to exist if humanity did not? Or worse, if reality itself broke down the middle? She could feel that, could feel it tearing at her. At her own reality, her own self.

She would die if this continued...no, she realized. Not die. Perhaps she had to choose after all, which she would be...human or more than.

No. The choice was being made for her. "Fuck you," she said, and she wasn't sure at whom she aimed it. Maybe herself. Her mother...her mother would have washed her mouth out with soap.

Fortunately, nobody heard her. Instead, the sounds of the city seemed to wash over her for a moment, then fall silent.

Had time stopped? She didn't know. She never had managed to get her watch working again. But her eyes scanned the area for Lucia.

No sign of her. Maybe she had gone deaf? No, because she could still hear voices from within the hospital. Maybe technology stopped working altogether.

As she had that thought, the lights went out, starting in the distance and coming towards her in a wave. "There's people in there on life support!" she found herself screaming at the air.

And the wave parted, leaving the hospital as a small, bright sea in a darkened Manhattan. "Thank you," she breathed.

Who was she to yell at the gods? Well, they had apparently listened. Apollo was the god of healing.

She felt restless, but she knew that if she left Branson he would only follow her on his own, and perhaps get hurt or killed.

Would she regret not killing Nancy for the rest of her life? Or would it be a Gollum situation, where the spared bad guy ended up saving the world? She laughed a bit, harshly, and just kept walking away from the hospital.

Somebody came up to her. It was Clark. "Well, you've done it now."

"Pissed off the dragon. She attacked me, in case you weren't aware of that." Laura was in no mood to deal with Clark, Lucia, or any of them. "And right now, I'm in the mood to find another punching bag. Please don't nominate yourself." She did not want to hit Clark, who had never directly done anything to her.

He snorted. "I don't intend to. I'm not born to war the way you are. Look. What do you plan on doing?"

"I'm trying to find a way to fix things. You can feel it too, can't you?" She tilted her head, turned towards him. The feeling was stronger, but she was starting to almost tune it out. Get used to it, as if one could get used to such a thing.

"And Nancy would say blood is the only way to repair the rift." Clark's tone sounded more skeptical than she might have expected.

"You don't agree with her. I thought you were her little lackey." It came out harsher than she intended. She bit her lip. Clark was Nancy's friend, not her lackey. Or was he?

"I don't know anymore. If bloodshed could do it, we've had plenty." He flicked his fingers to indicate the dark city.

As if to emphasize his words, another shot sounded. It said something about how tired Laura was that she just sighed and shrugged a little at the report, otherwise ignoring it. "It needs everyone to step back and really take a look at the situation, but nobody will. The mortals are terrified and the gods are stubborn."

"I wouldn't dare say that." He quirked a lip at her. "You might get..."

"I haven't been smited yet. Smitten. Smote...I think the word's smote." She was not sure. Smitten had to do with being in love. She was not in love.

"Who cares? But that may mean something, you know. The fact that you seem to be on their good side." He glanced up at the sky, and she saw a slight shiver pass through him.

"I don't know why. Maybe because I'm the only person trying to see both sides and it's tearing me apart and..." She felt her voice elevate, forced it back down to a reasonable volume. "Dammit."

"You need a break." His lips quirked again.

"I'll get one after it's over, one way or another." Probably six feet under, she thought. "Can you at least get Nancy to go after me, not my friends?"

"I can't control her. She's desperate, I think, seeing everything she tries fail. Why did you let her go?"

"Because I wanted to be better than her. And then she dumped my friend in the harbor. It's all so stupid. We should be working together, not at odds..." He had been controlling her? Or trying to? That had not been the impression she gained, but then, relationships could be very complicated. Not that kind of relationship. Clark wanted to date her, not Nancy. She had, at least, already let him down easy. What else could she do?

"Except you and Nancy..."

"We got on fine until I worked out what the three of you wanted." She wondered where Lucia was. "Now she wants me dead...and she wants me hurting first. Because I let her go."

"She might have been hoping her death would fix things." Clark sounded...even more skeptical. It was clear he believed no such thing.

Laura shook her head. "She's not that important. Heck, I'm not that important. What we need is..."

"What we need is to convince the gods to put reality back before the conflicts cause an explosion." Clark paused. "And I've tried talking to mine. They aren't listening. You have a better chance."

The sky was shifting from purple to green. "Too late. We need to contain the explosion first." Maybe only Manhattan would end up as shattered shards. Laura frowned. "And I can't do it. At least, I don't think I can."

Even if she was willing to sacrifice her existence, it would only slow down such a tearing. Of course, that might buy time...

"Where is Lucia?" That was what came out next. She was starting to realize she was worried about the time manipulator.

"I haven't seen her." Clark's face grew a frown.

"Find her," Laura said with sudden intensity. "She's the one person who can buy us the time we need to come up with...oh my gods."

The sky was actually beginning to rip apart. "Find her."

Laura stood outside the hospital as Clark ran into the night. Beyond the rip in the sky was golden light. She knew no mere mortal would remember this night. Either they would all be dead, or it would be forgotten. The wind had become warmer, and with it came a scent she could not recognize yet somehow remembered. What was on the other side? Olympus? Asgard? All of the realms of the gods together? Hell?

It could be hell, too. It could be some dark place, the world about to be taken over by demons. She had no way of knowing.

She would give everything she had for the survival of these people. For the future of the world. For now, though, she was not the one with the power to stop it, or even to slow it down.

The sky began to peel away, as if it was being drawn aside like a curtain. As if everything that had been seen and detected...planets and stars and galaxies...was the illusion, and this the reality. Gold.

Around her, most people fled towards where it was still dark. Others stood, looking up at it. Perhaps they were in too much shock to move. Perhaps they thought this was the Rapture.

Hell, maybe it was. As of yet, though, things at ground level had not been touched.

"Zeus and Apollo," she muttered, falling somewhere between an oath and a prayer. "Ares," she added, a little more respectfully. For good measure, as a friend of hers would have said.

She looked around for the supernatural creatures. For the first time, she saw none. They had all scurried into the otherworld at the first tear, she was sure of that. She became solidly aware that she could do the same thing.

She did not have to face this. If it was destruction, she did not have to die. Somehow, that emboldened her. She had the choice, and she chose to face this with the mortals. Chose to protect them. All she saw in the rift were golden clouds. It looked like the pictures she had seen of the atmosphere of Jupiter. It looked like heaven and hell rolled into one. It looked like...death.

Too pretty to be death, but it was that nonetheless. She knew that the gold would slowly expand, claiming everything. That it was the reality of the gods, impinging on the earthly plane.

She knew that had not been their intent.

"No, it was not." His voice came as if from behind her.

"Ares." He spoke to her as if she was a person. "I think I screwed up."

"This is bigger than you. It is bigger even than the gods." He sounded afraid.

"Then how the heck do we stop it?" She turned, but she did not see him, only a vaguely smoky form. He was afraid. If the gods were afraid, then what did that leave for her?

"I am not sure."

"If the gods don't have a clue, then we have a big problem. I sent

Clark to find Lucia." If he was not sure, then there was nothing anyone could do. This might be it, and everything everyone knew gone, erased. Would even the souls of the people survive? A little reassurance flowed into her on that front. Reality could be destroyed, but not rendered as if it had never existed. Souls could not be destroyed.

"She can slow it down. She cannot stop it."

"You can't stop it. Who can?" But he was gone, his presence fading away. She noticed the rift above them had widened, and especially where she was, the gold brightening. As if it was being drawn towards her.

He must have left because he was making things worse. Did that mean she was making things worse? If she stepped into the otherworld paths, would it help? She could do so, no longer needing a gateway. She could almost see into it in places. She could see into Faerie.

Then the rift stopped growing. "Lucia," she breathed, but she could feel...sense through her...the struggle.

Chronos' daughter was likely to give her life to this, and Laura felt a pang through her.

If her own life was the answer, would she give it? She looked up at the golden sky again. Then at the paths. She let her breathing slow, listening to her own heart. Her own instincts. Not yet, her heart seemed to say. Or was that simply her desire to live?

She had time. She had to make use of it, she had to make the sacrifices all worthwhile.

17

She did not see either Clark or Lucia. Branson, arm in a sling, came out of the hospital, watching her. She suspected Ares was helping her, somehow, supporting her. What she did see was people getting the hell out of Dodge. Whilst everything before had made the New Yorkers band together against it, this was too much even for them.

The streets emptied again, and it was not just people vanishing inside in the hope that they could wait it out. They were fleeing, not even taking stuff with them. The bridges would become riot scenes in no time.

She could not even spare a thought for them, and that hurt. Wasn't she on their side? But those fleeing masses... They were cowards, but she could not blame them. They ran because they did not know what else to do. She stayed because she could not bear to run. Was that too a form of cowardice? If she was a coward, she would already be dead.

She did something else, then. She found a church. Stepping inside, though, she felt that this place too was drawing more of the rift. Anywhere that was a focus of belief.

That could not be it, surely. The solution could not be for humans to turn their back on faith. On all gods. On anything but their own mundane lives. That could not be it, not just because it could not be done, but because...

...people could not live like that. Was there a point of balance? If it was that, then she would leave, she would abandon them as well. She could not go back to being Laura Maxwell, schoolteacher in training. As much as that that normal life, that chance to forget, appealed, she knew it to be impossible.

The gold was streaming, as she stepped outside, down over Liberty.

Either people continued to believe and the world ended, or they stopped and it became worthless. That could not be the choice. Laura would not allow it to be.

Bigger than her? Well, yes, but she could try. She started to head back towards the statue, knowing that there would be no ferry running now. Nobody was going to go anywhere near it.

Well, except for a few crazies that thought it was the Rapture. She began to wonder if they were right. If this was something like that, if their souls would at least be translated to some other plane. Souls could not be destroyed.

A shiver ran through her, instinct telling her it was not the Rapture. That their souls were not being pulled to some pleasant afterlife. It also told her to hurry. There was not much time. Time. It beat through her, she could still sense Lucia giving all the energy she had to just give enough time to try something. Before they all ended up wherever they were going to end up. Before the planet split apart. As she had that thought, the ground rumbled just slightly. New York did not get earthquakes.

The sense of something reaching out to her, of something being near her was remarkably strong. "Who are you?"

"You live."

She did not turn around. "I intend to stay alive."

"Stubborn." The voice was female, familiar and not at the same time.

"Is that a bad thing? Did you try to kill me, Athena?" She knew who it was with an odd kind of certainty. Perhaps the goddess was making sure she knew.

"What is done in the name of a god is not always that god's will. You should know that." The presence was gone.

Laura knew it was the nearest to an apology she was going to get. She found Branson again, outside.

They found a boat a bit away from the ferry port, already exhausted from running across town. Her vision was a little blurred...or was it reality? At least the boat had an engine. It even worked, starting up first time. She could not be sure what would work and what would not, but she did not have the strength, right now, to swim across the harbor. Earlier, she could have done it. Now, she was too tired herself. Tired, she grasped, from sustaining her own reality. From not making things worse.

At least she could rest, even if she could not remember when she had last slept. She knew no ordinary person could possibly keep up this pace. Well, she would use the advantages she had, darn it. The ocean seemed normal enough, but lightning in all the colors of the rainbow crackled on the horizon. Shapes stirred in the water, and she felt a sudden urgency. Not all would be as benign as the mermaids...and fortunately, if the legends were right, she was immune to sirens, but...

She heard no music, in any case, but drove the boat practically into Liberty Island. She jumped ashore, leaving Branson behind. "Go on," he said. "I'll turn off the boat and stuff."

To her shock, she was not the only person there. A group had gathered at the base of the statue, the golden light flowing over them. Their faces were tilted upwards and their arms spread, welcoming it.

"Idiots." She said it loud enough for them to hear, but was ignored. They were seeking salvation, as humans were prone to do, desperate for any way to shed their guilt that would not involve them actually doing anything.

She could not save them, but she could reach out and touch the light herself. It stung, and then it explored her being, she could feel it read the deepest heart of her...and then pull back. It almost seemed as if it did not know what to make of her.

"Yeah, friend. That's me." But had it accepted her...the circle of people standing in the light crumpled, one after another. She did not have to check to know that they were dead. Their souls had been taken, and she feared not to the heaven they expected. No, she feared they were in Tartarus.

She, however, seemed somewhat resistant to it. Or maybe it did not want to anger daddy dearest. Maybe it was not that intelligent, or yet strong enough. Strong enough to take her. She was, after all, not merely mortal. She had to be different at some level. It had feared her, and that give her hope. Her father, it had sought out, prepared itself to attack. Maybe there were advantages to being neither fish or fowl...well, she knew there were some. She had choices. Or did she? Had Helen really chosen to be the most beautiful of women, or Hercules the strongest of men? She had not chosen to be what she was. Her choice was how she used it.

The door to the inside of the statue was open, and the security guards were gone. She stood there for a very long moment. It had been broken in by somebody, somebody who no doubt now lay dead somewhere within it.

"What do I do?" This seemed a good place to ask, a place which was already half inside the rift. A rift inside which humans could not live. If she climbed the statue, she would be inside it...for it had already settled around the torch, the crown, was working on the head.

"What do you want to do?" This was not her father. This was a woman's voice. Liberty herself.

"Save everyone. I know...I know...it's bigger than me. But that's what I want." Liberty had not been strong enough to speak before. Or had chosen not to. Had tested her. Had implied she had wanted her to kill Nancy, when the truth was opposite.

"What if they don't want to be saved?" The voice remained soft, remained strong, remained sure.

"That's their problem. I'm pretty damn sure enough of them do." She knew she could do nothing for those who sought the end of the world, and there had always been those. That peculiar death wish pervaded human society. Some people would always be drinking Kool-Aid. Of course, Liberty would place freedom before even life. Something came into her mind and fled again, something she was unable to quite place, yet knew was important.

There was silence. A long silence, the golden light forming a sort of circle around her. It did not dare touch her, it seemed, did not dare reach for her. She was able to hold it back. She was focused entirely on her own reality.

Then, she heard footsteps. She turned. Branson, fresh from taking care of the boat, arm still in a sling. His face was serious, and he glanced up at Liberty, almost bemused. He was brave, she thought. Too brave. He cared for her. And he was determined to see it through. She respected his determination to protect. She made a decision.

"Branson. Leave now. This place is too dangerous." She could not have him here. She could not, would not, watch him die. Watch his soul pulled into what might be Hell or worse. Yet, she had not even tried to find and get rid of the tracer.

"You're here..." His voice tailed off. His eyes had become a little larger.

"Damn straight. Have you forgotten who I am?" She glared at him. "This is no place for you. I know I'm coming over as an arrogant bitch, but..." She indicated the fallen bodies. She had to get rid of him, had to chase him away. Had to reject him utterly, before he died for her. She could not and would not let him die for her.

As if seeing them for the first time, Branson rushed over, dropping to one knee to check a pulse. "Damn." His eyes clouded.

"Don't waste your time. Get out of here. Please...trust me." She did not need to check pulses, she did not need to look. There was nothing there anymore but meat, and the light was starting to reach for Branson. It hesitated. Unlike them, he did not seek it, embrace it, welcome it. He had more sense.

He frowned. "Laura...you're...I don't want you to die," he said, finally. "I already lost your mother. I *loved* her, Laura. I can't lose you too. You need me."

"I won't." She had to interrupt him, before he said the words. Her own sounded shaky even to her, she was not sure that she could survive this.

"You can't promise me that. Please, come with me." It was his turn to beg her, his turn to try and get her away from this place. From a place that was beginning to almost shimmer. Its reality was fading, and she suspected she was the anchor keeping it here even this long.

"If I do, then we will all die. Look around you, Branson. The world's about to end. I'm trying one last desperate attempt to save it. But if you stay here, you will definitely die." Not begging. Firm. Determined. She knew she was likely going to die. She knew that her soul was likely to end up somewhere unpleasant, although her father would do his best to prevent that. God of War or not, she trusted him.

The gold energy was starting to swirl around Branson again, reaching for him, closing in on him. She could sense its growing triumph. It wanted souls, it needed them. It was not intelligent, whatever it was. Maybe it was the real horror from beyond, that Lovecraft had glimpsed and given a tentacled form.

"Run." She did not shout. Shouting would have given her words less urgency, not more.

He started to...but he did not get very far.

Clark was standing on the dock, his ready grin on his face, his eyes flicking over Laura. "Hey."

* * *

For a moment, Clark's casual attitude infuriated her. Hey? At a time like this? She walked towards him, bent on slapping him. Then she restrained herself.

No violence. She had to control that instinct. "Hey yourself." She kept it to her voice.

He lifted a hand. "Whatever you are annoyed about, can it. Bad guys coming."

She saw them then. Two boats...two amphibious style landing craft.

Purely human bad guys, then. Those who had been trying to end her life from the start, still determined to do so. No doubt discipline kept them from falling apart with the rest of New York. And she was going to have to fight.

There was nothing else for it. Her hand closed around her gun. A cold, comforting weight, something that was more than just an object. She hated that feeling. Guns.

She hated herself for a moment, then pushed that to one side. "Thanks for the head's up, Clark. Branson? You may want to get out of the way, unless you can shoot one handed."

His answer was to produce his own weapon. She wracked her brain for a better way. The gold light blocked them from fleeing up the statue, constrained this to the ground. She wished for some kind of transportation, but no path to the Otherworld opened here.

There was nothing for it. As the first of them came ashore, slinging his rifle against his shoulder, she squeezed the trigger. He went down, but she saw the other effects immediately. Felt the world threaten to fade, to dim.

So, was this to be it? Was she to allow herself to die to save the world.

Clark stepped across, put a hand on her arm. They were preparing to fire. "I have an idea."

"Whatever it is, try it." She could maybe take all of them down before they nailed her, a bullet flowing past her. Slowly, it seemed, slow enough to dodge. Yes, she could. But if she did, she would finish the job. Would doom the world.

"Thank you, Laura." Clark turned to face them. He crossed his hands in front of them and was suddenly holding sword and shield. A bullet pinged off the latter.

He simply walked towards them. But him fighting could be no better than her fighting, surely. He was making of himself a threat to them. An obvious one, and she had seen the light in his eyes.

He was drawing their fire to give her time to think of something. She trusted him for the first time in that moment. Go in the water? It was full of monsters, she could sense them. Not mermaids and selkies, but something darker. Something that longed for the taste of human flesh.

They had Clark surrounded, which meant that some of them had their backs to her. They were focused on him, on the blade which spun through the air, blocking their fire. She doubted any merely mortal eyes could even see the weapon, so swift was its passage.

Then. He dropped sword and shield. Stood there for a moment, looking taller and larger than he had before. Then their fire ripped through him.

"Clark!" For a moment she wondered if bullets could kill him, if he really knew what he was doing.

No, he must. Yet, she sensed it, the power building within the circle. Power released. Power called. "Branson, get back!"

He stepped behind her, and she sensed that was enough. Enough as the air suddenly darkened and thickened. What came out of it was a nightmare in almost the literal sense, a woman in grey armor and black cloak riding a dark winged beast that was almost, but not quite a horse. A woman with bright hair and eyes that shone with terrible light. Fear radiated from her.

Branson actually whimpered, but stood his ground. The soldiers did, for a moment, then the brilliance of the power struck them down and away. Into the water, in several cases, the rest insensible on the turf. Not dead, but struck down.

Laura found herself stepping forward, meeting the rider's eyes.

"Not for you," the woman said. "Never for you."

"My father would not approve." She managed a smile. Clark's form, on the ground, torn and bleeding stole it away again, caused it to fall flat.

The woman dismounted, although her feet left no mark on the grass, nor did her mount's hooves. With almost a lover's gentleness she lifted the body and then placed it across the beast's back, just behind the wings, then sprung up behind him.

With a swirl of cloth and mane and the pattern of the rainbow arcing through the gold, she was gone.

And as the light cleared, Laura saw a small boat speeding across the harbor. Nancy sat in its prow.

18

Nancy stepped onto the shore lightly. Her eyes took in the downed troopers, and then she walked to the place where Clark had fallen. As she did so, the golden energy drew back, recoiling from her as if to give her space.

"What has happened here?"

"He took my place." She knew that truth. She also felt the residual power, the remaining energy, although most of it had departed with the Valkyrie. She had taken everything he was to Valhalla, even his physical form.

Branson stepped out from behind Laura, but stayed close to her. She reached out for his hand, as if hoping that she could, thus, give him some protection.

"See what you have wrought." Nancy's hands flicked to take in the entire scene, but most especially that place. Whatever quarrel had come between them, she still cared for him. She had loved him, it was obvious in her eyes.

"Not me. Or you. This is humanity's own doing. They're so stubborn, so set in their ways." Laura knew she was speaking the truth, but she found her words drifted into the dragon's style of speech. She shook her head.

Branson looked between the two. He closed his hand onto Laura's, and the gold retreated a little.

"Let him go, Nancy." Not begging. A simple request.

"You care too much about that one." She stepped forward. "He's only leaving here one way. That's the only way you'll be able to..."

Laura made a throat cutting gesture. "It's too late for that. Chronos' daughter can't buy us much more time."

"Gods," Nancy whispered.

"Didn't know, did you. Maybe you care too much about her." Laura felt tears prick at her own eyes. Maybe she cared too much period. "This ends here, and it ends now, one way or another. Tell me what you know."

"It's too late," Nancy said. "If you had cooperated..."

"...then more people would be dead and this would still have happened. You know that. You also know I can take you." She would have to let go of Branson to do it. Nancy might or might not call her bluff. On the other hand, he might get time to get clear. For what it was worth, as the light was starting to spread across the harbor.

"Then do it." Nancy's stance shifted, her eyes on her. Daring her to call her bluff.

"I chose to let you live before. I choose not to fight you now. If there's one thing I've learned...I still have free will. They don't, you know. The gods. They can only be what they are. Can you only be what you are, dragon?" She could choose to sacrifice her free will, and she might, if that was what it took. If she could live with the results of the decision. Yet, for now, she still had it.

At the word, Nancy tensed.

Then, as if the use of that word had been a summons, wings shadowed the bay. The dragon that had once been small enough to sit on Laura's shoulder had grown large enough to carry her aloft. Or possibly it was whatever size it chose to be and needed to be.

Nancy whirled, and then she sensibly stepped to one side, giving it space to land. The wind from its wings ruffled Laura's hair, sent with it an odd, not unpleasant scent.

"Half of the gang's here now..." She studied Nancy's face, the impression on it. They needed Lucia, but Lucia was still busy. Still trying to stop everything. To buy them time.

"But not Clark..." Genuine sorrow was in Nancy's voice.

"Truce?" she asked. She knew that she needed her, her support, her assistance. It took a lot to admit that, even to herself.

"Or you'll have him eat me?" Nancy inquired, flickering her fingers towards the dragon.

"No. Do you want the world to survive or not?" Maybe if they worked together. Maybe if she was really going to work towards peace...she had to start with her own enemies. She already had. Clark. Lucia. Now Nancy.

The light was becoming brighter. She could no longer see

Manhattan. The waters of the harbor were agitated, flowing upwards, choppy. As if the rift was drawing them in, or perhaps seeking any mermaids foolish enough to have lingered. Were the supernatural creatures safe? She thought not. Safer than the mortals. She had that thought and it disturbed her, a little. Mortals.

"Do you?" Nancy shifted her stance again, eyes flicking between Laura and the dragon. Branson had not let go of her hand.

"Yes. But not at the price of things not mine to offer. Let Branson go." That was the condition she had to place on it. He was not to be involved any more except of his own free choice. Except she knew what he would choose. Her eyes flicked to him. His face had paled under the dark of his skin, his eyes showed whites. Nancy frightened him. Or perhaps it was the form of the dragon...easily large enough to eat a human in one bite, now. Yet...

"No way." That was Branson. He released her hand and stepped around the dragon, regarding it warily. "Let me help." His fear was obvious, but so was his courage.

"You'll die." That came from Nancy. "She cares about you, and you *will* die." Dark eyes on his. A staring contest threatening to occur.

"I can't stop him." Laura shook her head. "His choices are as important as mine. I may want to, but I can't."

"But I can," Nancy said quietly. "I could remove him from this place." She flickered her fingers. "He is not strong enough to fight me, even if he was not injured."

"If you do that, I think you'll make things worse." Was Branson's life the actual sacrifice? She could not... "Dammit, Branson. Please." It had to be his choice.

"I'm not leaving you to deal with this shit alone. You need me." His color was returning to normal. He was finding a second wind of strength, although his eyes did occasionally flick to the dragon.

"Not for this." She didn't even know what she had to do. The dragon, though, stepped forward now, awkward on the ground, and lowered its head towards her. She could smell its hot breath. "Do you have any ideas?" Liberty had gone silent the moment Branson had shown up. Maybe she was letting them work it out themselves.

The dragon, though, seemed no more capable of speech now than he had before. All he did was nuzzle her gently for a moment, more like a horse than anything else. She could see his wings, the detail of them. Not quite a bat's wings, she thought. His shoulders were almost perfect for a human...maybe two...to sit astride, although one might prefer a saddle of some kind. Or maybe a harness. Beggars, not choosers.

"Guessing he doesn't have any bright ideas," Branson commented. His voice broke the spell. She glanced towards him for a moment.

"Well, it was worth a shot, because neither do I." The wind suddenly picked up. "And whatever we're going to try, we have to do it now."

She could feel things returning to what they had before. Lucia. Goddammit. She was tired of death, tired of loss, tired of everything. She held in her mind the vision of New York as it had been, of the world stable. That was not enough. She did not have the power to make her vision into reality.

What do I have to do? she asked silently, almost of the city itself, were such a thing imaginable. There was no response. She had not really expected one. "Branson. Do you have any ammunition? I'm out."

"This is a time to think about that?" he asked as he handed her a clip. At least the mention of such a mundane concern seemed to relax him.

"I suppose not, but...well..." She shook her head. She felt more secure with the gun loaded. "Call it a security blanket."

What kind of person had she turned into? She would worry about it later, if she lived. And there were worse things than feeling safer with a gun. She did not intend to use it.

Nancy frowned, then spoke, "This is the weak point. You were right to come here."

"What if we go through?" The weak point...why? Because Liberty was strong, or because she was weak? Violated truces, wars, terrorists. Was Liberty harmed by any of that? Maybe she was. Nancy was speaking again.

"He would not survive that. I might not. You probably would, but...no. I think we have to do it from here." The dragoness looked up at the sky again, at the golden light.

"Do we?" Laura glanced up at the sky, which seemed to be slowly but surely falling. She forced a focus on herself. How long did they have?

"Besides," Nancy half-whispered. "I do not wish to die."

Laura smiled. "You were willing to earlier."

"Willing and wishing are different things. You know that."

The dragon nudged her again. "What do you want? I don't have any dragon sized treats." Laura ran a hand along his muzzle. Warm from his inner fires.

Those people had gone through, she realized, suddenly. They had died in the process, but it was entirely probable their souls were on the other side.

Part of her questioned, for a moment. She envisioned all the dark side. The shootings, the prostitutes, the drugs. Could she be wrong about what was on the other side being worse than this? Worse than a world in which children starved while their fathers spent their pay on alcohol? In which women...and sometimes men...were beaten by those who claimed to love them? Could it really be worse than it already was?

Choice. It all boiled down to what people would choose. "Liberty," she whispered. "What do they want?"

The vision of New York strengthened, solidified, until she thought she might actually be seeing it. That illusion lasted only a moment. "Thank you." Yet, she did sense a weakness in the archetype, the goddess. But people wanted reality, most of them. Those who did not were likely already dead.

She felt as if she was presuming, still, as if she was taking so much on herself. But choice had to include the choice to take drugs and sleep with the wrong guy and screw up your life and join the army just to get out of the ghetto.

It had to. She had never had to make any hard choices until the day she found out her birth mother was dead. She made this one now, without hesitation. She would fight to the end.

The light drew back from her further. "Yeah, that's right. You don't belong here." Her words sounded far better in her head than before. More confident, more...aware of who she was and could be.

Nancy frowned at her. "Be careful, Laura."

"I don't think it has enough mind to piss off, not on its own." She reached up and touched the dragon's head. "But other things might. Hence our extra firepower here, right?"

"I wonder why he's here," Nancy mused, her tone soft.

"He likes me. I think." The dragon was actually making a deep purring sound. "Oh, come on. Let's get this done."

"I still have no clue how." It was clear that she did not wish to admit that, that she did not want Laura or anyone to know that even a dragon, an ancient being, did not know how to solve this.

"The gods do not know how, Nancy." That was an answer to that uncertainty, that self-doubt. The other dragon, the more obvious one, nudged Laura again. "I do know that we need as many people as possible."

"If you bring a crowd here..." Nancy tailed off, glancing at Branson. He was getting as close to Laura as he could without actually invading her personal space. Reaching for her hand again, but not trying to take it unwilling.

"Not here. Central Park. Branson...do you think you can handle that?" It was the perfect way to get him further away without angering him. To make him feel useful, as he so desperately needed. To get him out of the line of fire. Both of those were vital.

Did she love him? No. She thought not. Did he love her? She was sure of it. She shook her head, forcing her thoughts back to things that were more important.

War. How did she use that aspect, that attribute, to restore things? Did people have to fight?

Of course they did. It was human nature to do so. But how did you fight the end of the world? By asserting one's humanity. Which included fighting. It also included the choice not to fight. The choice to resolve things in a better way, or to walk away.

She felt that division within herself again. Was she human? If she chose to be human, to be nothing more right now, she would die. Was her death what would be required? She realized she was willing to give it. Not just because she had little life to go back to, but because it was the right thing to do. Because all of this really was bigger than her. Because Nancy did not want to die, and she could not ask it of her. Because she could not ask it of Branson.

But not right now. Not in this moment. Right now, she needed to be what she was. And perhaps that would be the sacrifice...to give up her humanity.

How did she know which was right? She glanced at Branson, who was heading for one of the boats. Then at Nancy, whom she knew for sure now was not human, did not have a soul the way others did. She was something else, and she stood there, the light flowing around her.

"This isn't what we think, Nancy," Laura said, suddenly. "The rift is not to Olympus or Heaven or even to Hell. It's something else, isn't it? Something that wants souls. Something that's taken advantage of the craziness."

Nancy shook her head. "Nice theory, but I think it's simpler than that. The veil between the worlds is failing. And it's going to take more than we have to put it back up, if it can even be done."

Laura forced herself to breathe. "I refuse to give up." She was stubborn. That was a good thing. "I'm a stubborn bitch and I refuse to give up." Sure, she was repeating herself, but it stood to be said.

Nancy shook her head. "We might have been..."

"Do you really think a lot of deaths would strengthen it? I think it would weaken it further..." Not that it could be weakened any further. The tips of the skyscrapers were now turning gold. She knew what would happen when it touched the ground. Possibly sooner, if there were more with a death wish for it to pick up on. Possibly sooner in the slums, in the brothels...in the places where people were more likely to despair. Or turn to God. She wondered about that woman, the one so strongly Christian. "Part of me wonders, still, if it's really a bad thing."

Nancy pursed her lips. "Perhaps not. But you will still fight."

"It's not time yet. I know that." She thought of Lucia. Was she really dead? Or just weakened into a mere shadow of who she was? She wondered if she would see her again, with that odd mixture of disgust and friendship. Maybe if she was alive, if all of this was over, if there was no reason to fight, then they could be friends in truth. She sensed the possibility, was entirely aware of it. Longed for it, but Lucia was most likely dead. Lucia was most likely on the other side. Her father...was supposedly imprisoned. Bound to ensure the order of the world. Was he now free? Was that what this was about? No. And if he was, Lucia had opposed him.

"No. It was not time for many thousands of years, but this is what we have." Cryptic, of course, and calm. The only emotion Nancy had shown was when she had admitted she did not, after all, want to die. At the same time, there was a faint hint of resignation to it...the calm having a different quality to it.

Nancy had given up, Laura realized. She might fight, but it would be half-hearted. "Dammit, Nancy. Don't you dare give up on me."

"Too late," she said, turning away.

Laura stared at the city for a moment, then she looked at the dragon. He had no ideas; he was looking to her to provide them. To provide some leadership.

Leadership that she did not have, not in that moment. "Dammit," she said again. She was cursing more, and it didn't surprise her. Everything had fallen apart, and there were no...

"Pieces."

"You have an idea?"

"No, but I have a thought. I need to chase it down." She moved back close to the dragon, running a hand along his scaled neck. She thought again, about riding him. He was more than big enough, if he was willing. "Why do you care about humanity? Who are you?"

The dragon simply regarded her with one slit pupil. He trusted her, and he wasn't the only one. Branson trusted her. Maybe Nancy. Simon. Debbie. She would have to disillusion them. She did not even trust herself.

The dragon rumbled.

"So, how do I fix this?" She was asking something that she doubted had any more intelligence than, say, a dog. But who else did she have to ask? Nancy had no ideas.

Choose, was the thought that flowed through her. Everyone had to choose. Herself included.

Did she choose to be human, to live out her life, get married, have children? Or did she choose to leave with the other supernaturals, to touch this world only when and where she could?

"I can't choose...I can't choose for myself, I'm too damn worried about the consequences."

The dragon nudged her again. "And the path needs to stay open for those who truly seek it." That was a decision she could make. How did she keep it open? She ran a hand along his muzzle again. "No. They have to keep it open themselves, each individual, as much as they need and want it." She thought of the Christian woman. Of Simon. Of Branson. Of all of the people in the city who had gone crazy because the door was too wide, not just for the world, but for them.

But then, she might be propping it open. Could she choose? She could not. She did not wish either path, so either way would be a sacrifice. Perhaps that was the point. She was being asked to sacrifice. So were they.

Nancy turned to her. "It always was...although I admit, leaving it a little wider would not go amiss. Your mother found it, though."

"I figured she didn't even know..." Or perhaps she had known at some level, and that had been why she had given Laura up. Sent her as far away as she could. "I wish I could ask her." She wished she could have known her, touched her. Her mother. She had had two mothers, they were both dead, and she wanted both of them.

But to try and contact a dead person would definitely... "I need to be alone," she said, abruptly, turning to walk away. The light almost touched her, but it was held off. If she chose to be human right now, she would die. The choice had to wait.

* * *

The other side of the island was empty, quiet, and she could hear sea birds. Were they aware? Were they affected? Were they an echo of reality, already gone but still touching her? Laura sat on the grass.

If she chose to be human, to give up her powers, she would die unless she did it at the right time, in the right place.

"I'll do whatever it takes to fix this."

"Even," said her father's voice, "if it means giving up some vital part of yourself?"

She did not turn around, she could see his shadow. "Do I have any choice?"

"You could go into the rift now, forget humanity, and be yourself on the other side." An offer. Even a promise.

"So, it's not a path to Hell?" He knew. And he was here, despite the fact that it had widened the rift last time. He had come to get her.

"It's a path to wherever the person truly believes they would go. It's always existed, the problem is..." Even the god sounded as if he had doubt. But if he spoke the truth, then this was a path to...where? Olympus?

"...that it's been torn wide open and is swallowing the world. And even the gods don't know how to close it." She spoke the words she knew to be true, letting out a breath. The breath that went in and out of her body reminded her she lived.

She could see shapes in the water, now. She knew they were a threat, but she could not find the energy to stand up. She rested one hand on the gun. "Maybe even the gods can't. Maybe it can't be closed."

The shapes were approaching the shore, rapidly, and she knew that the god could not help her actually fight them. "I suppose the fact that anything crossing over makes it worse means that me choosing to be human would make it better," she said as she stood, drawing her weapon.

"But so would you coming with me," he said, quietly. "I can't directly help you fight them."

"I know. It would finish the job. And that's why they're here. To try and finish the job." To kill her, at which point her soul would cross the rift...likely to Hades. Or would it? She had thought before dying might be a path to something else, for her.

"To kill you." He said it far more bluntly than she had. Yet gave her no answer on the consequences of that.

"Would that make things better or worse?" She had to ask.

"It depends." A non-answer. Or part of an answer, the start of one.

She shook her head. "On the when, the how, and the why." Would she have to die to end this? Was she willing to? Yes, she was. She did not want to...but wanting and willing, totally different things. Nancy was right. She was a little afraid of how much it would likely hurt.

Then somebody screamed. It was Nancy. She did not dare turn her back on the creatures, so she backed away from them, the pistol trained on them. It felt easy in her hand, light. "Nancy! What is going on?"

"I could use a hand here!" Nancy sounded alarmed, but not panicked. The scream had been surprise, not outright fear.

"Got problems of my own!" They were thankfully still within shouting range, albeit barely. Ally to enemy to ally again...oh pheh.

None of it mattered, and the gun fired almost of its own accord, seeking out the head of the nearest creature. She could almost feel the bullet now. Could sense its path through the air, tearing through it. It was more real. More real, perhaps, because it came from her hand. Touched by it. She was more real.

Except, that everything she did that spoke of war would strengthen the rift. Hell. Now she began to understand, but she could do nothing about it now. She couldn't play Gandhi with Nancy's life at stake...and then the dragon was swooping down from above her. She leapt. Her hand found one of his fore talons, and she was lifted above the fight. The rift was closing in on them. The air was different, it sustained her, but it smelled wrong. Felt wrong. Would she die if she breathed it? She had no choice but to take that risk. She had no choice but to trust the dragon would stay on this side. He still had no name. Puff, she thought, wryly. He didn't like the name, but she couldn't think of a better one.

"Nancy!" she gasped, and he banked around as she clung on with all of her strength. His wings made a lot of sound, their steady beat almost deafening.

She climbed up onto his shoulder, and then astride his neck before he swooped again, his other talon grasping Nancy by the shoulder. She could feel the beat of his wings, but it was easier to remain onboard than she had thought. No harder than a motorbike, and he was lifting upwards, reaching for the sky. The gold parted before him.

"Thank you." What did the dragon want? Nancy was a dragon too...but a different kind, so utterly different.

"What do you want?" she asked him, but all she felt was strength...the rippling of his muscles as he took off across the harbor.

Nancy was quickly behind her, no concern about falling from her. "Well, that was interesting. I suggest we let the beast take us where his instincts lead."

"I think he's more than..."

"This kind of dragon is, oh, a bit more intelligent than a dog, Laura. He's following instructions from somewhere or someone." Nancy's tone was gentle but lecturing. In the role of the sensei again, despite anything Laura could do.

"I think he's doing this because he likes me," Laura countered. They could not argue too vociferously, there wasn't room. Both women fell silent as the waters of the harbor fled by beneath them.

He was not taking them to Manhattan. He had turned further south, to skim past the south end of the isle. The rift was strongest over the city, outside it one could even still see a star or two. Drawn to the greatest concentration of souls.

"He's taking us to New Jersey. Talk about trading one hell for another." Laura was too much the New Yorker to resist the comment.

"Heh," came from Nancy.

The dragon, in fact, angled down towards a park. There was a baseball diamond, a small playground. Deserted, and looking very ordinary. Ordinary assuming the weather was inclement or it was night. It was night, she thought. Or was it? Was it simply that the sun had not risen, the world frozen on its axis? Had everything humanity had discovered been a false illusion? She wished she could say it had not been. Reality was consensus and consensus was reality. If every single human on the planet knew they could fix this, they could. If they believed.

For some reason, it reminded Laura of the start of Terminator. Probably how morbid she had been feeling. There was even a mesh fence around a playground. Should it still be night, or should morning be rising?

It did not matter anymore. "Okay. Now what?" she asked of the dragon, the air, Nancy, herself.

"We're here for a reason." Nancy had turned towards the city. She frowned in its direction.

"Branson's taking people to the wrong place." Laura frowned at that. They had to get back there.

The dragon sort of shook himself, then looked back at them.

"And he wants us to get off." Laura did just that, her feet touching the grass. She somehow still had the gun, and she wondered why she had not thrown it into the harbor. Because, still, she felt safer with it. A false illusion, given the likely effect of retaining it. Given what keeping it would do, how could she? Given she might have no choice but to fight again...

She glanced up at the sky for a moment. The rift was visibly spreading, but... "He put us at the edge for a reason."

As soon as Nancy was off, the dragon launched into the air again, his wings sending a wind over them.

"Careful!" she yelled after him. "Or I'll start calling you Puff again!"

Nancy snorted. "Puff."

"Well, he was about the size of a dog at that point. He's grown with the rift..." She tailed off.

"Then why is he helping us?" Nancy said it in the tone of one not seeking an answer, but rather to make her think.

"I don't know." Put like that, it made no sense. Why would a supernatural creature that had grown in power help them? What could a dragon want other than to... "He wants to survive, and whatever this thing is..." It would eat a dragon as quickly as a human.

"...doesn't like dragons much, of any kind," Nancy finished.

"Okay." She now owed the dragon one, and that perhaps was the real point. Ensuring his survival was now on her list of priorities. "I never did finish thinking."

Nancy laughed. "I'll be back in a few." It was a real laugh, surprisingly bright.

Nancy was no longer afraid of anything, including death. Her doubt on Liberty Island had faded away, vanished into the night. If this was night. Laura stood looking at the edge of the rift. It seemed ragged, uncertain, as if a fabric had been torn, rather than cut.

She felt as if she was stalled. She felt as if she could not make any progress, as if she was stuck reacting. It seemed that all she was doing was trying to think of a solution. With no success, at any level.

"Dammit," she said to the sky. "It's not time yet. You know it's not time yet." When would it be time? Thousands of years. Hundreds of generations. Humanity finally growing up...if that could ever happen. Humanity choosing to end their adolescence and join the gods. If they had chosen it, then the rift would lead to true immortality. Not destruction.

Then, the trees parted. Literally, they stepped to one side, as if commanded by a dryad. "Laura."

She turned. Ilorin, the centaur, stood there, his mane flowing over his back, his tail dragging on the ground. His bow was slung across the back of his torso, and his hands were empty and visible. He seemed the picture of dappled health.

"Ilorin." That was all she could think of to say. Now she thought she knew who was instructing the dragon. A little more intelligent than a dog, Nancy had said. But with its own agenda of survival nonetheless?

He stepped towards her, his hooves making prints on the grass. Proving his reality...and potentially annoying any groundskeepers. Now that was a banal thought to have at a time like this. Groundskeepers.

"Did you send the dragon?" She had to ask, had to know, even though she was certain of it.

"What is happening must be stopped." An answer without an answer.

"Even the gods don't know how." She regarded him. "Did you send him?"

"No," Ilorin admitted. "It was not I who had the idea to bring you to a path entrance at the edge of the rift. I believe it was one you think of as an enemy."

Athena? "Well, it has to have some meaning. Am I supposed to walk the paths again?" She stretched a little. The mystery would remain. Or would it? Ares might also have sent the dragon. At some levels, that should have been her first thought.

"Possibly." Ilorin frowned. "Even the gods do not know how to fix this?"

"So Ares claims. I don't think he has a reason to lie." At the start, yes. Not now. The gods wanted worshippers, not destruction.

"He would want a nice, healthy war. Not this." Ilorin tapped his bow, his tone very slightly amused.

Laura laughed. "Yeah. But as you said, it has to be stopped." Her frustration almost boiled over. "And I don't know how and right now..."

"Right now you would kill or die to do so." Ilorin's soft voice cut her off. "My family is safe. You too could leave."

"I choose to fight." She had to. She could leave, and what then? An existence, yes. Even a pleasant one, walking amongst the creatures of legend as one of them. They would accept her in a way humans might not. Besides, there was no murder rap against her in the Otherworld. No, she did not do this for herself.

"I know," he said, quietly, softly. "So do I."

"You? After those guys shot you up?" Her eyes flicked to Ilorin's scars, although none seemed to have been left by bullets. Arrows, more likely. Arrows fired by humans, a long time ago, certainly. He had been hunted.

"They are only a small subset of humanity," he pointed out. "I will help as I can." His voice had the tone of not just an offer, but a promise.

"You should leave. I don't want you to die. I'm tired of people dying." She just shook her head. "Tired of it."

He sort of leaned forward, so he could reach to rest his hand on her shoulder. "Yet, you want the world to be as it was."

"No, I want people to have the freedom to make the world what it should be." His grip was firm and warm on her. She felt almost as if she had passed a test, even if it existed only in her own mind. The wind seemed cooler and was the sky a shade darker?

"If we could get everyone to agree on that one thing, then perhaps we would have a chance. But humans are too stubborn." His voice remained rich, deep, and calm. His poise almost scared her.

"I noticed." She stepped back, away from the centaur. "Of course, I'm incredibly stubborn myself." Did that make her human? Maybe it just came from the human side of her.

She could see the entrance to the Otherworld. She could see her escape. Then she saw, out of the corner of her eye, Nancy.

Somehow, in all of this chaos, she had managed to find pizza.

19

By the time they finished eating, streaks of golden light were breaking the sky apart. Laura wanted to make them disappear, but she could not. "We gotta go back to the center. If it's not already too late."

"He brought us here for a reason." Nancy frowned a little.

"How do we know it was a good one?" Laura shook her head. "I trust that dragon, but I don't know..."

"Nobody's attacking us here," Nancy pointed out.

"That probably means it's not where we should be. Maybe he brought us here so we could catch our..." That was her theory. A safe place, but not to stay. Simply to rest, get food, and then return to the fight. Through the paths, or he would not have left them by an entrance.

And she saw wings up in the sky. The dragon flew out of the city, the light seeming not to touch or affect it, and she could see that it had a rider. A very nervous looking rider.

As it came to a landing, she realized it was Branson. "Okay. That is the last time...I do anything like that." He looked almost white.

Laura moved to help him down. With his arm still in a sling...she could see why he was having difficulties. "What, are you afraid of heights?" Okay, it was probably not fair to tease him about his nerve-wracking experience, but it might help him to feel better.

"People are gathering in Central Park. I couldn't get anyone to leave, then this fellow showed up." He eyed the dragon. The beast snorted at him, what might have been laughter.

"I'm amazed he persuaded you to come."

"So am I." Branson glanced at Nancy, then he saw Ilorin. "Oh my."

"What, never seen a centaur before?" Now she really was teasing, and this time he deserved it. His jaw was dropping more at the centaur than at the dragon. But he said nothing in response.

Laura realized that they were not going to be flying back. The dragon could carry her, Nancy and Branson. There was no way it could manage Ilorin as well. "Ilorin. Can you get us to Central Park?"

The centaur nodded, gravely, "If that is truly where you wish to go."

"It's not a matter of where I want to go. It's a matter of where I *need* to go." Laura brushed back her hair. "And what I have to do. Nobody has to come with me."

"We do," Ilorin said, quietly. "If only to stop you from doing something terminally stupid."

"What if I have to?" None of them answered that. The centaur merely turned and walked past the way he had come.

"Stay close to me," she told Branson. "No matter what you see or hear or, heck, smell. Just follow me."

"Don't worry. I won't run off with a dryad." His turn to tease, his turn to make the lighthearted comment. One that bothered her. She didn't want to hurt him. He said he didn't want to lose her.

"I'm more worried she'll run off with..." She tailed off as they made the crossing.

It seemed the same as it had before, yet there was a subtle scent she could not place that had been missing on her prior trip. Perhaps, though, that had something to do with Ilorin himself. She could not be sure, but it set her on alert, caused her hand to drift towards her gun. Still loaded. Would it even work here?

"Is something wrong?" Branson whispered, ignoring Nancy, who had moved up next to Ilorin.

"I don't know. I just don't..." And that was when the wind hit, rushing over them. A hot wind, almost as if somebody had set off a bomb ahead of them. "Oh hell." It was what she would have imagined people just outside the Hiroshima blast radius felt. That intense, that brilliant.

Ilorin stopped. He lifted both his hands to cover his face, although the wind did not seem to harm them.

"So much for coming here to be safe." The wind set the trees on fire; she heard a high, thin screaming that might have been a dying dryad. This part of the Otherworld was a great wood, but it should have been shielded. It was a different layer of reality, if it too was affected, then even the places to which souls fled might not be safe. If a soul died, then did that person cease to be? Or perhaps everything would cease to have ever been, return to primordial chaos. Chronos. But his daughter had fought and possibly died to preserve reality. Even the gods had choices.

"Indeed." Ilorin seemed uncertain. No, he actually seemed afraid, for the first time. If such a one could fear, then how could she find courage? She found it in a sort of mix of duty and hope.

Nancy stepped in front of him...and abruptly shed her human form. Laura had known, but seeing it was something else. She was blue and silver, a serpent with a frilled face and scales that seemed to reflect the rainbow between them. She was, perhaps, larger than the western dragon. It was hard to tell, for her body was long and thin, with short legs and no wings. No need for wings, Laura divined. The pearl necklace she always wore had become a pearl set into the scales of her throat.

"Whoah!" That was Branson. Had she warned him? She could not remember. Had he realized Nancy was something other than an enigmatic Chinese woman?

The dragon that had been Nancy turned away from them, at the path ahead, and...breathed. She had always thought of dragons as breathing fire, but what blasted through the woods ahead was water and ice, extinguishing the flames.

A storm dragon. Of course. "Nancy. Thank you."

"I have bought time only. Go." Her voice, in this form, retained all of its feminine quality, but was deeper and richer. Not a human voice, no, not at all a human voice.

Ilorin set off at a canter, Laura streaking after him. She could hear Branson's labored breathing. Nancy seemed to be staying back, as if to keep the road clear that way.

Clear it was, and then they were out...into Central Park.

Into hell. The fires had been a reflection of what was happening in actual reality. The sky was no longer gold, but rather burned, she could feel the heat...

...and Ares was a fire god. "Nancy. Shield the others. If you can." The hot wind had not harmed her, and this would not harm her. Who she was protected her.

There were indeed people, and Laura could feel their defiance. Could feel the way the flames reached out for them only to be blocked. Good. These people had made a choice, and they had made it with enough strength to build an oasis.

A fire god. The flames could not touch her, although they tried, licking around her. It almost felt good. She could, for a moment, feel what it would be like to fully acknowledge her heritage. To be the daughter of fire. Or, perhaps, it was only a part of her. Perhaps things were more complicated than that.

"This ends now," she said, knowing it to be the truth.

One way or another, win or lose, it ended now. Yet, she glanced at Branson. He was terrified. Ilorin looked grim. Nancy, still in her true form, held no expression she could read. She was still behind them, curling her form into great coils and radiating cool. She might be able to stave off the heat that way.

She needed the other dragon. He was a fire dragon. But no, if there was fire power needed, she held it.

Everything seemed to hold still, to freeze in place. She felt the weight of the world on her shoulders, like Atlas. Like him, she bowed, although she was not sure to what or whom.

The flames lit the faces of the people. She heard a faint beat. Somebody had a drum, somebody was trying to use it as some kind of focus. She reached for the music, felt it synchronize with her own heartbeat. Then she reached for the flame. At least she could end this, stop it...except she knew as she touched it that it was larger than her.

A wildfire. Could the others help? No. This was for her to do. For her to succeed or to fail. She opened her hands, spread her fingers. Her clothing was starting to singe, although she herself seemed unaffected. Why was it going sour?

Because people did not want heaven. Because people did not want to merely be...taken. Oh, a few did, but those here had come to fight. How did she use that? Use...them. No, not exactly. They would be the ones using her; they were the ones who needed her. Their belief flowed through her, and she was... If she was not careful, she would become what they needed.

Then Branson's good hand was on hers.

"Stay back. You're going to get burned," she told him. "I can take this, physically. I don't know about you." There was heat, but as yet there was no pain. The fire simply washed over her, but it came close to him, licking towards him.

Mentally, he could take it, she was sure of that. But if he stayed... "You'll die."

"If I must." He cracked her a smile. "It's okay."

"You'll go to Hell." She could not stay calm, could not stand the thought of losing another friend.

"I doubt that."

But she sensed it. That if he died right now, he would fall into the depths, because that, now, was what was reaching for them. He did not deserve that fate.

"Listen to her." Ilorin, turning towards them, looking back over his shoulder and equine parts. "She speaks true."

Branson lowered his hand. "Then what can I do?"

Dying he could handle. Ending up in Hell, apparently, was too much. His eyes flickered between the two of them.

"You can help me," came Nancy's voice, deeper yet still recognizable. "Please. Come over here."

Did she trust Nancy with a man she had only recently tried to kill? 'Nobody's side but your own'. But Nancy had had her own idea of what Laura's side should be.

Nancy wanted to live. What was going on was ripping apart all levels of reality now. There was nowhere for the dragon to run to.

There was nowhere for Laura to run to. Was she about to fall into the depths herself?

"No," came a voice, although this time it was inside her mind. "You need not fear Hell..."

"You think I could break out?" Could she? She had no idea, but at the same time...she was willing to take that risk. Why? Yet, the hint of her father's presence strengthened her. Not evil, after all, but simply a force. That was what a god was, a force of nature made sentient.

"You understand."

"I still will not let this happen." Because, dammit, humanity deserved a better epilogue, and because there were souls that would be destroyed or imprisoned eternally that did not deserve it.

She pulled out her gun. Why, she could not have said, except that weapons, violence, that was her power. For a moment, she stood there, the fire rushing around her. Then, quite deliberately, she set the pistol down.

"What are you doing?" Ilorin asked, softly.

"What I must." She knew in that moment that there was a very real chance that she would die. "I am not simply Ares' daughter."

"Then who are you?" the centaur asked.

Was he glowing, or was it a trick of the light? She shook her head. And there was no obvious answer. Laura Maxwell might as well be dead. She was nothing and nobody.

No. "Somebody who wants humanity to make its own decisions."

"Choice, then?" The Centaur turned to face her, pivoting on his forehand as neatly as any dressage horse. The scars across his shoulder seemed to be the center of the glow, his grey hair flowed into his mane and over his withers. He was not simply a horse with human parts, but a creature whole in and of himself...utterly graceful. Immortal. She knew that, too.

She could feel the intense interest of Liberty. "This city is the city of Liberty. She has the power to give choice, not me."

"What does Liberty need in order to survive?" Ilorin tapped a hoof on the ground. Sparks came from it, merging with the fire around, even though he wore no shoes.

She stooped to pick up the gun, slowly, "Eternal Vigilance." Which sometimes meant war. "She can stop this. She *can* stop this."

"Vigilance has been broken and cast aside in favor of greed," the centaur said. "And Liberty has been weakened, weakened to the core. You know that." He lifted that same hoof again, but this time, he did not bring it down, standing facing her on three legs.

"But not because of too little vigilance. Because of too much, and because of warriors sent into places where they were not needed. Vigilance needs to step to one side." She frowned, turning the pistol over in her hand. Examining it.

Nancy was building some sort of circle around them. Laura could see Branson 'helping' her by joining in the chant. She suspected it was the way a toddler 'helps' in the kitchen. "Nancy. Can I borrow Branson back for a moment?"

What was the right balance? If Vigilance was too strong, then... "This is giving me a headache."

Branson came over. "Giving *you* a headache? I have this feeling I'm about to be eaten."

"I won't let that happen. Branson...I just need you to help me think here. I need the extra set of eyes and the extra brain cells." She turned towards Ilorin. "I know he's only human, but..."

"But that makes him more qualified to find a way through this maze than any of us." The centaur actually bowed to Branson, dropping that hoof forward to lower his forequarters a little. To Branson. No, to humanity.

"Now, wait a minute. I didn't sign up for carrying the entire world on my shoulders." Branson sounded afraid, but he was trying to turn it into humor. Trying, with limited success.

"Neither did I." Laura knew she sounded grim. Yet, Branson had never shown that level of doubt before. It had not seemed to be in his nature. But then, he had not been standing amidst the fires of Hell. "But we have no choice. You know that. Everything we have done has angered the gods. Every broken truce, every lie, every treaty that turned out to be worth nothing. Liberty tried to fight back on your behalf, but she's not strong enough. We've sacrificed too much for security. How do we strengthen her?" A pause. "There can be no truce without freedom for everyone, but there also has to be protection. Safety."

Branson frowned. His face furrowing beneath his hairline, his eyes narrowing. He did not speak immediately.

Maybe weakening Vigilance was the answer? But how did they do that? She felt the pressure on her, and she did feel that perhaps she had been unfair passing even a small amount on to poor Branson. The man was out of his depth. He was simply a man. A man who cared about her because she was her mother's daughter.

She was thinking like something other than human, and she wondered if she had already made her choice. Yet, even the gods might be about to come to an end. She looked up, and through the fire...the stars were falling. "We have to do it now. We have no more time."

"Sacrifice," Branson said. "That's the only way liberty has ever been secured and maintained."

Bloodshed. Did it come back to that again? "But it has to be the sacrifice of those who choose to make it." The sacrifice of those who had a warrior's honor. Of those who gave themselves to Ares...and she, of course, was still his daughter.

"We conscripted during World War I, World War II..."

"...and Vietnam." She regarded Branson. Was he old enough? Old enough to remember a war that was history to her, a history of which she could have no memory and little understanding. The only wars she knew had been fought by volunteers but brought onto American soil. Had become something twisted, something not honorable warfare. A conflict in which nobody was safe or felt safe. A conflict that broke the truce and ate their freedoms at the same time, because there was no control on Vigilance. Because Liberty was represented, and through that image, the statue, had become real. There was no way that Vigilance could be formed, and if she was, she would be a dark goddess, darker perhaps than Ares.

He nodded. "Conscription only works if you convince everyone that their freedoms are threatened. Right now, everyone's existence is threatened."

"Which justifies any means, right?" She regarded him. "Nobody is going to be sacrificed. Eternal vigilance doesn't mean throwing innocent people on the altar." It had, lately. And it had in World War II, but that had been a different time. A different evil. Conscription versus no fly lists.

"Sometimes it has." Branson shook his head. "But I know that we can't restore liberty without sacrifice." His hand was moving to his gun. His left hand.

She sensed what he intended to do. "Wait."

"You said yourself, we don't have time. If sacrifice is needed, I'm willing to make it." There was only the slightest quaver to his voice.

Laura glanced at Ilorin. "Not that way. Don't you understand? It's not people's deaths that secure liberty. It's their lives. Every cop, every firefighter, every soldier who didn't sign up just to get three squares. How many years were you a cop?" It all fell into place. For however long it had been, she had fought for her own survival, but she had also fought to protect them. That had slowly come to the fore.

His hand lifted from the gun. "Fifteen."

"You've made yours." She glanced around. Nancy was now sort of hovering over the people. They were not sure which to be more afraid of, her or the flames. Yet, she was keeping them alive. With luck, they would forget. Was she, the dragon, Vigilance? No...

Then one of them spoke, softly. They had heard. "Ten years. Volunteer firefighter. Does that count?" He was definitely one of those more afraid of the dragon.

"It definitely does." Laura shook her head. "But apparently not enough." Her eyes scanned the crowd. She saw Simon...how had he got there? He threw her a grin, but said nothing. She even saw Barbara, the policewoman who had been so nice to her. There was somebody who had already paid the debt and made the sacrifice.

"People have to make new commitments," Branson said. "If that's the way of it. And they have to stop going too far. And..."

"Once, the gods guided people. But people have rejected them again." That was Ilorin.

"Not everyone." Laura kept her voice quiet.

"No, and for those who accept them, there will always be a way open." He extended one hand to her, only for a moment.

"Your name is not Ilorin. It's Chiron." The scars on his shoulder, the scars over a wound that had likely damaged his heart.

The grey centaur bowed. "So, you know."

"The most powerful of healers, who faced the deepest of wounds. Can you heal this?" She meant the world. She meant humanity. She meant the darkness.

"No. But I can heal those who need it. Including you, Laura."

She wanted, for a moment, to insist that she did not need healing. She knew it would be a lie. "To what end? The world is more important than me."

"You are part of it, woven into its fabric. The wars that should not have been fought." He had stepped towards her, was looking down at her.

"That's not my fault. Unless the people trying to kill me were right and I caused that kind of thing by existing."

"If you can cause something, if you truly have that power, then you can prevent it. You know the truth, Laura." Not talking in circles, now. But had he needed to wait until the last possible moment? Obvious answer, yes.

"That humans make their own choices and their own mistakes and the gods can only tell them what they are willing to hear." The stars were falling towards the city. The fire had entered into her, become part of her. She feared it would burn away everything human about her. "Tell me how to end this."

"They are the ones who must end it. All they have to do is know they can." Chiron turned to the huddled group.

"They lack the strength, most of them. They are too afraid." And her? She would become what they wished of her. She could feel that, and she could feel the knife's edge. Could she...no. War was what humanity made of it, but there was more than one god of war. Unless they were all the same god of war, under different names.

He stepped towards them. "Lung Mei-Xing," he said, looking up at Nancy. "You have done well to protect them, but I need to approach."

The dragon floated higher, giving space for the centaur's much taller form. She said nothing, nor did she retreat any further than was strictly necessary.

"It is time to heal the world. It had to be broken to know it needed healing." Had he set all of this up? No. He had simply known the answer, all along, and let it happen because it must.

The same man who had admitted to being a firefighter stepped towards him. "And will all this be..."

"Forgotten, except by those who choose to remember. All you have to do is believe. Laura."

She moved up next to the centaur. She could not help but rest one hand on his scarred shoulder. He had said he would heal her, but she knew what this was. Not a healing. A becoming.

"Who are you?"

The daughter of the god of war and a high-class hooker. A woman raised in the most secure place, in the heart of the American upper middle class, who had seen that all taken away from her. Who had been offered the chance to become a killer. Who had been offered the choice... And she remembered one person. Peter. The boy who had fancied he loved her, and thus died for her...unwitting, unwilling. The sacrifice that had been made for her, the one she had been forced to accept.

She wanted to take his place. She wanted to stand between all of them and the world, but at the same time she recognized that... "I *am* Vigilance. And I need to learn when to stand down. When to let people make their own mistakes. I thought I had, but all of this chasing around, all of this determination to fix it..."

Chiron merely bowed again. "You were still doing the very thing you were saying you were not. Of course, how many people do that?"

"Every mother. Every older brother. Half of the husbands on the planet. Most certainly..." She glanced at Branson. "Stubborn old ex-cops."

He quirked a grin at her.

"We still need to keep watch, but we need to make sure that the keeping watch...doesn't cross any of the other lines." The lines of tyranny. Of torture. The flames, though, were starting to pull away. "And the only way to do that is if absolutely everyone joins in the watch...including that on the watchmen."

But how did...then she realized. "And I can't get everyone in this city to watch. They have to make that choice. Some won't. Some will always hide in the shadows and refuse to take any part in the fight. There is nothing even the gods can do about that."

"They will learn. Most will not remember these days." Chiron turned to her. "Now you are not standing in the way of healing."

"But others are."

"Only if people let them." Chiron smiled at her.

She recalled her appeal over the airwaves. How had she been so...because she was who she was. Because she had the desire to kill and had channeled it into the desire to protect.

"I still want to protect them."

The fire within her had sort of settled into a knot. Was she a goddess? Not entirely, she knew, not yet. She had far more to learn yet, and for right now, it was best she remain...weak. Until enough people were willing to step forward. Until the time was right. Then, she knew what she would have to do.

"How about helping them learn to protect themselves?" He reached down with one hand, rested it on her shoulder for a moment.

Was that a strip of black sky? She dared let herself hope. "Talk to them, Laura."

There were not that many people here. A sampling. A couple of children. An old lady, leaning on a stick. "You heard what the man said. We each have to take responsibility for our own lives."

"What about her?" One of the young men jerked a thumb to the old lady.

"What about her? She's still got a working brain, right? A set of eyes, even if they might not be as sharp as they once were. And there's nothing wrong with asking for help. When it becomes wrong is when one person decides what's best for another."

"You're talking about ditching the cops." That came from a different voice, skeptical.

"No. I'm talking about keeping a leash on the cops, so they aren't crossing any of the lines. That means everyone here knowing when they're needed, knowing when they're not, and knowing when to stick up to them." Heck, it meant everyone in the city. "It also means that it's time we stuck up to the government, all of us, when it tries to do something stupid. Our constitution doesn't say 'The Government'. It says 'The People'. It also means that we have to acknowledge the gods, but not follow them blindly. Any of them."

The sky was darkening, as if clouds were crossing over it. She could still feel the heat on her. "As for me? If I have any kind of life after this, I'm going to dedicate it to teaching people how to protect themselves." She had always wanted to be a teacher. What she taught? That could change, that could...flex. If she got out of this. If she was allowed to do it...for she knew what she was very close to becoming something more.

"And I'll help you." That was Branson's voice from behind her. "Regardless of who or what you are, you don't know a bunch of stuff people need to know."

She knew that working with him was dangerous. He was at least fifteen years too old for her, and those feelings could easily awaken again within her. She knew that his had never slept. She also knew she needed him. "Got it."

"And I'll do my best." One of the young women in the crowd. "My husband's in the army. I'll support him and I'll make sure he doesn't do anything stupid."

"We won't have any more stupid wars." Cassie. When had she shown up here? "There's things worth fighting for, though."

"I never said there wasn't." A core, a seed, and then abruptly, the sky turned black. Completely black, there being no stars in it.

Then, it began to rain. The heavens opened, the water coming from them in cleansing sheets. "Thank you, Nancy."

But the dragon was gone, become a part of the clouds and the wind, perhaps, that being where she had come from in the first place.

The fires were gone. The stars came out again, one by one, as if turned on. Were they other suns, or were they something else? No. Earth had been, for a while, in a reality with different rules. And when Laura looked in the right direction, she saw Chiron's tail, swishing, as the path closed behind him. But the path was still there, for those who knew how to follow it.

20

Chiron had been right. Most people did not remember. Oddly, a certain selective amnesia seemed to have fallen over the police.

At least, nobody was trying to arrest her. Nobody recalled that Laura Maxwell was anything other than a rich kid who got shot at. Perhaps the gods had left that in there to give her an excuse to do what she was doing.

The old warehouse was a mess. She lugged another sack of debris out to the dumpster. Her strength was still there, her focus. She wondered, in the long term, what that meant.

Maybe it simply meant that she was what she was...and she no longer felt any conflict in it. She did not feel torn down the middle any more. Nor did she feel like jumping in bed with her best friend.

Not anymore.

Yet, there were other images...some of them her memories, some of them imagined things that might have been remembered. She knew, for example, exactly where Lucia was buried, even though she had not visited her grave. Yet.

She tossed the trash into the dumpster, making sure nobody saw how easy it was. Reality had fallen apart and then been put back together, and she still felt that she did not have the entire picture.

It had been larger than her. It had been people all over the world realizing who they were meant to be and pledging themselves to it anew. Perhaps it had been everyone on the planet after all...or at least everyone who had enough focus to choose a purpose.

Perhaps it had simply been those touched, in some way, by the gods and by the Others. Those in whose veins flowed the blood of the Sidhe. Those who's ancestor had once stolen a selkie's skin and fathered a child on her before she returned to the sea. Those who had, perhaps, a trace of dryad or dragon blood. One day, she would leave this world...but, if she was lucky, as an old woman, more than ready to join her father. She knew, too, what she would then become. She no longer feared it, yet was not ready to embrace it.

She stepped back into the warehouse. The floor was clear now, and she saw only what it would become. A sanctuary, but more than that: a place for people to set aside their need for the protection of others.

Above all, it would be the one thing she had always wanted, full circle. A school.

Author's Notes and Acknowledgments

As always, acknowledgments go to my husband, Greg Pearson, to my wonderful editor Jennifer Melzer. To Starla Huchton for the fantastic cover art.

For this book, I would also like to acknowledge Tim Ballew and the Solomon Slayers. They may or may not notice some cross inspiration here.

Also, I would like to inform my readers at this point that despite any appearances, I have never actually read any of the Percy Jackson books. (This was deliberate after somebody said the concept sounded similar). Ergo, any similarity in concept is entirely accidental.

About the Author

Jennifer R. Povey is in her mid forties, and lives in Northern Virginia with her husband. She writes a variety of speculative fiction, whilst following current affairs and occasionally indulging in horse riding and role playing games. She has sold fiction to a number of markets including *Analog*, and written RPG supplements for several companies. Her most recent novel, "Daughter of Fire," was released in the spring of 2019.

You can find her website at http://www.jenniferrpovey.com/.

To support this author check out her Patreon at https://www.patreon.com/poveyjr.

Other Books by Jennifer R. Povey

Transpecial — When first contact between humanity and aliens goes wrong, it is up to an alien diplomat and an autistic woman to broker peace.

The Silent Years — Three very different women deal with the zombie apocalypse and its aftermath.

Falling Dusk (Lost Guardians 1) — Anna McKenzie's life is changed by the death of her brother and the mysterious Victor Prince.

Fallen Dark (Lost Guardians 2) — As Anna tries to recover from the events of the first book, a bad guy of, in some ways, their own creation strikes.

Rising Dawn (Lost Guardians 3) — Anna and her friends (some of them) travel to London to talk to the one man who might know why no more Guardians are being reborn...

Risen Day (Lost Guardians 4) — To save the world, Anna and the others must face the realms of Death itself and somebody will have to make the ultimate sacrifice...

www.ingramcontent.com/pod-product-compliance
Lightning Source LLC
Chambersburg PA
CBHW022145240626

47153CB00007B/2524